SHADOWS

OF THE

HEART

* * * * * *

BOOK FIVE

* * * * * *

D.W. Neuman

ALSO BY D.W. NEUMAN

FICTION

Shadow Series
Shadows of the Mind – Book One
Shadows of the Soul – Book Two
Shadows of the Service – Book Three
Shadows of the Past – Book Four
Shadows of the Heart – Book Five

ISBN (978-0-9839446-8-3)

To my gorgeous wife, Connie.
Your endless selflessness
is truly unparalleled. I love you more
then you'll ever understand.

Carol, thank you once again
for your unwavering commitment
to these characters that you adore.

Love makes your soul crawl out from its hiding place.

Zora Neale Hurston

1
Saturday November 15, 1997 Early Morning
Cuba

"What happened? Somebody fucking talk to me."

"Sam?"

"What happened Laura?"

"I...I...there was so much shooting..."

"What about Julie, Kim and the kids? Tell me they're okay?"

Laura grabbed Gavin by the hand and slowly stood up. She saw the Marines extract Kim and the four children out of the Suburban.

Where's Julie?

She remembered that Julie got out of the vehicle right before Gavin got away from her.

"Julie? Julie, where are you?"

Laura walked over to the other side of the burning Suburban just as a Marine stopped her.

"Ma'am. I don't think you want to come over here."

"Why? What..." Laura saw Julie's legs protruding just out of view. "Get out of my way! Julie!"

Sam cringed as he listened to Laura call out his wife's name in desperation.

"Oh my God Sam." He barely understood her through her tears. "Julie's down. She's...oh fuck...she's dead Sam."

A single tear rolled down Sam's face from a world away. He'd never felt as helpless as he did at this moment.

Bill was stunned. He couldn't believe it.

Nikolay, on the other hand, just smiled as he watched Sam's demeanor change. "You could have prevented this by letting me go."

"Shut up," Sam hissed between clenched teeth.

"I'm guessing something tragic has happened to someone close to you."

"Shut up."

"Maybe you're a widower now?"

Sam punched Nikolay in the face. Nikolay fell over the log and landed on his back.

"Get up you piece of shit! Get up so I can kill you!"

"Godammit Sam," said the DCI in his ear. "I order you to return him alive.

"Fuck you sir. I don't take orders from you. You've already proven yourself to be a traitor in my eyes. Watch your fucking back, I'm coming for you!" Sam disengaged the comm channel and ripped his throat mike off.

"I NEED to get home right now."

"Easy brother," replied Bill. "Take it easy."

"Fuck easy! Everyone wants a piece of our family. I'm through. This motherfucker dies right now."

Sam pulled Nikolay up off the sand and stood him up.

"Going to kill me Sam? Shame. Well, at least I can say I'm the one responsible for your empty life now."

Sam pulled out his pistol and pointed it at Nikolay's forehead. His hatred burned through his veins.

"You sure you want to do this?"

"Don't fucking get in my way Bill."

"Wasn't planning on it brother. If anyone deserves to die it's him."

Nikolay stared at the end of the barrel. "I often wondered what my father's last thoughts were when I had my gun to his head."

Sam tightened his grip. "What the fuck are you babbling about?"

"My father didn't see it coming. I wanted his power; his influence. When I assassinated him in that alley I always wondered what the last thing that went through his mind."

Bill stepped back as Sam pressed the barrel deeper into Nikolay's forehead.

"You know what asshole. I actually met my dead father recently. It was one hell of a shock to my system. I have a strong suspicion that your father has been waiting a lifetime for this moment and will be very pleased to see you."

Nikolay's smile faded. He didn't understand.

"This is for Julie."

Sam's suppressed handgun ejected a single spent casing. It landed in the sand. A moment later Nikolay's corpse joined it.

* * *

Nikolay opened his eyes and watched as the two operators donned their own equipment and headed out into the ocean to meet up with the submarine.

What happened?

What the hell is going on?

Is that my body lying on the sand?

"Hello Nikki," said a familiar voice from behind him.

Nikolay turned and came face to face with his father.

"We're going on a trip, just you and I." His father's smile frightened him.

"Noooooo."

* * *

Sam's powerful arms propelled him through the ocean waters towards the rest of his team. Bill struggled to keep up but Sam

3

was on autopilot, his body and mind numb from the pain he'd just been dealt.

Julie's dead. I failed my wife. All she wanted was for me to be there for her and I couldn't even keep that promise. The love of my life has been taken from me. What the hell am I supposed to do now? Julie, I'm so sorry.

* * *

Goddammit. What the fuck happened to our families in Hawaii?

Bill dug deep while he continued to kick his flippers through the Cuban waters. Sam was ahead of him by a good fifty feet as they both closed in on the GPS coordinates they'd been given for their sub pickup. He could see the other five team member's heads bob up and down in the gentle sea a few hundred yards away.

The firefight he and Sam had heard over their earpieces continued to plague him. All Bill could hear in his head was the automatic gunfire and the sounds of explosions that were mixed in with the panicked screams and cries for help.

Laura didn't say anything about Kim and my children. Fucking hell, this is bad.

* * *

The five team members watched as Sam approached their position. Bill arrived thirty seconds later.

"Report," Sam ordered.

Alpha One spoke up. "We're at the coordinates. Our ride should be here anytime now."

"It's either that or one hell of a swim back home," Charlie Two quipped.

4

"Listen up," said Sam, his face ashen. "I've gotten you into something I'm not sure I can get us out of. The director of the CIA, Victor Bannon, is holding Thomas and his daughter hostage. On top of that, as you know, our families were just attacked in Hawaii by men sent by Nikolay, the man we just took into custody."

One of the men was about to speak up when Bill interrupted him. "Don't ask why he's not here."

Sam continued. "I just learned that my wife was killed."

The other operators silently glanced at each other. There was absolutely nothing they could say.

"In the heat of the moment I ended Nikolay's life. I killed the only bargaining chip we might have had."

"What do you mean?" asked Bravo One.

"The Director has quite a bit of power and influence."

Bill tried to lighten the mood. "The CIA Director has power? Who would've thought?"

"Not now Bill."

Bill lowered his gaze. "Roger that."

"Without Nikolay to bargain with we're left without any cards to play. I don't know what he wants with Thomas and Emily but he's now an enemy."

Bill knew exactly why they were being held captive but he kept his mouth closed.

Sam took a few seconds before saying anything else. "We're going to have to deal with him."

"Deal with him?"

"The DCI has overstepped all bounds. We all made a pledge to defend our country from threats, both foreign and domestic. I can't speak for any of you but what he's perpetrated will not stand."

5

Alpha One spoke up again. "You know we're with you Sam." There was a round of collective nods. "What do you want us to do?"

* * *

Eight minutes later the USS Seawolf rose out of the water one hundred feet from the seven operators. They made the easy swim over, climbed on the bow and pounded on the closed hatch. A few seconds later the locks disengaged and it swung open.

"Eagle One requests permission for seven to board," said Sam.

"Permission granted. Welcome home."

Sam clamored down the ladder into one of the larger spaces on the submarine followed by Bill and the other five SANDBOX team members. The hatch was secured behind them.

"Make our depth twenty feet and hold position," the captain of the boat ordered. He turned around to greet Sam and extended his hand. "Captain Scott."

Sam smiled and shook the captain's hand. "Sam Paige, sir."

Captain Scott briefly looked around before he focused his attention back on Sam. "Where's your cargo?"

"He didn't make it."

He gave Sam a hard stare. "I see." He turned, nodded and faced Sam once again. "I'm needed elsewhere. Commander Benson, my second in command, will see to your needs."

"Thank you sir," Sam replied.

Captain Scott took another long look at the men in the compartment before he left. Commander Benson stepped up.

"Sir, you and your team will immediately remove all your gear and place it on the deck."

"Excuse me?"

"Now!" the Commander said in a loud voice.

From the two adjoining hallways four men appeared. They were armed with .45 caliber semi-automatic handguns that were distinctively pointed at all seven SANDBOX members. The situation became tense very quickly.

"Sam, orders?" Bill requested. The other five team members were ready to rumble as well.

"Hold fast. Commander, what's the meaning of this?"

"I have my orders, just like you. You should have followed yours."

"Sam?"

So it's going to be like this. Goddammit.

Sam looked around at the four sailors that had them covered before he focused his attention back on Commander Benson.

"Safety your weapons and place them on the deck."

"Sam?"

"Do it!" Sam hissed. "Our fight isn't with these men."

Gear began to hit the grating until each man wore nothing but his wet suit.

"Good boy," said Commander Benson.

Sam gut-punched him before anyone could react. The Commander fell to his knees gasping for breath. The four sailors didn't know what to do other than stand their ground. A smirk appeared on Bill's face.

Sam bent over and whispered in Benson's ear. "I've had a really bad day. I dare you to push me again asshole."

The Commander found his breath, stood-up and tried to regain his composure but his face was beat red. His eyes locked with Sam's for a full ten seconds before he spoke up.

"Lock them up in the brig. Captain's orders."

"Aye aye sir."

Shadows of the Heart

<u>2</u>
Saturday November 15, 1997 Early Morning
Hawaii

Laura couldn't help but stare at Julie's still body on the ground. Gavin stared as well before Laura finally noticed and forcibly turned his head away. She hadn't been really listening to the loud conversation in her ear.

"My men will be there momentarily to take you into custody. I recommend that you surrender upon their arrival."

What the fuck?

"Thomas. Did I just hear that right? You're being arrested?"

He sighed. "It's bigger than that now. The DCI's been holding us hostage."

"What?"

"He knows...or he thinks he knows something. He wants Emily and he's prepared to take her by force."

"Oh my God!"

"I had to shoot the man holding us just so I could talk to you. He was going to kill me. Laura...listen to me. You have to get everyone out of there. You're not safe. None of you are safe."

* * *

The early morning light began to creep up out of the ocean. The aftermath of the attack, that they'd just survived, was all around them. Shell casings, scorch marks and bodies from both sides still littered the road. Rebecca needed medical attention.

Laura knelt over Julie's body and cried. She saw that her friend had two entry wounds to her upper chest. One of the bullets had torn through her heart. Due to that injury alone there wasn't a terrible amount of blood around her body because her heart had stopped pumping.

Kim had mostly collected herself until she realized that she didn't know where her sister was.

"Where's Julie?" she asked Oscar. "Where's my sister?"

He shook his head and didn't answer.

Kim looked over and made sure the kids were being looked after. She began to walk around and it didn't take her long to find Laura and Gavin. Kim rushed over and before she could say anything she saw her sister's outline on the ground.

"Julie?"

"Kim...I'm...I'm so sorry."

"No! I don't believe it!" She crashed to her knees next to her sister. "Julie's fine." She began to shake her sister. "Come on Jules...stop faking it. It's not funny anymore."

Laura tried to pull Kim away but she resisted.

"She's fine. You'll see. Come on Jules. Time to wake up."

"NOOOOO!"

Everyone jumped as Gavin screamed.

"Honey..." Laura started.

"NOOOOO! Get away from her!"

Kim backed off. Partly from shock and partly because she was scared of him.

Some of the Marines, as well as the security personnel, came over to see what the new commotion was all about.

Gavin knelt next to Julie's body. He placed his hands over her wounds, closed his eyes and concentrated.

The bird had been easy. This time is different. This time there is something new to cross.

Reviving Stir had given him hope and new strength; strength and depth he didn't know he had or even what it meant.

A thin line of sweat appeared on his brow.

Gavin grunted and concentrated harder.

Out of the ground rose a shimmering doorway right next to him and Julie.

Laura and Kim fell over in shock. Everyone else took a step back. They had no idea what the hell was happening. No one had ever seen something like this.

Gavin opened his eyes and stood up. Without even glancing at his mother he stepped through the portal and disappeared from the face of the Earth.

"Gavin!" she screamed.

* * *

Gavin stepped through and appeared in a different place of existence.

"Why hello dear."

Gavin turned and saw his grandmother Betsy.

"What are you doing here?"

"I'm looking for someone," he explained.

"Oh, I see. You know that you're not supposed to be here."

"I'm not?" he responded. "How come?"

"It's complicated dear."

"Can you help me find her?"

"Maybe. I think I know just where to find who you're looking for. Come with me."

Gavin took Betsy's hand and they flew. In no time at all she had taken them to a large arena. Below them a swarm of people aimlessly sat around. Betsy landed and looked at her grandson.

"Be quick."

"I will grandma. Thank you. I'm...I'm sorry I can't stay."

She laughed. "There will be plenty of time for that later."

Gavin turned and walked up a few of the arena steps. He saw her immediately and approached.

"Come with me."

"Where am I? Who are you?"

"Take my hand."

"Okay." She placed her hand in Gavin's.

* * *

There was even more confusion and disbelief as Gavin reappeared. However, in his hand he held onto a corporeal form. Laura and Kim stared, mouths wide open as Julie, very translucent, stood over her unmoving body. The portal lowered into the ground and disappeared.

Gavin looked up at her. "Here you go."

"Oh. Is this for me?"

Gavin nodded and let go of her hand.

Julie's form lay down over her body and faded away.

Julie coughed and abruptly sat up.

What the hell? What did my son just do?

Kim immediately moved forward and hugged her sister. "Jules! I knew you were okay."

Julie stopped coughing and opened her eyes. They were no longer brown. They were now black.

Laura spoke up. "Are...are you alright?"

"I don't know."

Laura pulled Gavin to her. "Do you know what your name is?"

"What are you talking about," said Kim. "Of course she knows what her name is."

Julie looked at both of them. "I have no idea. Who are you?"

Thomas was awestruck. "Uh..Laura? Are you still there?"

12

"I'm here."

"What the hell is going on?"

"I literally have no fricking idea. I can't begin to describe what just happened."

"Neither can we. But you need to do me a favor. Run and hide. I'll find you. I love you Laura."

"I love you too."

The earpiece went dead and Laura took it out of her ear. Gavin squirmed in her arms but she held on to him tight. *Run and hide.* Her husband's words sent shivers down her spine.

"Jules? Jules?"

Kim kept shaking her sister as if doing so would somehow wake her up from what they'd all just witnessed.

"Stop that. I don't know you. Leave me alone."

The shock on Kim's face said it all. "How can you not know me? I'm your sister. It's me, Kim."

Laura looked around at the jaws that hung open from the Marines and the SANDBOX security personnel that had witnessed what her son had just done. *I still can't believe that he brought Julie back from the dead.* She tried to concentrate. *I need to focus.* Laura looked around. Delta and Foxtrot stood by her side while Hotel, Oscar and Yankee were looking after Kim and Julie's four kids. Whiskey was nowhere to be seen. Gavin was still squirming in her lap.

"What? What is it Gavin?"

Her son stopped moving and looked up at his mother. "Becca." Laura let him go and he scrambled over to where Rebecca lay on the ground. The sounds of ambulances and police sirens could be heard in approaching in the far distance. Laura stood up and started giving orders.

"Foxtrot, check on Rebecca. Delta, what's our sitrep?"

"Whiskey's down," he replied.

"Dead?"

"Yes Ma'am."

"Damn." Laura looked away and then turned back. "We're not out of danger yet. Thomas told me to run and hide so that's exactly what we're going to do."

"Are you telling me that there are more men on the way to us right now?"

"I just don't know. We need to protect our own. Who's in charge of these Marines?"

"That'd be Gunny Malloy," Delta said.

"Point him out."

"Ma'am?"

"First thing. Call me Laura. Secondly, what is it?"

"Um...what happened with Sam's wife?"

"I don't know that either. First thing's first, okay? Where's the Gunny?"

Delta pointed him out and Laura bee-lined right to him. Gunny sized her up as she approached around the wreck of one of the destroyed Suburban's, spent brass and fires.

"Are you Gunny Malloy?" Two Marines stood behind him.

"Yes Ma'am."

"Sometimes the military politeness drives me crazy. My name is Laura Clark. Call me Laura, okay?"

Gunny nodded.

"Anyway, I wanted to thank you for your help."

"I only wish we had arrived sooner. Are you okay?"

Laura replied with an odd stare.

"Of course. My apologies. Let me rephrase. Is there anything you need?"

"I have reason to believe we're not out of danger. I'd like to request transportation to the closest hospital and one other thing."

Malloy slightly cocked his head to one side. "Shoot."

14

"That you run interference with the police for us. I have five catatonic children, two very confused adults and seven operators, one of which is lying dead on the road because he took an oath to protect us while the other one needs immediate medical attention. Can you do that for me?"

"You remind me of my wife. She doesn't take any shit either."

"So that's a yes?"

"Of course Laura." Gunny turned around to the two privates behind him. "You heard the lady. Round up a third driver and get them all to the fucking hospital. GO!"

"Aye Aye Gunny!" The two Marines took off like a shot. One headed towards one of the Humvees while the other one went to grab a third driver.

"Thank you."

"I have to ask....who were these men that wanted you and your families dead?"

"You want the no shit answer?"

"That's the only currency I deal in," Gunny replied.

"Russian sleepers."

"No shit."

"No shit Gunny. I have to get my family organized to leave." Laura began to turn away.

"Laura. Ma'am."

She winced and stopped.

"I don't know how to describe what I saw here."

Laura didn't make eye contact as she replied. "Neither do I. It's better if you make sure that stays out of any report that's filed."

"No one would believe me anyway."

"No, I don't suppose they would." Laura hurried back to where everyone was gathered just as the three Marine Humvees pulled up.

* * *

The police and ambulances arrived just as the three Humvees pulled away from the scene. Gunny Malloy began to handle the multitude of questions the police asked after he ordered that Rebecca be transported to the hospital asap. He also told them to call ahead and let them know that three Humvees full of injured were inbound to the hospital. No one questioned him. Lives were at stake.

Castle Medical Center was a large ten acre hospital and multiple staff were outside and ready to assist the three military vehicles as they pulled up. The doors flew open as five heavily armed men exited. The medical staff hesitated.

"We're private security and these women and children need medical attention," Delta tried to explain while attempting to appear relatively non-threatening.

The staff kicked into gear and began to do their job. Doors were opened. Unresponsive children were extracted, placed on gurneys and wheeled inside.

"Oscar. Yankee. Go with the first group and secure the area."

"Roger that."

"Leave me alone! I'm fine." A nurse was trying to help Julie out of a Humvee. Her shirt was covered in blood.

"Go with the nurse Julie," Laura commanded.

"Who are you? My mother?"

"They're just doing their job," she replied as gently as she could muster. "It's important that you go get checked out. Okay?"

"Okay, I guess." Julie let them lay her down on another gurney and they headed inside. Delta instructed Hotel to follow her inside.

Kim's head emerged and she stepped out.

16

"Are you feeling any better?" Laura inquired.

Kim gave Laura a hard look before she answered. "What the fuck is going on?"

Laura leaned in so that only Kim could hear her. "Listen to me very closely. This isn't the time or the place. Your kids need you right now. Your sister is alive somehow and needs you right now. Get your shit together Kim. Nod if you understand me, otherwise you and I are going to have one hell of a problem."

Kim's mouth hung open. She'd never heard Laura talk like this before. Kim nodded in compliance.

"Good. Go watch the kids. It looks like I have to handle something else now."

Kim looked over her shoulder as a police car drove up. She headed inside under Foxtrot's watchful eye.

Delta remained next to Laura by the three Humvees. His weapon was slung across his chest. He kept his arms down and slightly away from his body. Two officers pulled their side arms as soon as they exited the police car and pointed them at him.

"Drop your weapon!" one commanded.

"Hands up!" yelled the other.

Laura stepped in front of Delta.

"Lady, get out of the way!"

"I will do no such thing," Laura calmly replied. "My name is Laura Clark. This man is a member of my personal security detail and has authorization to carry and use the firearms in this state. Furthermore, he and I were just part of the massive firefight which must be all over your radio. We have injured being treated in the hospital right now. Please lower your weapons."

Two of the three Marines stepped out of their Humvees with their rifles. "It's true officers. They were attacked. We were there. He's one of the good guys."

Both officers looked at each other and then holstered their weapons. "I don't like this. I'm calling it in." He got back inside the police cruiser and picked up his radio.

Just then an ambulance pulled into the drop-off area and squealed to a quick stop. The back doors popped open and they all watched as the unmoving form of Rebecca Cross was unloaded and taken inside.

Laura turned to the officers. "That's one of my security detail that was critically injured in the firefight. My security and I," indicating Delta, "are going inside now to check on her condition and rejoin my family."

* * *

It wasn't every day that armed men, other than the police, were seen guarding patients. Therefore, to alleviate any panic, a section of the hospital was immediately cordoned off just for them. Regardless, word started to spread through the staff that victims of the firefight were being treated in a private section of the hospital.

Shortly thereafter a nurse took it upon herself to call a local news station.

* * *

It'd been five minutes since they'd arrived at the hospital. The remaining five members of the SANDBOX security detail had the private area locked down and closely watched the staff and the families. They were all still coming down off the adrenaline from the fight and the realization that two of their team members were down; with one KIA and the other currently was being cared for began to hit them.

Kim had finally risen to the occasion and had corralled her two kids, Sarah and Edward, along with Julie's kids, Amanda and Craig on a couch in the opposite corner of the waiting area from Laura and Gavin. Julie was currently being examined while Rebecca had been immediately wheeled inside to the trauma unit.

"Is Becca going to be okay?" Gavin asked.

Laura held her son on her lap and looked down at him. "She's a fighter sweetheart."

"What does that mean?"

Laura smiled. "I think she's going to be just fine."

"But how to you know?"

I forget how much he's been through already in life. "You're right honey, I don't know for sure."

"I could help her. I'm stronger now."

Laura's smile faltered. "What happened out on the road with Julie? What did you do? Where did you go?"

"I went to the other place."

"The other place? I don't understand."

"I saw grandma. She helped me."

"You saw Grandma? How?"

Gavin shrugged.

"But..." Before Laura could continue she was interrupted by Delta.

"Laura?"

She adjusted her head and looked up at him. "Yes?"

"There's a Detective Zikes here that insists on speaking with you."

Laura sighed and lowered her eyes. "Of course. Tell him I need a few minutes. I need to make a phone call first."

"You got it." Delta turned on his heels and disappeared around the corner.

Laura spoke to her son. "Will you be alright for a few minutes sweetie? Mommy's got to make a phone call, okay?"

"Kay."

She got up and headed over to the hospital phone on the wall. She looked around as she picked up the receiver to make sure no one else was within earshot. She dialed a number and tt was answered after the first ring.

"SANDBOX. This is Roberta, how may I help you?"

"Roberta, its Laura, Laura Clark."

Roberta's demeanor changed immediately. "You sound frazzled. Is everything alright?"

"No, not even close. Our families were just attacked here in Hawaii. There's been one casualty and Rebecca is down but being looked at right now."

"Oh my God!"

"I can't talk right now but Thomas told me to take our families and run. Run and hide. I didn't know who else to call. Can you help us?"

"Of course. Absolutely. You're in good hands. What hospital are you calling from?"

"Castle Medical Center."

"Got it. And let me know if my math is correct. There are a total of three female adults, five children and six operators?"

"Five. Rebecca's in the trauma unit right now."

"Okay. I need to get to work on something for all of you. Just don't leave the hospital. I'm going to send over a lawyer to run interference for you. I'll call you back later this evening."

"Thank you Roberta. You have no idea how good it is to hear your voice."

"You hang in there Laura. Be strong. Let me work my magic." The line went dead.

Laura slowly hung up the phone and tried to compose herself. *Where are you Thomas? Where's our daughter? Are you both alright?*

"Mrs. Clark?"

Laura turned and saw two men dressed in suits. Delta stood behind them. "Yes?"

"I'm Detective Zikes and this is Detective Harrison. Would you mind if we asked you some questions?"

"Sure. Seeing what my family and I have been through today I'd like to see some identification first."

Both detectives shared a glance and missed Delta who smiled behind them. "Of course."

They pulled out their credentials and Laura scrutinized them before nodding. They put their ID's away.

"I want to talk someplace else. As you can see the children are still reeling from this morning's events and, quite frankly, on top of that I'm exhausted, frazzled and pissed off."

The two men shared another glance before responding. "Sure. Why don't we step around the corner and into the hallway?"

"Fine." She turned to Gavin. "I'll be right around the corner if you need anything sweetie."

"Kay."

Laura led the way followed by the detectives and Delta taking up the rear. Oscar was at the end of the hall and guarded that entryway. She stopped and turned. The detectives looked over their shoulder at Delta and then back at Laura.

"Do you always have this much security with you?" asked Detective Harrison.

Laura avoided the question. "Detectives, first off I want you to know that I want to cooperate."

"That's good because..."

21

She cut him off. "I wasn't finished." Detective Zikes closed his mouth. "As I was saying I want to cooperate. However, try to imagine the traumatic events my family and our security team just experienced. We're on edge. We're raw. I understand you're just trying to do your job so for now all I'm going to do is give you a statement."

"Which is?"

"Early this morning my family and I were ambushed by a number of men with automatic weapons. In the ensuing firefight two of our security detail was injured. A group of Marines arrived and turned the fight in our favor. If it wasn't for the heroic actions of both the Marines and our SANDBOX security we would not be having this conversation." Laura paused for a few seconds. "My family needs to rest and begin to deal from this morning's ordeal. I hope you can understand that Detective."

"Yes Ma'am. We have a few follow up questions. Who would want to attack you and what exactly happened out there?"

Laura's eyes hardened. "You don't listen very well. I get it though, I really do. However that's going to cost you in the long run. Right now I'm going to tell you this. Go out to where this all happened and talk with Gunny Malloy. Take a walk through the fucking carnage and take in what those bastards did to us."

"Mrs. Clark, there's no need to get hostile."

"Fuck you Detective. You had your chance to do the right thing. You'll only get one more word out of me."

"And that is?"

"Lawyer," she replied. Laura motioned to Delta. "Show the detectives out please before I really start to lose my temper."

Delta moved to block the hallway as Laura turned and walked back around the corner to join Gavin.

"Gentlemen, you heard her. Please leave."

Detective Zikes eyeballed Delta. "We could have you detained for carrying those weapons, you know that right?"

Delta didn't budge. "Yes, you probably could. The problem with that happens to be your short sidedness. Our lawyers would have a heyday talking to the press about how the police focused on disarming the same individuals that were brutally attacked. SANDBOX is globally known gentlemen and we have permission to operate in the state of Hawaii with these weapons. We're the victims here Detective. We did our job today. Why don't you make yourself useful and leave these families alone. You're not helping the situation by being here."

"Let's go Zikes," said Harrison. "We've hit a brick wall here."

The two detectives retraced their steps down the hall with Delta close behind. Oscar opened the door and let them out. A sea of reporters turned and cameras began to flash.

"Great."

"Detectives! Detectives!" yelled one eager female reporter. "What can you tell us about the victims of this shooting? Are they alive? Are they talking? Why is security so tight..."

Oscar closed the door behind the two detectives.

"This is turning into a madhouse."

"I don't like it either," replied Delta. "I'll talk with Laura. You okay? Need to be relieved?"

"I'm good. I just keep thinking about Whiskey."

"Me too. But we'll deal with that later. Stay alert."

"Copy that."

Delta walked back down the hallway and turned the corner. Kim had four kids around her on the other side of the room. They were all quiet although a couple of them were crying. He turned his attention to Laura who had Gavin back on her lap. He seemed to be coping better than anyone. *What the hell did I see out there on that road? Julie was dead and gone. She took two in the chest with one going right through the heart. There's no way she should be up and walking around. What the hell did Gavin do to her? More importantly, how?*

"Laura."

She looked up at Delta.

"Two things. The press is here in full force. Pretty soon this place will be a security nightmare."

"Okay. I'm working on a plan to address that. What's the second thing?"

"You handled those two detectives really well. I don't think they knew what hit them."

She let a small smile pass over her lips before it vanished. "Thanks. Hey, tell me you've heard something from Sam, Bill or my husband?"

Delta shook his head. "I'm afraid not."

"Yeah…" Laura spaced out for a second before she refocused. "Delta?"

"Yes?"

"Thank you for saving our family today."

"It's our job."

"Nevertheless, thank you."

"You're welcome. Get some rest; it's going to be a long day."

3

Saturday November 15, 1997
The Other Place

Michael Clark suddenly appeared. Just moments before he'd stood next to his son Thomas in the Tactical Operations Center as a number of heavily armed and very serious looking men had barged in. He'd watched as the attack on the families played out on the large overhead monitor and witnessed his grandson open the portal, come through and then reappear. He'd felt the tug immediately and there hadn't been enough time for proper goodbyes.

I'm sorry son but I can't stay anymore.

Thomas' face was a mixture of disbelief and surprise.

What? I don't understand. What are you talking about?

The transition from Earth, to what some people believed was the afterlife, was seamless. Michael appeared and Betsy was waiting there for him.

"What did you do?" he demanded. "What in the hell did you do?"

"What did I do?" she replied indignantly. "I'll tell you what I did. I did what any mother would have done and helped our grandson. He's young and doesn't understand his power. The children needed their mother."

Michael scoffed. "Dammit, you're playing with fire. You have always pushed the boundaries."

"Oh really. And what about you? What our son and his family are going through is directly tied to your actions. Don't you dare begin to lecture me on what I've done until you stop and take a long look at what you've done and the choices you've made."

Michael turned. "I don't want to talk about this. I'm heading out for a while."

"Running away from our fight dear?"

Michael paused. "I just need time to think. And, if you haven't noticed, there's a new addition that's just arrived. I wouldn't want to pass up on at least saying hello to Nikolay personally."

"You do that," Betsy replied. "Say hello to him for me before he's taken away. And while you're out there do me a favor and figure this all out. Our family, our son, needs our help. The hell with the rules and damn the consequences."

4

Saturday November 15, 1997 Early Morning D.C.

Thomas was awestruck. "Uh..Laura? Are you still there?"

"I'm here."

"What the hell is going on?"

"I literally have no fricking idea. I can't begin to describe what just happened."

"Neither can we. But you need to do me a favor. Run and hide. I'll find you. I love you Laura."

"I love you too."

Thomas killed the link and removed his headset.

"Um," said Hobbes. "I'm sorry to tell you this Mr. Clark, but there are visitors outside. They're coming in right now."

Thomas nodded and walked over to his father and Richard. Michael placed his hand on his son's shoulder.

"I'm sorry son but I can't stay anymore."

"What? I don't understand," Thomas replied. "What are you talking about?"

Michael disappeared along with the weight on his shoulder from his father's hand.

What the fuck pop?

The door to the TOC opened and a number of tough looking men rushed in. They pointed their weapons at Thomas.

"Drop the weapon or die where you stand!"

Thomas was thoroughly exhausted from the entire ordeal. He let the rifle slip from his hands and it clattered as it hit the floor. His raised his arms.

"I'm going to walk slowly to the couch now. My daughter is sick and I don't know what the hell is going on."

As the men continued to cover him, Thomas walked over to the couch, sat down and pulled Emily close to him. It was at that moment he finally started to cry. His tears bore down his face and a few droplets fell on Emily's cheek. He whispered in her unconscious ear.

"Everything's going to change Em. I'm so sorry. I'm so very, very sorry."

The team leader spoke into a radio. "We have them sir."

"Give me specifics," was the sharp reply.

"Three individuals. Two men and a little girl. The girl appears to be ill."

"You're useless," said the DCI over the radio. "Give the radio to Calvin."

The unfazed soldier in camouflage tossed his radio to the first tech that stood up from his computer.

"Sir, this is Calvin. Richard, Thomas and Emily are here."

"What the hell happened to Michael?"

"He just…um…disappeared sir."

Victor Bannon didn't respond right away. "Very well. Anything else to report?"

"Yes sir, but I think you'd rather talk offline about that."

"I understand. Let me speak with the Sergeant."

Calvin tossed the radio back to the soldier. "Sir?"

"Sergeant, transport the three prisoners to Facility Thirteen using protocol Five Beta. Acknowledge."

"Yes sir, right away."

"Also, get a unit to come by, retrieve Curtis' body and scrub the TOC down."

"Wilco."

"I'm sure Calvin and Hobbes can hear me. The two of you hang back so I can talk with you. I'll contact you very shortly."

Facility Thirteen was located in the heart of Washington D.C. in a non-descript office building. The facility itself was located two stories underground that was only accessible via a large secured elevator large enough for vehicles. The black van that contained Thomas, Emily and Richard pulled into the underground parking structure, turned the corner and came to a stop at the edge of a wall next to one of the many support pillars. This pillar, however, had a card swiping unit attached to it. The driver rolled down his tinted window, extended his card and used it. A moment later the wall in front of the van swung upwards which allowed the van to drive into the large elevator. The floor began to descend and the outer door swung back into position above them.

Thomas and Richard's hands remained secured behind them in the back of the van. They had no idea where they had been taken since black hoods had been placed over their heads back at the TOC. Thomas began to struggle against his bonds when he'd seen one of the men pick up his unconscious daughter off the couch. A moment later the hood had come down over his head and his world turned into darkness.

The elevator ceased its downward motion. The van moved forward and came to a stop. Thomas heard the sliding door open next to him. He was yanked out backwards and landed on the cold concrete.

"Get up!" a gruff voice said.

Thomas rolled onto his side and struggled to right himself before he was hauled to his feet.

"My daughter. She needs me. I have to see my daughter."

A sharp blow to the back of his skull sent Thomas back to the ground. Pain shot through his head and all he saw was stars.

"Thomas?" Richard asked.

"No talking!"

One of the men pulled Thomas up by this arms which only added to the intense pain he felt already. He took baby steps as he was led deeper into the facility, pushed and jabbed at along the way by the same men that took them prisoner. Thomas heard a door hiss open. Another set of strong hands grabbed his upper forearms while his restraints were removed. He was then pushed forward and landed on the floor just as he heard the hiss of the door closing behind him.

Thomas tore off the black hood and blinked quite a few times as his eyes adjusted to the bright cell he'd been tossed in. The cell was ten by ten, painted white and contained a basic bed, sink and toilet. Thomas shifted his gaze towards the door and realized why he'd heard it hiss. It was a hydraulic door and seemed very out of place for a prison. There was a small square of reinforced glass that allowed him to view a small section of the outside hallway. Thomas pressed his face against it in hopes of catching a glimpse of his daughter. The only thing that stared back at him was the guard and his smirk.

Thomas turned away from the door and sat down on the edge of the bed. *What the hell do I do now? What have I gotten my daughter and myself in to? What's going to happen to us now? Why did my father abandon us?* Thomas' left hand began to hurt. He looked down and realized he'd been squeezing the black hood as hard as he could. He relaxed his hand and the black cloth fell to the floor. *Won't this nightmare ever end?*

* * *

The phone rang and Calvin picked it up. "Yes sir?"

"You said you needed to tell me something," replied Victor Bannon, the DCI.

30

Calvin nodded his head. "There's something you have to see."

"I don't have time for your games. This is a secure line, tell me."

"Um...actually sir I wouldn't know how to effectively describe this to you. I'd like to send over a video file."

The Director sighed. "Fine. Do it."

Calvin cupped the phone and spoke to Hobbes. "Sync it."

Hobbes nodded. "It's already in progress. I just need a few more seconds." He worked the keyboard. "Okay. It's ready."

"Sir, you should see the new video on your screen?"

"I see it. What am I looking at? A gun battle?"

"This is from the satellite we tasked over Hawaii during the attack on the three families."

"What's so important about it? You'd better not be wasting my time."

Calvin swallowed and pressed on. "No sir. The snippet of video you're looking at is at the tail end of the attack. The Marines had just arrived and took down the northern attackers."

"Get to the Goddamn point Calvin."

"As you can see two of the adult women, after exiting the Suburban, each took out a target on their own. The next part is where it gets interesting. Watch closely sir."

The DCI watched as the last attacker shot one of the women. As she fell to the ground a small, and very fast form, shot out from underneath an abandoned Suburban. The attacker's body fell to the ground as the man's head flew several feet further.

"What the hell was that? What did I just witness?"

"We don't know sir," replied Calvin. "We haven't had time to analyze any of it. But let me skip forward a minute. There's something else that will definitely warrant your attention."

"Very well." The DCI watched the overhead satellite video fast forward on his screen. It suddenly began to play at normal speed again. On it he watched a little boy run over to the fallen woman and place his hands on her chest. Shortly thereafter something appeared out of the ground and the boy walked through it and disappeared.

What the hell?

Before he could open his mouth Victor watched as the boy reappeared with something translucent in his hand.

What is that?

The ghostly shape lay down over the woman's body and she sat up.

"Play that again!" he demanded.

The screen rewound and he watched wide-eyed as a shimmering doorway rose out of the ground, the child walk through it and reappeared.

"Calvin."

"Yes sir?"

"You and Hobbes have just been promoted. Your first thing you'll do is transfer all records, videos and recordings to a secure server."

"Yes sir."

"After that you'll scrub the logs. I don't want a trace of what you just showed me, along with the Cuba incursion details, to be made available to anyone but myself. Is that clear?"

"Of course sir. We'll get right on that."

"Make sure that you do." The line went dead.

"What the hell did he say?" Hobbes asked.

Calvin relayed the conversation. "We're in deep now. It's about time."

"You're really enjoying this aren't you?"

Calvin smiled. "Why shouldn't I be? We've got an 'in' with the Director of Central Intelligence on a project that will blow open people's perceptions all over the world. How can you not be as excited as I am?"

Hobbes nodded towards Curtis' body that lay dead on the floor, shot to death by Thomas Clark a bit earlier. "Don't kid yourself Calvin, we're expendable. In time we'll become liabilities."

"Don't be such a pussy. He needs us."

Hobbes nodded. "Maybe. Just keep telling yourself that."

"Hold it. Are we going to have a problem?"

Shit. "No, no problem. I'm tired and just running my mouth. We're good. I'll start to migrate the Hawaii data to the secured server if you want to work on the Cuba portion?"

Calvin gave Hobbes a long look before he turned back to his own bank of computers. "Good."

Hobbes took another glance at the dead man on the floor before he got back to work.

<u>5</u>
Saturday November 15, 1997 Afternoon
Hawaii

Julie appeared through the trauma unit doors led by Doctor Goodman. Amanda and Craig both saw their mother at the same time and cried out in unison.

"Mommy!"

They dislodged themselves from the couch and raced over to embrace their mother. They both wrapped their arms around her and held on for dear life. Julie didn't know what to do and just patted them gently on their backs.

"We missed you!"

"Are you okay?"

"Can we go home?"

"I want to go home!"

Doctor Goodman, Kim and Laura watched the interaction with great interest until the doctor motioned for the two of them to join her. Kim got up from the couch and Laura stood up from the chair she and Gavin shared and walked over.

Doctor Jenny Goodman greeted them as they approached and then got right down to business.

"Kim, your sister is experiencing a form of amnesia. She knows how to talk, write, eat, etc. but clearly doesn't recall who she is and the life she's created with her husband."

"What does that mean?" Kim replied. "It's temporary, right?"

"At this point all I know is that she's been through a traumatic event. You all have. I'm seeing similar symptoms to individuals with PTSD."

"What's that?"

Laura answered. "PTSD is post-traumatic stress disorder. It's commonly seen in soldiers. Although amnesia, in this case, would be a rare side effect."

"Exactly," said Dr. Goodman. "Are you familiar with PTSD Laura?"

"I'm a psychiatrist. Well, to be more exact, I used to be one. I treated a number of patients with PTSD."

"I see. That's good actually. Julie's going to need time and she'll be much better off with you in her corner."

Kim spoke back up. "But what about my sister's injuries?"

Dr. Goodman shuffled her feet. "That's another topic altogether."

"What do you mean?"

"I can't account for all the blood that was on her clothing."

"She was shot," Kim insisted.

Dr. Goodman shook her head. "No. She has no entry wounds of any kind. An x-ray revealed nothing out of the ordinary. She's in perfect health other than the fact she's lost her memory."

"No. That's not possible."

"Why?"

"I saw her lying on the ground. She was dead."

A confused look appeared on the doctor's face.

"Excuse us for a second." Laura pulled Kim by her arm to the side. "Look. I don't know exactly what happened out there either. What I do know is you need to stop asking questions right now."

Kim was frazzled. "You can't tell me what to do. That's my sister we're talking about."

"No shit Kim. And if you didn't notice that was 'my' son that somehow brought her back to life. So get a fucking grip."

"How dare…"

"We have our families to protect. That's our main concern right now. You want to scream and yell and tear me a new asshole

later on, once we're out of this place and somewhere private, you
go well ahead and vent anything and everything to me or at me
then. But right now our children, and your sister, have no one else
to look after them but you and me. You keep making 'crazy'
statements and they might take your kids away. I don't want that
and I know you don't want that."

Kim's eyes flared. "I don't know what happened out there on
that road and I'm confused as all hell about it. But our kids need
us."

"Good."

"Don't think for a second this is over Laura."

Laura sighed. "I didn't think so."

They moved back over to Dr. Goodman. "Sorry about that,"
said Laura.

"Sure." She gave Kim one last odd look before she continued.
"Anyway, like I was saying, your sister checks out physically."

"What about Rebecca?" Laura probed.

"I was just getting to that. Rebecca's another story. She's still
under observation."

Laura didn't like where this was going. "How bad is it?"

"Once we removed her bullet proof vest the team was able to
probe the extent of her injuries. She has a cracked rib and some
shrapnel cuts that were cleaned and stitched up. There's a long
gash that starts above her right eye and comes down her mid
cheek. Unless she gets plastic surgery in the future that scar's
going to remain."

"Is that it? That doesn't sound too bad."

"She took a hard hit to her head and is concussed. There's
some swelling on her brain because of it. Right now we are
keeping her in an induced coma."

Laura and Kim both covered their mouths with their hands.

"It's just going to take some time but I'm sure she's going to be okay."

Laura had to take a few seconds to collect herself before she could say anything else. "So Rebecca won't have any permanent damage?"

Dr. Goodman sidestepped the question. "It's too early to tell. We'll keep a close eye on her and let you know if there are any changes."

"Thank you doctor."

Dr. Goodman turned and headed back in to the ER. Kim didn't bother to look at Laura as she walked back to join her confused sister and the children. Laura sat back down in the chair and Gavin climbed in her lap.

"Is Becca going to be alright?"

Laura stroked his hair. "I hope so sweetie. They made her sleep because her head hurts."

Gavin tried to wrap his mind around that. "Maybe I can fix her."

No time like the present. "Is that what you did with Aunt Julie? Did you fix her?"

Her son nodded his head.

"How?"

He shrugged. "I dunno. It was like helping the bird that hit the window or when Stir got hurt. I just did it. Are you mad at me mommy?"

"No. No, of course not sweetie. You're an amazing young man with a special gift."

"Then why are you and Aunt Kim fighting?"

Kids don't miss a thing. "Aunt Kim is worried. She doesn't understand your power is all."

Gavin chewed his lower lip. "My power scares me too sometimes."

Laura pulled her son close and hugged him. "It'll be okay. You and your sister have a lot to learn. We'll figure it out together."

"Really? When's daddy and Em coming home?"

Damn. Stuck my foot in that one. "Pretty soon. But right now we need to take care of each other. Can you do that for me? Can you watch out for all of us and we'll watch out for you?"

Gavin pulled back from his mother and nodded. "I can do that. But when are we going home?"

"I don't know sweetie. The bad men that tried to get us might be there. We might have to find a new home."

"But Stickers is there!"

Shit. "It's okay. It's okay. I'll make sure we get Stickers before we go anywhere."

"Promise?"

"Yes Gavin, I promise."

"Kay." He smiled and cuddled in. Within seconds he had fallen asleep.

This is one hell of a mess. Her thoughts were interrupted as she heard her name.

"Laura?" Delta motioned for her to come with him.

She gently got up, with Gavin in her arms, and headed over.

"Is everything alright?" she asked.

"It depends on your point of view. There are two things. The first is that the story has hit the television. The local stations started broadcasting it and CNN has already picked it up. They've got pictures of the scene somehow. It shows body bags being carried away and they've already traced the license plates. They know who was involved but its still speculation at this point. On top of that the news crews are camped out here at the hospital waiting for any word on your condition. You're a global story now and they're not going to stop."

"Wonderful," she said sarcastically. "That didn't take long. What's the second thing?"

"A man claiming to be your lawyer is here. He says he's from SANDBOX and that Roberta sent him. What do you want me to do?"

"Send him in."

Delta motioned to Oscar who was preventing anyone from entering their private wing of the hospital. He edged open one of the doors and started to talk to someone. A man, carrying a briefcase, was let in. Oscar patted him down and told him to head to Delta. Suddenly the second door opened and before Oscar could react a number of flashbulbs went off. Delta swore and rushed down the hallway to help Oscar.

Shortly thereafter a picture appeared on television that clearly showed a woman clutching her child that stood next to a large armed man. The picture left little doubt he was her security. The caption read, "Supposed victim's holed up in Hawaiian hospital."

The population of the story grew even larger and naturally the world demanded more details.

<u>6</u>
Saturday November 15, 1997 Afternoon
D.C.

Victor Bannon, the director of the Central Intelligence Agency, watched Thomas Clark as he paced around his cell via the closed circuit television monitors. Thomas couldn't stay still for more than a few seconds at a time as he moved from one end of his cell to the other and back again.

There is no escape.

Victor shifted his eyes slightly to the screen that showed Richard Moore's cell. The old man, once Michael Clark's mentor, sat quietly on his bed with his eyes closed.

Interesting.

He moved his eyes once again and the young six year old girl came in to view. Emily Clark lay on a table, covered with a white sheet, and had numerous medical leads attached to various parts of her body. Victor watched as two men in surgical attire observed and recorded her vitals. Her fever was still present and she had not recovered consciousness.

Hello dear. What secrets do you hold for me?

Victor picked up the phone, dialed an extension, and spoke. "Escort our two adult guests down to the lab."

He hung up the phone and followed along as cell doors were opened. Moments later another camera angle followed two armed guards, along with Thomas and Richard, walk towards the lab area. Victor watched Thomas immediately bee-line to his daughter as he began to shout at everyone around her. *That's my queue.* Victor turned and exited the security room. As he walked down the long corridor he heard Thomas' shouting become louder and louder.

41

"What the hell do you think you're doing!? Why do you have us here!? We're American citizens Goddammit! You can't hold us here against our will!"

The DCI turned the corner and boldly walked into the lab. He saw that Thomas stood between his daughter, the two doctors and the two armed security men; while Richard had taken a seat and took everything in.

"Quite the contrary Mr. Clark," Victor began as Thomas suddenly focused on him. "You killed one of my men in cold blood."

"Curtis?" replied Thomas. "You have got to be shitting me. I was defending myself. You made us prisoners long before that ever happened. His death is on your hands."

Victor smiled. "Details, details." He walked farther in to the lab and past the two security men towards Thomas and Emily.

"What the hell do you want from us?" Thomas hissed between clenched teeth.

Victor stopped a few feet from Thomas. "Please. Continue to play coy all you want. However, we both know what powers your daughter possesses, don't we?"

Thomas' head tilted ever so slightly. *Fuck. Not again.*

The DCI smiled again as he picked up on Thomas' discomfort. "That's right. You and your daughter are here because I have quite a number of unanswered questions."

"Go to hell."

Victor dismissed the comment. "Irrelevant. You're here. Your daughter is here. The two of you aren't going anywhere anytime soon. Trust me when I say that we'll have plenty of time to get to know all about you and your family's secrets."

"You bastard. We came to you to take down Yuri and this is how you thank us?"

"You're right. That will be a nice feather in my cap. Thank you. However, you only have yourself to blame." He paused for a few seconds. "Your father is really dead isn't he? He didn't disappear for thirty years and then come out of hiding. No, he's dead and somehow your daughter has the ability to bring him back. I can't help but to wonder if she can bring anyone else back? Care to comment on my speculation?"

"Fuck you."

"Fair enough I suppose. However, your current reality is quite different. Look around you Mr. Clark. If you haven't noticed, this is your new reality whether you want to accept it or not."

The overhead intercom interrupted the conversation. "Sir, you might want to check out CNN."

Victor motioned to one of the doctors who nodded, pivoted and turned on the television that hung from a wall. He found CNN and punched the volume.

"...it's still not clear what happened outside Oahu, Hawaii. If you're just tuning in there has been a brazen attack, early this morning, on three families that were traveling with security provided by the private military contractor company called SANDBOX, based out of Marin, California."

The reporter vanished from view as a camera panned around the scene of the attack. A number of Marines, Firefighters and Ambulance were mixed in with police who were fighting to contain the scene. Filled body bags were lined up next to the side of the road.

"Currently a motive for this attack hasn't been established, but the SANDBOX personnel fought back against an unknown number of men. Early reports indicate they may have lost at least one of their own during the firefight. Initial speculation as well, based on a check of the three destroyed Suburban's license plates indicate that two of the three families attacked belong to the owners of

43

SANDBOX. It's unclear whether those owners, Sam Paige or Bill Nicholson, happened to be in those vehicles during the attack but what we do know is that surviving members of those families have been seen at the Castle Medical Center."

The picture changed once again. A woman held on to what must have been her son. Next to her stood a rather imposing man with a weapon. The caption read: Supposed victim holed up in Hawaiian hospital.

"The hospital remains tightlipped about this woman's identity or even whether she belongs to one of the families that were involved in the attack. However, it would appear that a lawyer was allowed access to the private wing where this woman was photographed."

"Turn it off," said Victor and a second later the television went quiet.

Thomas couldn't stop staring at what he'd just seen. His wife and son were still safe but well out of his protective reach. *Why hadn't they run?*

"I'm happy to see your wife and son survived Nikolay's attack."

Thomas didn't reply to Victor's comment.

"You know. A saw the strangest thing on the satellite feed before I came over here. Do you know what that was Thomas? No? You don't want to answer? That's okay. I'll tell you what I think I saw but quite frankly I don't even know how to properly describe it. I saw something small and fast take down a heavily armed man. The man's head just popped off. Just poof and off it went. Can you imagine that? But that wasn't the most surprising thing. No, the shock came when I saw something shimmering rise out of the ground and a small boy then enter it. Not a moment later he reemerges with who knows what in tow and then a deceased woman just comes back to life. Just like that. Creepy."

44

Victor looked around the room at everyone before focusing back on Thomas.

"Now, I don't know about everyone else here and what they believe but I think I saw something straight out of a science fiction movie. Would you care to comment on that?"

"Go to hell."

"You know it doesn't matter right this second if you talk to me or not. In time I'll know your entire story. But you know what Thomas? You should be thankful."

"And why's that?"

"Your wife and son will be joining you here at this facility shortly."

Thomas grimaced and sprung at Victor with outstretched hands. One of the guards quickly intercepted him and he ended up on the floor with a sore cheek. "I'll...kill...you."

"Temper temper. I'm not a bad man Mr. Clark, just an enterprising one. I have to think of our country's security and best interests. Your family is a threat but if I can harness what I've seen then the next evolution of intelligence gathering will be at hand. And I'll be the one that gave our side the necessary edge."

"You don't know what you're doing," Thomas said from the floor.

Victor nodded. "I agree. I don't know anything yet, but very soon I'll know everything I need to. Now, if you'll excuse me, I have Sam and Bill to visit."

"They're alive?"

"Alive, but in custody. I have a few jobs for them to do for me."

Thomas scoffed. "I guess you don't know them like I do. They'll never do a damn thing for you."

"No, I believe you're right, I'll give you that. But with the correct incentive I'd be willing to think they'd do just about anything I asked."

Victor motioned to one of the guards who then pulled Thomas off the floor and back on to his feet. The DCI produced a digital camera from his pocket and made sure both Thomas and Emily were visible before he took the shot.

"You can follow along with my logic now, can't you?" Victor smiled. "Put them both in one cell for the time being." Both guards nodded as the DCI excused himself.

As the guards took Richard and Thomas away, Thomas turned back and asked one final question. "What's wrong with my daughter?"

He didn't get an answer as he and Richard were taken back down the long corridor and placed in Thomas' cell together. The door's lock clanked loudly as it was engaged.

Thomas sat down on the bed with his head in his hands. He started to murmur to himself. "I don't know what to do. I don't know what to do. I don't know what to do."

Richard knew about the powers the children possessed but he'd remained quiet as ever while the Director continued to boast. Richard had seen and held his own dead daughter recently thanks to Emily. He knew what Thomas' daughter could do and was determined not to let the DCI get away with his plan for the Clark family, no matter what. Richard quietly sat down next to Thomas.

"It's going to be okay."

"You don't know what you're talking about."

"Maybe not. But I do know that you don't want to lose it in here. Not when your family needs you to be strong."

"What the hell do you know about family?"

"Thomas. I lost mine in a car crash. Everything in the world that meant something to me was taken away in an instant. You still have yours. And yes, the situation is dire, but it's not over. You need to fight and remain hopeful. I lost my way when I lost my wife and daughter. So believe me when I know something about family because you still have yours."

"I'm...I'm sorry. I didn't mean..."

"Forget it. We're in this shit together so we need to help each other keep our heads screwed on straight. It's either that or let that sonofabitch win."

"Fuck that shit," Thomas replied instantly. "That's never going to happen."

"That's the spirit," Richard said as he placed his hand on Thomas' back in support.

Shadows of the Heart

7

Saturday November 15, 1997 Late Afternoon Hawaii

The hospital wall phone rang shortly after five o'clock. Laura disengaged herself from Gavin, who was sleeping on her lap, and walked past Jerold Smith, the lawyer, to answer it.

"Hello?"

"Laura. It's Roberta."

"Oh thank God," she breathed into the receiver.

"How are you all holding up?"

"The media is going crazy. Everyone's exhausted. Kim and I are not seeing eye-to-eye. The kids have no idea what's wrong with their mother. The SANDBOX personnel are professionals but they haven't had a chance to rest at all since the attack this morning."

"I hear you Laura. The good news is that I've got a plan that's practically ready to go."

"Practically?" Her tone had a slight edge to it.

"I can hear the worry in your voice. Trust me. Your family is going to be safe."

"I'm sorry Roberta. I didn't mean…"

"I know. You've been through so much already. Can you just hold on for another thirty minutes or so?"

Laura nodded. "I can do that. What's the plan?"

"I'll fill you in momentarily. I need to talk with one of the SANDBOX men, the lawyer I sent over and then I'll fill you in. Okay?"

Laura looked over her shoulder and spotted Delta watching over them as usual. She motioned for him to come over and he approached.

"Problem?"

Laura handed him the phone. "It's Roberta. She needs to talk with you."

Delta let his weapon hang from its sling across his chest and took the outstretched phone. "Roberta? This is Delta. I mean, you're talking with Tony O'Neill."

Laura watched Delta closely throughout the conversation looking for telltale signs. Other than his 'Yes, Ma'am' or 'No Ma'am' replies she couldn't gleam a thing. After a few minutes he handed the phone back to her.

"Well, this is going to be interesting." He turned, walked ten feet away and got on his radio. "All team members report in."

Laura looked after him and then back towards Mr. Smith. "Roberta. I'll get Mr. Smith for you now."

"Thank you."

"Mr. Smith?"

The lawyer had been watching the recent events expire. He promptly stood up and joined her.

"Roberta would like a word with you." She handed him the phone. It was then that she noticed that Gavin wasn't where she'd left him. The chairs were empty.

He nodded and took it. "This is Jerold Smith."

Laura looked around the waiting area for her son but didn't see him. She looked over at Kim, Julie and their kids but didn't see him over with them either. *Where have you disappeared to Gavin?*

"Mrs. Clark?"

A few seconds later it was repeated again.

"Mrs. Clark?"

Laura turned back to Mr. Smith who held the phone out for her to take.

"Roberta would like to talk with you now."

Dammit Gavin. She walked over and took the phone from him.

"What the hell is going on Roberta?"

"The plan is that you're all getting out of there and somewhere safe."

"Where?"

"I'm getting to that part dear. First thing's first. There is quite the contingent of reporters out there that would like nothing more than to hound you and your family. In a few minutes Mr. Smith will walk out and announce he has a statement to make. This will naturally focus all attention on him while all of you exit out the back and leave the hospital grounds. Delta has assured me he and the rest of the team can pull this off covertly."

"Okay. And then what?"

"Two members of the five man team will head back to your houses and gather some clothing, etc. and then meet up with you at your final destination."

"Where's that supposed to be?"

Roberta filled her in on the final part of the plan.

Laura's mouth hung open. "Seriously? Do you think that will work?"

"It has to. You're way too exposed right now."

Laura contemplated the upcoming events for a few moments. "No, you're right. We need to stay together. The only thing that comes to mind is Stickers."

"Stickers?" Roberta replied. "What's that?"

"Stickers is Gavin's cat. It's at the house."

"I see. I don't think that will be a problem. After I get off the phone with you I'll make a quick call and make sure cat supplies are made available. Just tell Delta that Stickers needs to be picked up."

"Thank you so much Roberta, for everything."

"You hang in there Laura."

"I'm doing my best."

"Is there anything else you need?"

"What about Rebecca? We're just going to leave her here in the hospital?"

"Delta told me she's been placed in an induced coma."

"Yes, that's true."

"The best place for her is exactly where she's at Laura. I don't want to sound callous but your security team all knew the risks when they signed on with SANDBOX. Your family needs to be protected right now. Rebecca will be in good hands."

"I...I know. It's just all too much. I just can't believe that Whiskey's dead and Rebecca is in a coma all because of us. It's just not fair."

Roberta got stern. "You listen to me and hear what I'm about to say. There will be plenty of time for you to feel remorse for them. However, this is not that time. You need to focus and concentrate on getting your family to safety. After that, and only after that, you will allow yourself to grieve. You'll have plenty of time to think about anything and everything that transpired today, believe me. Laura, are we clear?"

Laura got a hold of herself and a small smile appeared on her lips. "You remind me of my mother Roberta. Thank you."

"Anytime Laura. Now, are you ready?"

"I am."

"Good. I'll talk to you again once you're all in the clear. Safe travels."

Laura slowly hung up the phone and closed her eyes. *I can do this.*

"Ma'am?"

She opened her eyes and turned towards Delta.

"We're nearly ready to go."

"Listen. I don't know who you're sending to our houses but Stickers needs to be picked up from my house, okay?"

Delta smiled. "Already ahead of you on that one. Oscar and Yankee have been briefed."

"Thank you. You've all been so wonderful to our families. I'm sorry about Whiskey. He..."

Delta put up his hand to stop her. "Another time. Right now we need to get everyone to safety. I need you to talk to Kim and Julie. Get them ready to go and make sure they do it quietly."

Laura nodded and then looked around again. "Have you seen..."

"I watched Gavin sneak into Rebecca's room. He's safe. Why don't you go prep them because once I give the signal to Mr. Smith we're going to be moving straight down the back corridor together. I'll go round up Gavin for you so we can get this show on the road, okay?"

"Thanks."

Laura headed over to Kim and Julie and started talking to them. Delta headed down the hallway towards Rebecca's room and stopped outside the observation glass. Inside Gavin had pulled a stool over to the bed and was standing on it. Both of his hands were on Rebecca's chest. Delta opened the door and startled him. He pulled his hands back.

"Hey bud," said Delta, "your mom's been looking for you."

"I just wanted to see Becca."

Delta walked over and joined Gavin. "She's tough. She's going to pull through and be just fine. However, you and I need to get ready to leave."

"So the bad men can't get us?"

"That's right. So the bad men can't get us."

"Can't Becca come with us?"

Delta knelt down on one knee so he was face to face with Gavin. "She needs time to rest so she can get better bud. You'll see her again soon enough."

"Promise?"

Delta smiled. "Yeah, I promise. Now, are you ready for an adventure?"

Gavin nodded.

"Good. Let's go find your mom and get everyone out of here."

He picked Gavin up and watched him wave goodbye to Rebecca on their way out of the room. Delta walked back to the waiting area and handed him off to Laura.

"And where did you run off to young man?" she asked her son.

"I wanted to see if I could help Becca."

Laura knew what that meant and immediately changed the subject. "I think we're ready."

Delta pulled his radio out and checked in. "This is Delta. Sitrep."

"We're good to go back here. Ready when you are."

"Roger that. We're one minute out." Delta turned to Mr. Smith. "Sir. You're up."

Mr. Smith nodded and stood up from his chair. He walked down the hallway to the outside door that was guarded by Oscar. Oscar let him out and then quickly closed the door behind him. The crowd of reporters surged when they caught sight of the lawyer stepping up to the podium.

"I have a statement to make on behalf of the families that were attacked earlier this morning."

He waited thirty seconds before he continued as additional reporters joined the group, cameras were readied and tape recorders were rapidly switched on.

"Earlier this morning a group of unknown men brazenly attacked my clients a few miles from here on North Kalaheo Ave.

54

Automatic gunfire erupted and the seven personnel from SANDBOX, who were assigned to my clients, immediately responded in kind to protect everyone trapped in the deadly crossfire, especially the small and innocent children traveling in those vehicles. During the firefight two members of the SANDBOX team were injured. One expired at the scene and the other has been placed in an induced coma. Currently the families are requesting that their privacy be adhered to during this obvious trying time for them. They are attempting to deal with this violent act the best that they can."

As Mr. Smith finished his statement numerous questions filled the air simultaneously.

"Do you know who the attackers are?"

"Can you confirm that the families attacked were the owners of SANDBOX themselves?"

"How many children were in the vehicles?"

"How did the Marines know to come to their aid?"

"What are the names of the two personnel that were injured and killed?"

Mr. Smith put his hands up to quiet down the crowd of reporters. "At this time I am not at liberty to discuss any additional particulars. My clients are traumatized, as you can imagine. I am, however, able to say that my clients are cooperating fully with local investigators. Thank you."

As Mr. Smith stepped back from the podium the reporters continued to badger him for new information. While he ignored them he looked over their heads and observed two vehicles exiting the parking lot. One held two men dressed in hospital scrubs. The other was a transport vehicle that the hospital used when it took elderly patients back and forth from their rest homes. The two vehicles separated at the stop light. The single passenger car headed north while the transport van headed south.

* * *

Delta looked in the side mirror for the first mile and didn't see anyone following them. He talked into his radio.

"We're clear."

"Ditto on this end," replied Oscar. "We'll rendezvous as soon as possible."

"Roger that. Out."

Delta spoke up to the families he, Foxtrot and Hotel had clandestinely escorted out of the hospital while Mr. Smith began his statement.

"You can all get up now."

Laura, Kim, Julie and the five children rose up off the floor and took seats in the large transport van.

"I don't like this," said Kim. "Why are we sneaking away?"

"Take it easy," Laura replied. "We don't know if there are more people out there that want to hurt us. The last thing we need to do is continue to advertise is exactly where we are, no thanks to the press."

"But the hospital was safe."

Laura shook her head. "I don't think anyone of us is going to feel safe for a while. Those men who attacked us, those men were coming to kill us in our homes. This is the only way we know for sure we'll be safe."

Kim didn't reply. Even Julie didn't have anything to say, but that hadn't really changed since she'd emerged from being looked at by Doctor Goodman.

"Sit back and relax," said Delta. "We'll be there sooner than you think as long as we don't run into any real traffic."

* * *

Oscar and Yankee wiggled out of their scrubs after leaving the hospital behind them. The station wagon they'd managed to 'borrow' might have enough space after they were done ransacking the three homes.

Oscar took a right and then a left onto South Kalaheo Ave. The plan was to approach the homes from the south and hopefully not run into anyone since the attack was half a mile north of the three properties. They arrived and parked across the street. After a full minute of observing the three houses they agreed they looked clear. Oscar backed the station wagon into Sam and Julie's driveway and they both stepped out.

Oscar and Yankee walked next door to Bill and Kim's house, let themselves inside and began to gather adult and children's clothing as quickly as they could. They took the luggage to the station wagon and placed it inside and then repeated the process at Sam's. The last house they entered was Thomas and Laura's. After scrounging up a variety of clothing they had two tasks left. One was to resupply their small arms from the hidden armory cache. After everything was packed in the car they headed back inside. Their second task was a little more daunting.

"Here kitty kitty," said Oscar.

"Seriously? The cat's name is Stickers," said Yankee.

"Yeah yeah. Sue me. Let's find the damn cat and get out of here. It hasn't been fed all day so where the hell is it?"

"Mew."

Both men stopped and listened.

"Mew."

Yankee bent down and looked under the low table in the foyer. Stickers had wedged himself underneath it.

"Hey Stickers."

"Mew."

"Get the carrier ready." Yankee reached for the cat. "Hey Stickers. Come on out will ya?"

"Mew."

Yankee grabbed hold of Stickers and gently pulled him clear of the foyer table. Surprisingly Stickers didn't put up any fight as Yankee placed him in the carrier Oscar was holding.

"Well that was easy," said Oscar.

"More so than the shit we've all been through today."

"Don't remind me. Let's lock this place up and head out."

"Give me a second," said Yankee. "I'll check the street and make sure we're still clear."

Yankee headed out the front door and out to the street. He looked around and finally gave the thumbs up to Oscar who brought Stickers outside with him and locked the door behind as he left. The two of them got into the station wagon and pulled out of the driveway heading south. Oscar pulled his radio out.

"This is Oscar. Nothing to report. We're inbound plus one."

"Roger that. Good job. We're waiting on you. Out," replied Delta.

* * *

Traffic was fairly non-existent for a Saturday evening so Delta made better time than expected. Roberta had been spot on with her directions as he pulled into the private residence and drove down the long driveway towards the estate. The property, like theirs, was directly on the water. The view was breathtaking.

"Is this where we're staying?" asked Kim as she looked out the van windows.

"Not exactly," Laura replied.

Delta drove past the large house and parked in the rear. Foxtrot and Hotel exited the van and began to scout the area.

58

"Well, if we're not staying in the house then what are we doing here?" Kim insisted.

Laura looked out the left window and pointed at a very large yacht moored just outside the breakwater in the distance and pointed.

"That's going to be our new home."

Delta's radio chirped and interrupted the moment. "We're clear out here."

"Roger that." He turned to the five children and three mothers. "We're going to head down to the dock together. Once we're there we'll board two boats that will take us out to the yacht. I hate to ask this but does anyone have a cell phone on them?"

Kim and Julie shook their heads. Laura spoke up. "I still have Rebecca's phone."

"I'll need it please."

Laura pulled it out of her pocket and gave it to Delta who pocketed it.

"Lets go."

Laura led Gavin by the hand down the front exit steps of the van and began to walk towards the dock. In the distance she could see two females, one in each boat that wore identical outfits. Laura surmised they must be part of the yacht's crew. Julie, Amanda and Craig exited next followed closely behind by Kim, Sarah and Edward. Behind them Foxtrot and Hotel appeared and watched the family's backs as they were helped aboard both small boats. They each joined them while Delta remained behind on the dock. He took off his tactical gear and weapons and handed them all over to Hotel. The only thing he kept was the radio.

"Aren't you coming?" Laura asked.

Delta nodded. "I'll be there shortly. I need to move the van and wait on the other two to arrive with the supplies from your houses."

She nodded. "Thank you."

"Don't mention it." He unhooked the ropes that held the two boats and tossed them onboard. "Cast off!"

The two boats revved their engines and slowly pulled off the dock and out towards the open water. Delta watched them go and then turned and headed up the hill to the van. He climbed in, started it up and drove back up the driveway. He hung a right and drove one mile down and parked it at a public beach. His radio came to life as he exited the van.

"This is Oscar. Nothing to report. We're inbound plus one."

"Roger that. Good job. We're waiting on you. Out," replied Delta.

He pocketed the radio and began to jog the mile back to the estate.

*   *   *

The yacht grew larger as the boat Laura was in slowly approached it. *Wow. That boat is big.*

Gavin tugged on his mother's pant leg. "Is this where we're going to live now?"

She reached down and picked him up. "For the time being we're going to be living on it. Is that okay?"

"Cool," he replied as he nodded.

Laura let a small smile appear again. *Maybe everything will work out.* On the side of the yacht she made out the words 'Slice of Heaven'. Her boat docked at the back of the yacht and the female who had piloted it secured the craft before helping the passengers out. Foxtrot exited first and secured the area. The female had remained quiet the entire time and still only smiled as she helped Laura, Gavin, Amanda and Craig off. Once the boat was empty the female reversed the process and pulled away from

60

the yacht and back towards the dock to make room for the trailing boat that contained Julie, Kim and her children. The second female then began the process of securing the boat back onboard the yacht. The children couldn't help but to watch in amazement.

A man wearing a captain's hat approached the group and spoke up.

"May I ask which one of you is Laura?"

Laura stepped towards him.

"If I may, I'd like to talk to you in private."

Laura nodded. "Give me a second." She turned to the two SANDBOX personnel. "What's the protocol now?"

"I'll start clearing the ship," said Hotel, "if Foxtrot wants to watch the group for the time being."

"Fine by me," Foxtrot responded.

"Thank you," replied Laura. She turned back to the captain. "I'm all yours."

The captain smiled and led her up one level via the rear stairwell. When they were alone he extended his right hand. "My name in Captain Bob."

She shook it. "Laura Clark."

"Very nice to meet you Mrs. Clark. Roberta gave me specific instructions and told me to go over them with you as soon as you boarded."

"Very well. Go on."

"Thank you. First off, welcome aboard. This yacht is new and just came off the assembly line. It's an Oceanco yacht at one hundred and sixty eight feet in length. It's an Accolade style with four levels, one master, four doubles and one twin room. On top of that we have many entertainment zones, a dining room, exercise room and other options for our guests. Slice of Heaven maxes out at eighteen knots per hour but her real cruising speed is around fifteen knots. Without stopping we have enough fuel to travel thirty five hundred miles. Secondly, Roberta insisted that the crew, which consists of myself, Ginger and Felicia, not engage any of you unless instructed otherwise. The three of us are cross-trained in everything from piloting, cooking and any emergencies that may arise. Although, if I may say so, it appears that Roberta wasn't kidding when she stated professional soldiers would be coming onboard. In any case, we've been paid to be very discrete and I assure you that's the kind of service you will receive."

"What else did she say?"

"We were a bit rushed but there is a fresh compliment of supplies that will last two weeks before we need to resupply. We have enough to stay out longer but, as you know, vegetables and fruits only last so long before going bad I'm afraid. As for sleeping quarters, additional cots were brought on board to make space for the extra people Roberta said would be joining us. And cat food and a litter box made it onboard during our final trip so no worries there."

Laura smiled. "Good. Anything else?"

"No, Mrs. Clark, I don't believe so. Our duties, as instructed, are to see to your daily needs and stay invisible. We will stay out in the ocean and on the move during the daytime as much as possible. If contacted via radio I have been told to reply with an entirely different story of who's on board. Your anonymity is my top priority and by the looks of things I don't want to know anything else. More to the point, Mrs. Clark, we've been well paid to keep our mouths shut and our eyes averted. With all that being said is there anything I can do for you?"

"Thank you for your candidness Captain. I'll let you know if we have any needs that aren't being met."

"Very well. Thank you for your business. We look forward to serving you." Captain Bob changed his stance and pointed towards the shore. "It looks like the rest of your group is on their way."

*   *   *

Delta made it back to the estate a few minutes before Oscar and Yankee arrived. Oscar backed the station wagon down by the dock and everything was unloaded. He then moved the vehicle to the estates garage where it would be picked up by someone else after they left and brought back to the hospital grounds. The local lawyer had seen to that part of the plan.

"Any problems?" inquired Delta.

Oscar and Yankee shook their heads. "Not unless you mean how uncomfortable it was to go through female underwear drawers."

Delta chuckled. "You'll live. Let's load this stuff and get onboard. Once we're on our way everyone's ordered to get some rack time, understand?"

"Roger that."

Delta continued. "We'll go through the plan of attack after we're all rested and thinking straight."

"No arguments from me."

"Looks like the precious cargo wasn't that hard to find," Delta said as he pointed at Stickers' pet carrier. "Gavin's going to have two new best friends because of it."

Oscar and Yankee smiled as they hauled the luggage to the awaiting boat. Once everything was onboard Ginger pulled away from the dock and made a heading towards 'Slice of Heaven'.

8

Sunday November 26, 1997 Middle of the Night Miami

The USS Seawolf briefly docked in Miami, Florida, just long enough to expel Sam, Bill and the other five SANDBOX operators from its belly before it disappeared into the night. Their wrists were secured as they were met by a contingent of CIA officers that were well armed and seemed to be looking for one of the seven men to start a fight. They were led to two windowless vans, placed inside and driven to an unknown location. When they arrived it was still too dark out for anyone to get a bearing on where they were other than it was somewhere in an industrial area.

One of the officers unlocked the door to the safe house facility and they were led inside. The seven operators hadn't said a word to their captives or each other since departing the submarine. However, during their underwater trip from Cuba to Miami they had all quietly conversed with each other and decided that their best course of action would be to wait for the exact moment they could break free.

Sam, Bill and the other five men stopped and looked around. The group had entered an enormous cement room that was devoid of any windows. Florescent lights littered the ceiling and shone down on seven military cots. At the back of the room they all immediately noticed that there was only one other exit and that was clearly marked as the latrines. A monitor hung on the wall protected by a metal grate with a video camera mounted directly above it.

"Find a cot and take a seat."

Still bound at their wrists, and under the watchful eyes of the other armed guards, they complied and each found a cot to sit on.

"So what now?" Sam probed indignantly.

"Hold that thought." The officer dialed a number on his satellite phone and waited for the connection. "We're ready here sir. No, no problems so far. Yes sir." He lowered the phone and the monitor on the wall blinked to life. Victor Bannon appeared on the screen.

"Good morning gentlemen. I hope it's not too early for all of you." A broad smile appeared on his face.

"Go to hell Bannon," Bill replied.

"Ah...Mr. Nicholson. It would appear the submarine trip hasn't dampened your spirits. Good, you'll need all your energy for the next task I need you for."

Sam spoke up. "I have to agree with my colleague here, go to hell."

"Now now Sam. You disappoint me. Clearly you couldn't follow my simple directions and bring Nikolay back from Cuba alive."

"That sonofabitch attacked our families and countless others have lost their lives because of him. My wife died because of him. He deserved to die."

"Yes, you're right Sam," replied the DCI as he completely skipped over the Nikolay issue. "My condolences on the loss of your wife, Julie. My apologies for not having said so earlier."

Sam stood up abruptly. "You lying piece of shit. You don't have the right to breathe her name."

Victor leaned into the camera. "Sit down before I have them put you down."

Sam hesitated a few seconds before he complied.

"Good. Now, just so you are up to speed, the playing field is different and the rules have drastically changed."

"What the fuck are you talking about?"

66

"Initially, I wanted Nikolay alive to mine his brain for delicious amounts of information he could provide me. However, you defied my orders and executed him. Tragic."

"And I'd do it again," Sam added.

"Nevertheless, as it turns out I apparently don't need him alive to get the answers I need. Nikolay's body was recovered shortly after your team was picked up and is on its way back to D.C. as we speak. Once there his corpse will cohabitate the same space as the rest of your families currently do."

"That's bullshit you fucking asshole!" exclaimed Bill.

"Temper, temper Mr. Nicholson. That's no way to treat the man who holds the future of your loved ones in his hands."

"You don't have them. There's no way."

"You're right of course. Thomas, Richard and Emily are my guests already. The rest of your family members are on their way to me as we speak."

"Impossible," said Sam. "You're lying."

"That's understandable. Here, why don't we watch the latest CNN report."

The face of Victor Bannon was replaced with an earlier recording from CNN. A man, dressed in a suit, had just stepped up to a podium. The caption beneath said this was all taking place at the Castle Medical Center on the island of Oahu.

"Earlier this morning a group of unknown men brazenly attacked my clients a few miles from here on North Kalaheo Ave. Automatic gunfire erupted and the seven personnel from SANDOX, who were assigned to my clients, immediately responded in kind to protect everyone trapped in deadly crossfire, especially the small and innocent children traveling in those vehicles. During the firefight two members of the SANDBOX team were injured. One expired at the scene and the other has been placed in an induced coma. Currently the families are requesting that their privacy be

adhered to during this obvious trying time for them. They are attempting to deal with this violent act the best that they can."

"Do you know who the attackers are?"

"Can you confirm that the families attacked were the owners of SANDBOX themselves?"

"How many children were in the vehicles?"

"How did the Marines know to come to their aid?"

"What are the names of the two personnel that were injured and killed?"

The lawyer put his hands up to quiet down the crowd of reporters. "At this time I am not at liberty to discuss any additional particulars. My clients are traumatized, as you can imagine. I am, however, able to say that my clients are cooperating fully with local investigators. Thank you."

That video clip faded and was replaced by a CNN reporter.

"That was a statement made by the family's lawyer, a Mr. Jerold Smith, a few hours ago. However, during that time a member of the hospital staff leaked the news that the family, and their protective detail, have suddenly vanished from the hospital grounds without a trace. We'll bring you more to this story in our next update."

Victor Bannon's face once again filled the monitor.

"So, like I said gentlemen, the rest of your family is on their way to me right now."

Sam and Bill shared a glance before turning back to look at the DCI.

"That report doesn't prove a thing. It could easily mean they got away on their own," Sam challenged.

"Oh, I agree wholeheartedly," replied the DCI. "That kind of positive thinking is what you should really hang on to right now, especially after I show you this."

The monitor dissolved and a still photograph of Thomas came into view. Behind him they could make out Emily strapped down to a table with medical equipment filling out the rest of the picture. Victor appeared once again.

"So you see gentlemen, I'm not bluffing. Your lives are mine to do with as I want. And you know why? It's because I hold all the leverage."

Sam and Bill remained silent.

"Now, let's take a quick step backward so I can finish my story. Nikolay's body will arrive and I'll be able to glean all the information from him that I want."

"You know he's dead, right?" said Bill.

"I think you know exactly where I'm going with this. I believe the two of you know 'exactly' what little Emily is capable of."

Sam and Bill exchanged a glance. *Oh fuck.*

"So here's the bottom line," Victor continued. "Your company, SANDBOX, will do a few jobs for me. Failure to comply will result in, well, I guess you don't need me to spell it out for you." Victor couldn't help but to watch Sam and Bill squirm on the other side of the camera. "Enjoy your stay and take this time to rest up. You're going to need it."

The monitor blinked off.

Shadows of the Heart

<u>9</u>

Sunday November 16, 1997 Crack of Dawn
Facility 13

The light hurts…but…but my eyes are closed.

"Her vitals are changing."

"Let's check in on our patient."

Patient? What does that mean? Where…where am I? Emily cracked open her eyes and the fluorescent lights quickly forced her to shut them.

"The lights hurt."

"You got it," she heard as a reply.

Ah, much better. She opened them again and slowly moved her head to look around. She saw two men, dressed in doctor attire, standing over her.

"How are you feeling?" one of them asked her.

"Thirsty," she squeaked back.

The other man disappeared from her sight but returned less than ten seconds later with a small paper cup. Emily tried to raise her arm to take it from him but she couldn't move. She lifted her head and looked down the length of her small body. *Why are my arms tied down?*

"Here, let me undo your arms," said the other man.

"I don't know if that's a good idea," the man with the cup said.

"I know what I'm doing," the first man insisted. He unclasped her left arm and then walked around to the other side and repeated the process for her right arm. Emily slowly sat up and accepted the cup of water that was handed to her. She started to sip it.

"Slowly…not too much at once," said the first man.

She finished off the small cup and handed it back to the second man. "May I have some more please?"

"Yes, of course."

The second man turned. As he started to walk away Emily suddenly grabbed the first man's exposed hand that still stood next to her bed. His eyes immediately glazed over.

"Where am I?" she demanded.

"A hidden medical bunker called Facility Thirteen in downtown Washington D.C."

"What the hell…" The second man turned around when he heard his colleague. He saw that she had a firm grip on his associate's hand. *Fuck.*

"Where's my daddy?"

"He's being held in a cell on the other side of the facility."

"I don't want to be here. Let me go."

He started to reach for Emily's leg restraints when a needle plunged into her neck from behind.

"NOOOOoooooo……" She couldn't control herself as she lay back down and her body began to relax. Her eyes fluttered and then closed. Her grip opened on the first man who snapped back to her senses. He moved away from Emily and the table.

"What in the hell just happened to me?"

"I believe we just saw exactly what we were warned about. Maybe you'll listen to me next time, eh?"

* * *

Victor Bannon turned in his office chair away from his monitor.

"Very interesting."

He hadn't gotten very much sleep, if any at all, these past few days. It didn't matter, he couldn't have slept anyway, certainly not with the endless possibilities that Emily could provide him.

The power of persuasion. The ability to make the dead appear. What won't I be able to accomplish when her powers are harnessed? And the son, Gavin. Bringing the dead back to life. Just amazing.

Victor stood up and walked around his office as his mind worked over everything. He stopped and stood still.

If both children have powers then it's logical to think they must have originated from either the mother or the father. I have the father. I wonder what secrets Thomas' body holds?

The private phone on his desk rang. Victor walked over and picked it up.

"Yes?"

"The family is gone sir."

"I know that already. I watched it on fucking CNN. Where did they go?"

"I don't know sir. They're just gone."

"Explain to me how a large group of people, and children, walk out of a hospital surrounded by reporters and medical staff. Start pressing people you moron. Somebody knows something."

"There's something else sir. There's one SANDBOX personnel left here. A Rebecca Cross. They still have her in an induced coma."

"Put a guard on her and find out where they all went." Victor slammed the phone down and then picked it back up. He dialed and waited for it to be picked up.

"Sir? What can I do for you this early in the morning?"

"If I'm awake then you can damn well be awake too Calvin."

"Yes sir. Sorry sir."

"The families eluded the mob of reporters and are no longer at the hospital in Oahu. I need you to covertly track down where they went, and more importantly, where they are right now."

"Yes sir."

Shadows of the Heart

10
Sunday November 16, 1997 Noon
Offshore Hawaii

A small tone emanated on all decks aboard 'Slice of Heaven'. Everyone had heard the same tone that morning and had wondered what it meant. Soon afterwards the smell of bacon, pancakes, and other delicious smells had invaded their senses. They all stumbled into the dining room tired and hungry. They'd all eaten in relative silence, attempting to regain their strength and come to terms with the fact that just the day before they'd nearly been killed. After breakfast some of them meandered around the ship while others drifted back to sleep in their beds.

And if breakfast was any indication of the quality of food and service they were going to expect, then it was no surprise when all five children beat their parents to the punch and arrived to lunch before they did. And lunch was not disappointing in the least. BLT's, cold sandwich meats and fresh fruit were available, along with an impressive dessert area that had ice cream, Oreo cookies, popcorn and assorted wrapped hard candies. Laura, Kim and Julie followed their children inside and watched as all five headed straight for the dessert buffet.

"Not too much you guys," said Kim as the three adults sat down at the table.

"Awh mom," replied Sarah.

"You'll be bouncing off the walls if you eat too much. You can have a couple of cookies but then come and eat some fruit."

"Mom, can I have some candy?" asked Amanda, Julie's daughter.

Julie didn't acknowledge the question.

"Maawwmmm," her daughter pleaded.

75

Laura placed her hand over Julie's to get her attention and Julie looked over. "Your daughter is asking you a question."

"Oh." She turned towards Amanda. "Go ahead. Whatever you want."

"Hey, that's not fair!" Sarah exclaimed. "Why does Amanda get to eat candy and I can't?"

"Don't start with me young lady," Kim retorted. "Get some real food and go sit down at the kid's table. We're not starting a scene."

Sarah pouted but let it drop. The kid's helped themselves to a variety of cheese and meat slices and ended up sharing it all together at the kid's table. Stickers followed Gavin wherever he went and when Gavin sat down Stickers begged for some meat.

Kim turned to her sister. "What is up with you? You can't just tell your daughter she can have candy like that."

"Who the hell are you to tell me what I can and can't do?" Julie snapped back.

Kim was shocked. "Cause...I'm...I'm your sister."

"So both of you keep reminding me. Listen 'sis', I don't remember you. I don't remember Laura. I don't remember a husband or those two kids over there. I'm not used to being called mom. I don't know what's going on and I don't like that feeling, okay?" Julie's tone softened a little. "Is that okay?" She sighed. "I look down and see that I have a ring on my finger which means I'm married...but I have no idea to whom, or even who that person is. I have two children that keep looking to me for comfort but when I hold them it's like I don't even know them. You asked 'what's up' with me and that's what's up with me. Who am I? Why don't you tell me what the hell happened and why we're on this boat?"

Laura watched the interaction and knew it was time to step in before Kim exploded with even more frustration, anger, concern and disbelief that Julie not only had amnesia but had been raised from the dead the previous day right in front of her eyes. *Oh yeah, this is going to be quite the challenge. Fun for me.*

"Kim?"

Kim turned her head slightly and looked over at Laura. "What?"

"Why don't you go grab some lunch and see what the kids are up to while I have a chat with your sister? I'll bring her up to speed and see if I can't jog her memory, okay?"

Kim got up from the table. "You do that. I don't know what's going on around here anyway. It's only our lives that have been turned upside down." Kim abruptly retreated outside and disappeared from view.

"What's her problem?" Julie asked.

"She's been through a lot. We all have."

"Is that why we're running?"

"That's one way of looking at it I suppose. Another way would be to look at this yacht as refuge. We need to keep our families safe and that's what we're doing."

"Safe from what? I just don't understand. You seem like a nice person Laura. Can you tell me why can't I remember what happened to us?"

Laura smiled. "Tell you what. Why don't we get some lunch and I'll try to explain just that?"

A few minutes later they were back at the table working on hand made sandwiches while they drank freshly squeezed guava juice.

"Do you want me to detail everything or just give you the condensed version?" Laura asked.

"Start with the short version if you don't mind. I'll stop you if I have any questions that need a further explanation."

"Fair enough. You have to realize that you and Kim have always been close. You're twins. You actually like to spend time with each other."

"That seems to have changed."

"I'll get to that part, but let me talk about the history between you two. You both met and fell in love with military men who, for all accounts, should have been brothers. You had a joint wedding eleven years ago and two years after that both of you had daughters, only two months apart. Nearly two years later, in ninety-two, each of your sons was born."

"How did you come into the picture?"

"My husband, Thomas, is best friends with your husband Sam, and Kim's husband Bill. They were the three musketeers growing up and have been through some rough shit together. Anyway, seven years ago Thomas and I met when he was a patient of mine."

"A patient? Are you a doctor or something?"

"Psychiatrist. Well, I was a practicing psychiatrist back in the days. Ever since I met Thomas my life has changed. We fell in love and had children of our own. But that's another story."

"So you're a shrink? Hmmm. Guess that's why it feels so easy to talk with you."

Laura smiled. "I'll take that as a compliment."

"I suppose the reality could be that we've never gotten along because you're still a complete stranger to me."

"Are you getting any inclinations about me one way or another?"

Julie shook her head. "No. I think I was just trying to lighten the mood with an attempt at a joke."

"Well, that's a good thing actually."

"Yeah?"

"It means you're more comfortable now than you have been. I mean, look at what you've seen. You woke up on the pavement with your sister hysterically blubbering all over you. We're surrounded by carnage, men with guns and crying children. You don't know who you are, who we are or what's going on. Now fast forward through the hospital and our trip to this yacht. The fact that you want to talk about what happened and can make a joke is a huge improvement."

"I guess. I just want to know who I am and the life I had."

"You mean the life you have. It's not gone. It's only been forgotten for the time being."

"If you say so. So what's so special about my husband?"

Laura finished off her guava. "Sam and Bill were Army Rangers. They met you and your sister at a bar one night and things just took off from there. Anyway, you were always the more forward of the two when it came to vocalizing that your man was always away and in harm's way. Long story short, Sam and Bill didn't re-enlist and instead worked on their idea for a new company."

"Company? What kind of company?"

"A private security company based out of Marin. The goal was to provide VIP security services to a select group of clientele. It started off small, with my husband's help, but grew larger and very reputable."

"What's the name of it?" Julie asked.

"SANDBOX."

"They named the company SANDBOX? That's a ridiculous name."

"It was in homage to their youth and the crap they went through. Anyway, each word in SANDBOX stands for something but I can't remember what they are at the moment."

"Okay, so let me get this straight. I'm the reason my husband left the military and started a private protection company?"

"More or less."

"And he was okay with that?"

And down the rabbit hole we go. "For the most part. You have to understand that SANDBOX had become their baby, Sam and Bill's baby that is. As the company grew he was away more and more and took jobs that placed him in potential danger. You were silent about it for a long time but earlier this year you made sure he knew exactly how you felt. You told him he was never around and that you waited by the phone for that inevitable phone call. Things came to a head when there was an incident..."

Julie leaned forward. "What do you mean by 'an incident'?"

"Okay, sorry. I'll be more specific. There was a firefight back in Marin. Sam and Bill were shot."

"Shot? Seriously? But I don't understand. You said we used to live in Marin. Why would they be involved in a gun battle so close to home?"

Laura had a quick flashback before she squeezed her eyes shut. Julie caught it immediately.

"Oh crap. What did I say?"

Laura composed herself. "It's okay Julie. Everything's happened so quickly this year that all the scars haven't had time to heal. The attack. Our move to Hawaii. Thomas' father and his crazy history. And now the blatant attack on our family."

"You don't have to talk about it."

"The funny thing is that you already know all about this."

Julie paused for a few seconds. "Maybe you should tell me again. I seem to have this problem with remembering things lately."

Laura cracked a grin. "Cute. You got me there." But then her smile faded. "The reality is that our husbands were all being shot at because my children had been kidnapped."

"Kidnapped? Oh my God, that's horrible."

"It was."

"But why your kids? Were they after money or something?"

"Or something is absolutely right. The fact is…you only recently found out about our biggest secret."

Julie leaned in yet again. "Secret?"

Laura let out a huge breath. *And the rabbit hole doesn't seem to have a bottom.* "My children have special gifts."

"Gifts? What do you mean?"

"They have…powers."

"I still don't know what that means. You're just messing with me now, right?"

Laura shook her head. "I assure you I'm not. You learned all about this a couple of weeks ago. And it was quite a shock to your system."

"I see. Okay. I don't necessarily believe you but I'll go with it. I don't have anything to lose at this point and apparently we've already been down this road together. Explain it to me."

Laura looked Julie straight in the eyes. *Oh what the hell.* "Emily, my daughter, can summon people that are no longer with us anymore. On top of that, if she holds on to a part of someone's body, she can make them think, do or tell her anything."

"And you're being completely serious with me right now?"

"Yes."

Julie chewed on that for a bit. "Alright. And what about your son? What can he do?"

"We thought Gavin had only the one ability. It's just until very recently, yesterday to be exact, that we experienced his second one first hand. Although technically it's his third power now that I think about it."

"What's his first ability? Is this something you can have him show me?"

"You sound skeptical."

81

"A little I'll admit. I'm actually intrigued at this point. I mean, this all sounds a bit 'Star Trek'ish', if you know what I mean."

"Oh, I hear you there. We're alone, and the kids know about this, so it should be safe to show you."

"The kids know?"

"And Kim knows. You both found out at the same time."

"And our husbands?"

Laura nodded. "They've known for a while."

"And my husband didn't tell me? I'm guessing I didn't take that very well."

Laura smiled. "No, not so much. Anyway, you ready for the demonstration?"

"Sure. Wow me."

"Gavin. Sweetie."

Gavin looked over from the kid's table.

"Come over here please."

He scooted his chair out and made his way over to his mother. Stickers, who had been curled up on the floor, got up and followed Gavin to the main table and lay back down. Laura picked her son up and placed him on her lap.

"Julie, this is Gavin."

"Hi Gavin."

"Hi. You remember me?"

Julie was taken aback. "What? I...no. I'm afraid I don't."

"Oh," he replied. "That's not good."

"Why's that?" she asked.

"It was my first time. I only wanted to help you. I didn't mean for it to happen."

"What's he talking about?"

"It's okay Gav," said Laura. "You did a good thing. Julie's not mad at you and neither am I."

"Auntie Kim is."

"No. No, she's not mad at you."

"But she yells a lot," he insisted.

"She's confused and hurt. She'll come around."

Gavin shrugged. "I hope so."

"Anyway sweetie. Would you mind bringing Stir out so Aunt Julie can see him?"

"Really?"

Laura nodded. "He's still our secret so what I said last night about no one else finding out about your powers on this ship still goes. Just bring him out for a little bit right now, okay?"

"Okay! I know Stickers has missed him and so have I."

Julie looked confused. "What's a Stir?"

Laura took Gavin off her lap. "Stir is the name of his imaginary pet. It's short for 'Monster'."

"You just said it's imaginary."

"Well, we used to think it was. You'll see." She turned to her son. "Okay sweetie."

Gavin stepped back and stood next to Stickers. He looked up at his aunt before he did anything. "Promise you won't be scared?"

Julie wasn't prepared for that. "What? What does that mean?"

Laura put a hand over hers. "Just don't scream, okay?"

"Okay I gu…"

Julie's words stuck in her throat. Out of nowhere a small black and wispy creature appeared on the floor next to Stickers.

What the hell is that? Where the hell did it come from? What is going on?

Stickers and Stir immediately began to preen each other. The kids at the other table saw him appear and got up from their own chairs.

"Stir!"

"Oh cool, it's Stir!"

They ran over and joined the group on the floor. Julie watched in horror as they began to pet both the cat and the creature with red eyes. But not one of the children displayed an ounce of fear and Julie soon overcame her own as she knelt down and joined them.

"May I...um...touch it...him?"

Gavin nodded. "You're not scared Aunt Julie?"

"A little."

"It's okay mom," said Craig. "Stir's cool."

"Yeah mom," added Amanda, "he's awesome."

"Well, okay then," said Julie. "What do I do?"

Laura watched on as Gavin gently took Julie's hand and brushed it over Stir's back, who began to purr. She watched as a smile formed on Julie's face.

"He purred!"

"Uh huh. He likes you."

Tears formed in the corners of Julie's eyes but she forced them back. *This is amazing. I've never felt anything like him before. It's like soft smoke but it's tangible. It's just amazing.*

The sliding glass door opened suddenly and everyone snapped their head up to see which person had just walked in on them. Thankfully, it was only Kim and they hadn't blown their secret with a member of the crew. Kim had a stern look on her face.

"Hey sis," said Julie. "I'm glad you came back."

Kim's face loosened up. "Wait...what? You are?" Kim closed the door behind her.

"Come over here. Have you petted Stir yet?"

It was then that Kim noticed the small black animal amidst the gaggle of bodies on the floor.

"I was beginning to wonder what the fuss on the ground was all about." Kim joined in, petted Stir and Stickers and then gave each of her kids a hug.

Julie stood up and retook her seat at the table. Kim did the same.

"Can we please play with him some more?" Gavin asked.

The rest of the children joined in. "Pllleaaassse?"

"Just be careful. If anyone comes around he needs to go away immediately. Okay?"

"Promise."

"Okay then. Have fun."

Five children and two animals headed back over to the small kid's table area. It wasn't long before both animals were knee deep in lavished attention.

Julie looked over at Kim. "Listen. I might not know you right now, because of my memory problem, but I'm glad you're my sister. Laura's been filling me in on the highlights and it sounds like we've always been there for each other."

Kim gave her sister an odd look. "You're sure there isn't alcohol in that juice you're drinking?"

"What?"

Kim relaxed. "I'm just joking with you sis."

"Oh."

"Listen. I came back because I wanted to apologize to both of you. I've been a complete jackass."

"Everyone handles stressful situations differently," said Laura. "This situation has been tough on everyone."

"I wish I could handle it more like you. You're a rock."

"Hardly," Laura replied. "I'm a complete mess on the inside."

"Bullshit. You took control of the situation and got us all to safety. I lost my fucking mind, much like my sister here." Kim cracked a grin. Julie and Laura couldn't help but smile.

"Overall I did what I had to, that's all."

"Well I just wanted to thank you. I felt like everything was suddenly taken away from me all at once."

"Are you talking about the attack on the family yesterday?" Julie asked.

"You remember it?" Kim inquired.

"No actually. Laura hadn't gotten to that part yet. I take that it was bad?"

"Goddamn horrible if you ask me," Kim replied. "I'm going to have nightmares for a long time."

"You sure you want to talk about this?" Laura probed.

"I dunno. I was walking around on the decks all pissed off at the world. But then I realized I'd been directing it at you rather than at the assholes that attacked us. So yeah, I think we should talk about it."

The trio was silent for a few seconds before Julie spoke up.

"So…um…what happened? Did I get hurt or something? Why can't I remember anything?"

"Maybe I should start," said Laura. "Sam, Bill, Thomas, Emily and Michael were away in Washington D.C. working on a case, for lack of better words."

"Wait. Who's Michael?" Julie asked.

"That's Thomas' dead father," Kim answered.

"Dead father? You mean…and Emily used her powers…"

"Exactly," Laura confirmed. "Anyway, they're away and we're here. Thomas and I talk all the time until I stopped receiving his phone calls. Then, yesterday morning the phone rings and Thomas frantically tells me to get out of the house. I immediately alerted the security personnel and we rushed to get the hell out."

"It was insane," Kim added. "We were roused and told to get dressed right away."

"We loaded everyone into three Suburban's and headed off north towards the Marine Base as instructed. A half mile up the road four vans bore down on us. Two pulled around us and cut off our escape while the other two blocked the road in front of us. It seemed that before we could do anything our vehicles were being rocked with automatic weapon's fire."

"The kids were screaming. I was screaming. I couldn't think straight. It was chaos."

"What did I do?" Julie asked.

"It looked like you got pissed off," said Laura.

"Pissed off? I don't understand."

"You and I were both armed with Glock seventeen nine millimeter hand guns. All of us had been taught how to use them. Quite frankly, I saw you exit the vehicle and move towards the danger with a purpose."

"Shut up. That doesn't sound like me."

"I screamed for you but you didn't hear me. Before I knew it I heard two pistol shots from your direction. Right after that I had a bad guy appear around my side of the car and I continually pulled my trigger until the bastard fell down."

"You...you killed someone?" Julie asked.

"Shot him dead just like you did to the other guy."

"You're saying that I killed someone?"

Laura nodded.

"I don't remember any of this."

"I wouldn't expect you to."

"Why's that?"

"Well....because you died yesterday."

Julie's mouth hung open. "Come again?"

"I heard the assault rifle shots. Stir took off like a bat out of hell and then everything stopped."

"Stir? We're talking about the cute little imaginary animal, right?"

"Let's just say he's not so cute when he needs to be," said Laura.

"Oh." Julie paused. "So back to the part where I died then. What the hell are you talking about?"

"It's true," said Kim. "Laura knew you were dead and tried to stop me from seeing you just lying there on the pavement. I…I remember how much I begged you to wake up….but you wouldn't listen."

Julie looked back and forth between Laura and her sister. "You two are absolutely serious."

They both nodded.

"I was shot…"

"Twice in the chest," said Laura.

"So I was shot, in the chest, and died. Is that what you're telling me?"

They nodded again.

Julie didn't know where to begin. "So how am I even talking to you two right now if I'm so dead?"

"And that's the question of the year," said Laura. "Remember when I said that my son has a second power we weren't aware of until yesterday?"

"I do."

"Well…here you are."

The seconds ticked by as Julie worked that thought through her head. "Really?"

"I don't know what I saw sis," Kim blurted, "but Gavin screamed and scared the shit out of me. He put both hands on your chest. Suddenly there was this shimmering portal thingy that came out of the ground and he walked through it."

"Come on."

"I'm not lying to you. I'd never seen anything like it before, ever. After he went through he reappeared holding something's hand."

"What do you mean…something?"

"It looked like a ghost form," Laura added. "Corporeal. Floating."

"Yes, exactly. The damn thing floated and settled down over your body."

"It just settled over my body, just like that?" Julie was credulous.

"I couldn't make this shit up if I wanted to, okay? Cut me some slack."

"Easy everyone," said Laura. "Let's keep our voices down."

"Then what?" Julie asked.

"What do you mean, then what? You fucking popped up like a damn spring."

"Shit," Julie said softly.

"What?"

"I remember that part. You were hysterical and all over me. I didn't know where I was or who was around me."

"Whatever happened to you, and whatever my son did to bring you back, it has to have something, if not everything, to do with your amnesia."

Julie placed her hand on her t-shirt. "It's weird. When I took a shower this morning I didn't have any pain or and scars on my chest. I don't feel any different."

"But you have changed sis."

"How so?"

"Well, aside from the obvious memory loss there is one significant alteration."

"What's that?"

"What color are your eyes?"

"They're brown," was Julie's instant answer.

Kim nodded. "You're right. They should be brown, just like your twin sister's."

"You're saying they're not?"

"Get up and look in the bar mirror."

Julie hesitated before she got out of her chair and walked over to the bar. She leaned in close and stared at her own face. What she remembered didn't add up. Her eyes were pitch black now. *What the hell?* She pulled herself away and rejoined them at the table.

"I don't understand."

"Welcome to the club sis."

"Don't worry," said Laura. "We're going to get to the bottom of this. The first thing I had to do was get us all safe. Now that that's happened we can concentrate on you and the wellbeing of our children."

"Sonofabitch. This is all starting to really sink in now."

"Weird, right?"

"Very. But I haven't heard the part of the story about what our husbands were doing at the time."

Laura didn't want to think about that. The unknown was always worse because the mind could and would play awful tricks on her.

"Rebecca's phone was on. Thomas....Thomas told me he and Emily were being held hostage."

"What!? You didn't tell me that part," said Kim.

A tear began to roll down Laura' face. "How could I? You were so out of it and needed my help. What else could I do? I had to stay strong."

Kim grabbed Laura's hands. "I'm so sorry. We're going to get them back. Bill and Sam will rescue them, right?"

"I just want my family back together. I don't even know where Sam and Bill are right now."

"They'll come through," Kim insisted. "They always do."

11
Sunday November 16, 1997 Late Evening
D.C.

The rules they'd been informed of were very simple; don't ever cross the white line. The single door that led in and out of their holding area had a broad white line painted on the floor ten feet beyond it. Cameras watched the men from multiple angles as a group of armed guards removed the remnants of the evening meal without incident. The guards retreated and the exterior locks loudly engaged once again, and left the seven men alone.

Sam, Bill, Alpha One, Alpha Two, Bravo One, Charlie One and Charlie Two had just finished up their evening meal, which had been surprisingly delicious. And even though they were 'guests' of Victor Bannon, and his security detail, they had all been treated with respect, provided they didn't cause any problems.

Everyone had crashed out ever since their arrival earlier in the day. There was nothing they could do at the moment other than to conserve their strength and wait for an opportunity to present itself. Besides that, the team of men had been on the go since Cuba with very little rest. During the submarine ride to Miami they had talked amongst themselves. But so far they hadn't been presented with a method to escape yet. That was even more difficult after Victor's heartwarming welcome message about having their families under his thumb.

The group had been woken up around noon and eaten lunch. Store bought sandwiches, but freshly made. They ate two each. After that they quickly determined that even though they were under surveillance they couldn't locate any audio devices. However, not taking anything for granted, all of their conversations had been held facing away from any camera, conducted at a low volume and with hands covering their mouths. The rest of the afternoon and evening had been spent exercising, showering, and conserving energy as they tried to stay positive.

After dinner Sam and Bill broke off from the rest of the men to talk in private.

"What the fuck are we going to do Sam? This is bullshit." Bill forced out from behind his hand.

"I know brother. This isn't right on so many levels. Holding us here is illegal as hell," Sam replied from behind his own hand.

"I've been thinking about what his game plan is."

"Me too," Sam added.

"And all the outcomes don't favor us whatsoever."

"Tell me about it. If he's indeed stumbled onto Emily and Gavin's powers then we're unnecessary witnesses."

"Expendable," said Bill.

"Exactly, which is why we should be very concerned about what 'jobs' he wants us to do."

"So we're playing along then?"

Sam gave Bill a 'what do you think' look.

"Okay, okay," Bill replied. "I know what's at stake here, I just had to make sure we're on the same page."

"It doesn't mean I like it Bill."

"You're preaching to the choir. I will tell you one thing, that fucker has got to pay, one way or another."

"No shit. And he's got to be counting on that, and you know what that means."

"Indeed. When you think you're safe double check to actually make sure you really are. Bullets aren't the only thing that can kill you."

"Bingo."

Bill shifted his feet. "What do you think he'll do to our families?"

"I don't know. He could be bluffing. We only saw a picture of Thomas and Emily."

"And if he's not bluffing?"

"I don't want to think about it. It's our job to protect them and we're failing at that every second we're sitting in this fucking place."

Bill balled his other hand into a fist. "Not knowing is the worst. If he's hurt Kim or my kids, so help me."

Sam's eyes told a different story. "At least you have a wife."

"Dude. Stop. That's not what I meant and you know it."

"I'm...I'm sorry. Part of me can't stop thinking about it. My Julie. My Julie is dead." Sam put his back against the wall and slide down to the floor.

"Come on man...snap the fuck out of it. This isn't the time or the place. We all need you to be strong right now. I need you to be strong right now."

"I don't..."

"Fuck that shit, Sam. Turn that despair into rage. You've already killed Nikolay so think about what you're going to do to Victor. We need to plan this shit together, just like the old days."

Sam met Bill's eyes.

"That's it brother, Bill pushed. "Fight it back and let's do this shit together."

Sam held out an arm and Bill grabbed it to help him up. Sam leaned in close to Bill's ear and whispered.

"This shit's going to get ugly."

Bill smiled. "And that's when we do our best work."

12
Monday November 17, 1997 Early Morning
D.C.

Victor Bannon had an early appointment with the President of the United States, Bill Clinton. He knew that the President was going to not only inquire about the recent Cuban activities, but whether or not the United States' ass was properly covered. The DCI knew that he'd come out looking like a hero one way or another to the President because he held all the cards.

Victor's car passed the outer White House gate's security check and his driver proceeded up to the door. The driver parked, got out, and opened the back door for the DCI, who then made his way up the stairs as he'd done numerous times before. He didn't have to wait long before the President had him admitted into the Oval Office.

"Good morning, Mr. President."

"Morning Victor. How's my Director of the Central Intelligence Agency today?"

"Just fine sir, thank you for asking."

President Clinton paced a little. "Good to hear. Now, why don't you have a seat and tell me exactly why I woke up to Castro blaming the U.S. for invading their country?"

Victor did as he was told and sat down on one of the couches. "Your sources are better than mine Mr. President."

Clinton waved his hand in dismissal and sat down on the opposite couch. "Don't give me that shit. You have the same sources. Let me be clear. You assured me this operation was in and out. Clean and simple."

"Mr. President. I'll be frank. We're clean."

"Then why is Fidel screaming that American soldiers invaded his country?"

"He has to scream at someone. He's guessing, so it makes sense to blame America, sir. Let me break down the mission for you. The seven man team was inserted via parachute from a known commercial flight path. Radar will show that no aircraft passed over Cuba. The team splashed down on the southwest side of the island and proceeded to their target on foot. Once they reached their objective they surgically began to eliminate enemy combatants. Now, those enemies were Russian ex-military and KGB, not Cuban. Once the element of surprise was lost a firefight broke out. In the end all the Russian combatants were killed, including our primary target, Nikolay Dmitriev. There were no team casualties."

"How was he killed?"

"He died by a self-inflicted gunshot to the head, sir," the DCI lied.

"Damn. And all that information we needed went with him."

"For the moment, yes sir. There was minimal time to stop and collect any additional information onsite I'm afraid. The team had to evacuate the location in order to make their pickup rendezvous."

"I see. So the United States hasn't been implicated in this whatsoever?"

"I don't see how we could be sir. For all intent and purpose Nikolay's compound could have been attacked by anyone, even Castro. We have complete and plausible deniability"

"Well, that's good news indeed. It sounds like this country owes you a debt of gratitude for what you've done. Taking down that murdering sonofabitch is all I care about. I'll make sure the proper credit is added to your file."

"Yes sir, thank you sir."

"So what do I tell the American people? Nikolay is responsible for masterminding the bombings that took so many American lives. The country needs to be reassured that these acts of terrorism have come to an end."

"I agree. However, without the ability to interrogate, I mean question, Nikolay on the remaining cells in existence, we can only speculate that these horrific events are going to stop. By cutting off the head of the snake, so to speak, the ability to communicate plans and activation codes has been thwarted. In that same breath, I think it's time I step back and let the FBI take over. My work is done."

"So you just want to take the credit and run, is that what I'm hearing Victor?"

"In a manner of speaking Mr. President. The CIA isn't mandated to operate on US soil. I'm merely handing off the responsibility to the appropriate agency. But here's an idea. Why not leak to the press that the head of the terrorist organization has been captured by the FBI? In the name of national security the identity of that terrorist will remain classified. However, the FBI is confident that additional attacks will not occur. In the same breath the FBI Director can take credit, while at the same time take future responsibility for any terrorist actions while his people run down the sleeper cells."

The President smiled. "You have the heart of a politician."

"I do what I can sir."

"Very well. I have another request for you."

"Sir?"

"I'd like to personally meet the men who took down this threat to our country. I need you to arrange that."

Shit. "I'll pass your thanks along sir. However, those men have already been tasked with another mission."

"I see. No rest for the wicked. They must be a tough group of men."

"Yes sir. That they are."

"Very well. At some point in the future then."

"Absolutely sir."

The President stood up and the DCI followed suit.

"Is there anything else you have to report?"

"No sir."

"Until next time, Victor."

"Yes sir, Mr. President. Have a good day sir."

<u>13</u>
Monday November 17, 1997 Early Morning
D.C.

On the outskirts of D.C., in a quiet neighborhood, James Pearlman and Charles Hillburg had already been up hard at work since six that morning. For the most part they worked from home unless they were called into the office, or a remote location, to work their magic. Computer equipment of various sizes littered the main room of the house. Data and electrical cables were painstakingly cable-tied and accentuated the analness of the environment they loved to work in. They had their workstations situated on either side of the room as to not crowd each other. The two had been concentrating on their current task ever since the order was given. It was 'the' priority.

Charles's hands paused on the keyboard he was using. "Hey, Calvin."

"What?" James replied.

"Are we doing the right thing?"

Calvin stopped what he was doing and swiveled in his chair to look at Charles. "Hobbes, whatever you do…do not go pussy on me now."

"I'm just saying. This doesn't feel right at all."

"Listen to me. We work for the U.S. government. We're the good guys."

"You could have fooled me," Hobbes replied.

"We're knee deep in this and you know it. Right and wrong doesn't even compute anymore."

Hobbes didn't let up. "I can't stop thinking about Curtis. He got shot right in front of us."

"So what?" Calvin retorted. "You really want to get on the bad side of the Director? You'll end up buried in some unmarked grave faster than you can imagine. You need to get on board with all of this Hobbes." He paused. "Just think about it. We're going to be rich. Let the Director have his power, I just want the money."

"But that girl...Emily. She's so young. I..."

"Shut the fuck up already."

That started Hobbes. "Wha..."

"Shut the fuck up Hobbes!"

Charles closed his mouth.

"Now listen to what I'm about to tell you. Are you listening? Do I sincerely have your attention?"

Hobbes nodded.

"Good. It's too late to get a conscious about this. Flat out, it's just too damn late. You know how the Director gets. I don't want to admit it but we might not make it out of this thing alive. And you know what, that scares the hell out of me. I want my money and to get out. You should want the same thing. Let's just do our fucking job and pray he doesn't view us as expendable, that is, unless you have a better idea?"

Hobbes slowly shook his head.

"Yeah, well shit, neither do I right now." Calvin turned back around. "Now back to business. What do you have on our friends in California?"

Hobbes went back to his monitors. *This sucks.* "I've traced a call from SANDBOX to the hospital. External security cameras have them leaving in two hospital vehicles, which is probably why it wasn't noticed before. I initially followed their progress via traffic cameras but they split up and I lost them both. There aren't too many cameras where they're at."

"Good work and welcome back to reality. What about utilizing the satellite we had overhead?"

"No can do. That bird continued its orbit and was out of range long before they left the hospital. I couldn't locate another eye in the sky during the window we're looking at."

"Shit. Okay. I'll see what I can dig up by backlogging all calls made by SANDBOX during the time the families were all at the hospital. Right now that looks like our only lead, and trust me when I say we'd better come up with something for 'him'."

"I still don't like this," Hobbes whispered.

"I heard that bro. Please stop with that shit or I might end up just killing you myself and save the DCI the trouble."

Shadows of the Heart

14
Monday November 17, 1997 Late Morning
D.C.

Emily slowly opened her eyes. The light above her was bright and she blinked a few times to try and clear her vision. Remnants of sleep filled the corners of her eyes and she instinctively moved her hand to her face only to fall well short of her goal. *What's pinching my arms?* Emily raised her head ever so slightly and looked down her body. Not only were the leather braces that held her arms secured still there, but she saw new additions as well. Tubes ran in and out of both her arms, right above the elbow. She watched as blood pumped out of her right arm, into a machine and then back into her left arm. It didn't feel very good and Emily began to cry.

"Ahh, I see that you're awake."

She turned her head towards the voice as a man approached her bed. She'd never seen him before. He was older and of Japanese descent. She could still see two other men working behind him.

"Who...who are you?" she asked while her tears fell.

"And a good morning to you too, Emily. How are you feeling?"

"It hurts," she whimpered.

His face turned sympathetic. "I understand but I'm afraid it's necessary."

"Why?"

He smiled and pointed a finger at her. "Because you're a very special young lady. I'm here to figure out exactly how to replicate that. And to do that I need to take tests."

"I don't understand. Please make it stop." A large tear formed and raced down the side of her face. "Please."

The man ignored her pleas and began to inspect the connections on her arm. She could only watch him work.

"Please. I want my daddy."

The man stopped and looked at his watch. "You're right. It's time to visit with your father. Thank you for the reminder." He got up and abruptly left the room.

* * *

Thomas and Richard had shared the same detention room ever since the talk with Victor Bannon. Food trays had come and gone many times over the past two days. Rage fueled tirades mixed with extended emotional episodes had filled Thomas's time. Richard tried to keep Thomas focused and calm but it was becoming more difficult with each passing hour.

Thomas sat with his head in his hands when the cell lock clanked and the door swung outward. Richard swung his legs off the cot and onto the floor. Thomas looked up as two guards entered their room and took flanking positions on either side of the door.

One of them immediately spoke up. "Remain seated. Any overt movements will result in punishment."

A few moments later someone they'd never seen before entered the small cell.

"Good morning gentlemen. My name is Yamato Takuma Matsushita."

"What's this, the Director doesn't have time for us anymore?" Richard chided.

Yamato took it in stride. "You know how it is. The Director can't be everywhere at once. Now, as I asked young Emily this morning, how are you feeling?"

Thomas shot to his feet and pointed a finger. "Where's my daughter!?"

One of the large guards was already in motion. He reached Thomas and with his left hand grabbed him by the throat. He then used his right hand and forcefully bent one of Thomas' arms behind him.

"Ouch! Dammit, you're hurting me!"

"Leave him alone!" Richard cried out. "What the hell is going on here?"

"Calm down everyone," said Yamato. "I'm afraid we've gotten off to a bad start." He motioned to the guard to relax his grip a bit. "Thomas, do I have your attention now?"

"Yes," Thomas hissed.

Yamato smiled. "Good. Very good. To answer your question, your daughter is just fine. In fact, I just came from chatting with her. She wants to see you."

Thomas struggled with the guard's hard and unrelenting grip to no avail. "I want to see her too."

"I'm sure you do. But before I can allow that I need to know more about you and your family's history. You see, I'm in agreement with the Director. He and I have come to the conclusion that something extraordinary must have happened to you or to your wife that would allow two mutations into this world. I need to know what that is."

"I have no idea what you're talking about."

Yamato grinned. "I may be old but I assure you that I'm very good at what I do Thomas. You see, I use unorthodox methods to get the job done. I'm genuinely intrigued with you and can't wait to get started with this project."

"I'm not going to tell you a Goddamn thing."

"Oh? You'll find that that's where you're quite mistaken."

Yamato turned and exited the room. The guard holding Thomas began to force him out of the room when Richard jumped on his back and put an arm around his thick neck.

"Get this idiot off me."

The second guard moved in, plucked the elderly man off the first guard's neck in no time whatsoever and literally tossed him across the room and into the far wall. Richard's right shoulder took the brunt of the impact as he slumped to the floor in tremendous pain.

"I warned you old man," the second guard said.

Richard could only watch as Thomas was led out and the cell door closed and locked behind them.

Thomas' arm was practically numb as he was marched to a room with a metal chair. It looked like something out of a dentist horror movie with the addition of the restraints attached to the table. *Oh shit oh shit oh shit. This can't be good.* Yamato followed the two guards into the new room.

"Go ahead and release him."

The death grip around his neck was removed and his right arm swung down by his side. As the blood rushed back in Thomas gritted through the pins and needles. The two guards remained right next to him as Yamato walked in and sat in his own chair that was situated next to the metal dentist's chair. Thomas could only watch.

"Have a seat."

"I don't think so."

"I'll be as candid as I can be with you. I understand your reluctance but time is not on our side. You can either sit down or I can have them make you."

In Yamato's eyes Thomas could see that he hoped he'd resist.

D.W. Neuman

Fucking psycho. "Fine." Thomas relented as he walked over and sat down.

"Lie back."

Thomas hesitated for a few seconds before a guard took a step towards him. Thomas lay back. Yamato stood up and secured the four restraints before he sat back down.

"You can leave." The guards exited the room leaving them alone. "Now that we have some privacy I can fill you in on what the plan is. I've been instructed to expedite this process. So you'll understand when I don't ask you the same question three times and then use your daughter as leverage to force you to talk. It's not worth my effort, my time or the headache it would give me."

"You really like to talk a lot, you know that."

"Indeed I do, Thomas. And that's one thing we'll have in common very shortly. As I was saying, I'm going to go right to the drugs to bypass all the bullshit."

Yamato made a motion and the door to the room cracked back open. Thomas looked over as one of the doctor's came in with a tray of syringes and put it down.

"Thank you."

The doctor left and all Thomas could do was stare at the tray. Sweat began to form on his brow. Yamato picked one of them up, removed the protective cap and depressed the plunger ever so slightly until some of the liquid squirted out the top.

"Now, this will sting a bit as it works its way through your system."

Thomas's eyes widened as he struggled to escape from the needle that descended towards his upper arm, but there was nowhere to go and it found its mark. He could feel the warmth start to spread. His heart began to pump the cocktail throughout his system.

"This is what I want you to concentrate on Thomas. I want to know about your childhood, your parents, your schools, the books you've written. In essence Thomas, I want your entire life history."

Thomas started to get fuzzy. "Eat shiiit."

"You can't resist Thomas. This concoction I invented myself."

What the hell? Why would he...?

Thomas opened and closed his mouth like a fish while Yamato checked his watch.

"It'll take effect any time now."

"Why?" Thomas asked.

Yamato leaned over. "Why what Thomas?"

"Why tell me your name?"

Yamato grinned. "Why not?"

Thomas' eyes darted back and forth and then closed halfway. "You....you told....you told us because there's no reason not to. It means....means...we're never.....leaving...." Thomas' eyes closed.

"Relax now. I'll know everything I need to know very shortly."

15

Tuesday November 18, 1997 Early Morning
Miami

For the past day and a half the seven member SANDBOX team had had nothing better to do than sit around and wait. The only upside to their incarceration was that they had been able to rest. Unfortunately, the obvious downside was that they had nothing better to do but to stew. Bill had kept a constant watch over Sam and continued to lend his shoulder to his best friend. The men had just finished their breakfast when Sam cracked a smile. Bill caught it.

"Something funny I should know about?"

Sam cocked his head at his friend. "Not really. It's just a flashback."

"Do tell. It's not like there's anything better to do while we wait."

"Okay. Remember that time we came back from the mission in South America and went out to the bar in Walnut Creek to talk more about our business venture?"

Bill nodded. He knew where this was going.

"We were drinking and in the door they walked. I remember how your face changed when you saw them too."

"Guilty as charged brother."

"It didn't take them long to notice us in our dress blues and shortly thereafter they joined us at our table."

Bill's eyes softened. "I remember it like it was yesterday."

"It didn't take us long to fall in love with them, did it?"

"Not long at all. Hell, we didn't even know they were sisters right away. I think they enjoyed keeping that secret from us."

Sam chuckled. "Yeah, that took us by surprise, but at the same time it made the bonds we shared even stronger."

"What's your point with all this?"

Sam looked Bill straight in the eyes. "I fell in love with Julie and made my first promise to her. I broke that promise when I went back out in the field."

"She made that choice."

Sam shook his head. "It doesn't matter. What matters is that after all these years she's gone because of me." Tears formed in his eyes. "It's because of me that she's dead Bill....it's because of me."

"Easy brother. Take it easy." *Fuck. Here goes nothing.* "Better yet Sam, pull your shit together. We've got to get the fuck out of here first so we can issue some fucking payback. This memory lane shit isn't helping."

Sam eyes instantly widened and his nostrils flared out. "You sonofa..."

"Really brother? You're going to take your anger and hate and all the rage building inside of you and you're going to turn it on me? I'm not the fucking enemy. We need to work together. Our families are depending on us. So, go ahead and take a swing at me if it'll make you feel any better. I won't stop you."

Sam's fists tightened until they hurt. He wanted and needed to explode. His thoughts were interrupted as the door to the holding area audibly unlocked. He and Bill turned their attention to what might be coming next; their escape.

The door opened and six armed men entered the room and fanned out on the white line. They held their weapons at the ready. Behind them a familiar man strolled into the room. Sam bolted towards Victor with only one purpose in mind, to kill the man. Victor flinched but six raised weapons made Sam stop short long

110

before he could have managed to get his hands around the DCI's neck.

Bill put a hand on Sam's shoulder and pulled him back a few steps. "Take it easy. Now's not the time."

"I'd listen to your friend Sam," said Victor. "The next time you pull a move like that I won't hesitate to have one of your men killed. Tell me you understand what I've just said."

Sam controlled his breathing. "I understand."

"Louder. I didn't hear you."

"I said I understand you prick."

The DCI smiled. "Better. Now, on to business. First off I must apologize for the delay. I had some last minute issues I needed to deal with. Family stuff. You understand. I also took that time to finalize a mission plan that you two," pointing at Sam and Bill, "will carry out."

"And why would we do that?" asked Bill.

"I'm disappointed Mr. Nicholson. Would you like me to cover what I'll do to your families, or to these five men, if you refuse?"

Bill remained silent.

"I thought not."

Sam spoke up. "What do you want?"

"Good. Straight to the point. I have a job that's suited for you two. You'll be on a plane this evening. In the meantime these remaining gentlemen," sweeping his arm out in an arc," will continue to be my guests. This will insure your cooperation."

"We heard you the first time. But I have one question."

"Only one question Sam? Color me surprised. What is it?"

"Other than holding our families and our men hostage, what makes you seriously think we'll do anything you say?"

Victor turned deathly serious. "You don't want to go there. I hold all the cards."

"For now."

"Keep pushing Sam. Oh, and by the way, in case you were contemplating calling or talking to anyone while you're out in the 'real world', don't bother. I have eyes and ears everywhere. I'll know what you've done and the consequences will be swift. Test me on that, I dare you."

Sam didn't like that. "You don't know what kind of animal you're unleashing."

"Actually, on the contrary, I know exactly what you're capable of." Victor turned and started to walk back out the door. "See you two tonight. And please make sure not to think about your loved ones until then."

16
Tuesday November 18, 1997 Mid-Morning Hawaii

Oh fucking hell am I sore.

Rebecca Cross had shown drastic improvements over the past few days and had been taken out of her induced coma state. This was the first time she'd woken up since the attack three days prior.

"Good morning. It's nice to see your eyes open. Well, at least one of them."

Rebecca turned her head slightly and looked at the nurse who'd just walked in her room. Her nametag said her name was Nancy.

"Morning Nancy. I'm thirsty."

The nurse nodded. "I'll be right back."

Rebecca took the time to get familiar with her surroundings. She was in a private room that seemed somewhat isolated due to the lack of activity outside her door. She wasn't groggy but pain did emanate from her face and her ribs. She lifted her right hand up and felt the bandage that covered a portion of her right face, including her eye.

What the hell?

She then moved her hand down and prodded her ribs.

Tender but not too bad.

The nurse took that moment to return.

"Here you go sweetie. They're ice chips until you're up for something more."

Rebecca nodded as Nancy slid a few into her mouth. As the cold ice melted the soothing water trickled down her parched throat. *I don't remember water ever tasting this good.*

"More?"

"Yes, please." Rebecca worked on a few more in her mouth.

"And you're polite too, just like the other ones."

"Can you sit me up?"

"If you're up to it." The nurse put the cup down and worked the bed remote until Rebecca was more or less vertical."

"Thanks."

"You're welcome. How're you feeling?"

"Good I guess. My face and ribs hurt, but other than that I feel fine. What happened? Where is everyone?"

"You've been in an induced coma. What's the last thing you remember?"

Rebecca closed her eyes and multiple images flashed across her eyes. She opened them. "We were in a firefight. There was an explosion. I must have been injured." She suddenly sat up even straighter. "What happened to the families? Are they okay?"

"Easy. Don't put too much strain on yourself."

"Why aren't you answering my question?"

Nancy looked behind her and then back. "We're not supposed to talk about it but I don't see the harm in it. Your friends, or family, they were here with you."

"Were? They left?"

The nurse nodded. "It was the strangest thing. One minute they were all here and then next, ghost town."

"I don't understand."

"That's the thing, no one around here does either. The word is that maybe you'd have the answer for that."

Rebecca shook her head. "But you said I've been in a coma. How would I know?"

The nurse smiled. "Exactly my point."

Rebecca frowned. "So let me get this straight. They were here. Then they were gone. And through all that they left me?"

"That's pretty much how it was. I must say though, you had a fan while you were out."

"A fan? What do you mean?"

"The little boy. I don't remember his name. Every chance he'd get he was in here or looking at you through the glass."

Gavin. He's alive! "Was anyone else hurt?"

"Nothing life threatening. Just cuts and scrapes really. Although one of the mothers does have amnesia. It's the strangest thing."

"And the men?"

"The five that showed up were in good health."

"There were six."

"Oh. Well the news said that there were a number of bodies at the scene."

Goddammit!

The nurse caught her reaction. "I'm sorry. I didn't mean…"

"It's okay, really. Everything's just so raw right now."

"I understand sweetie. You've been through a traumatic experience. Is there anything I can do for you?"

"What are the extent of my injuries?"

"Right now you had a cracked rib, which seem to have practically mended, and a nice shrapnel gash over your right eye that runs down your cheek. The good news is that you're not going to lose the eye. You're lucky if you ask me."

Damn grenade. "I need to get out of here."

The nurse shook her head. "You'll have to talk to the doctor about that."

"I see."

"Why don't you lay back and rest a bit. I'll go find the doctor and update her on your condition."

"Thank you."

"You're welcome dear."

Rebecca watched Nancy leave and head down the corridor. She pulled the covers down and abruptly stopped. *Oh no.* She scooted to the edge of the bed and dislodged the catheter that had been inserted with a grunt and discarded it on the floor. Barefoot, and only wearing a hospital gown, she opened the room's closet door and breathed a sigh of relief when she discovered the clothes she'd been wearing hung there. The pockets still had her identification, other cards and some cash. She grabbed everything and hurried into the bathroom, closed the door behind her and got dressed as fast as her body would allow.

Why would they leave me? Because they didn't have a choice. Why didn't they have a choice? They didn't feel safe. Where would they go? Home? No. No way. Someplace safe. But where's safe? Headquarters? Maybe Roberta knows. She must know.

Rebecca looked at herself in the mirror. She was a mess. Her hair was out of place. The bandage on her face was large but not extensive. The worst part was that it limited her field of view. Her clothes were ripped and torn where the grenades shrapnel had torn into her. *Time for something new.* At least my shoes weren't damaged.

She opened the bathroom door and peered out. Her room was just as she'd left it. Rebecca walked across the room and looked down the corridor. It was still relatively quiet. A single man sat in the waiting room and didn't look up as she made her way past him as she followed the sign pointing out the gift store. Once there she bought a new shirt and exited the hospital through the front door. Not many people paid attention to her or the bandage on her face. It was a hospital.

Rebecca walked a block north and finally looked behind her. *Nothing.* Her ribs hurt a bit but it wasn't anything she couldn't handle. She saw a gas station in the distance and walked towards

116

it. Once she got there she entered the bathroom and quickly changed out her ruined shirt with the new one. She threw the old one away and walked out the door, around the corner past the payphones and inside the mini-mart. She bought a sandwich, a drink and some fruit. She paid for it in cash as the teller kept staring at her out of the corner of his eye. Rebecca ignored him and headed back outside. She stopped at the last phone, picked it up and hit 0.

"Operator. How can I help you?"

"I'd like to make a collect call."

* * *

The phone rang and Roberta picked it up on the second ring.

"This is SANDBOX. How can I help you?"

"I have a collect call from a Rebecca Cross. Will you accept?"

"Yes."

"Roberta, it's Rebecca."

"Don't say another word. We can't talk on the phone. I hope you're okay but whatever you do get back here as soon as possible. Head to the airport, I'll have a ticket ready for you."

"I understand." The line went dead.

Rebecca hung up the phone and smiled. *Now I have a plan.*

* * *

The private cell phone vibrated and was answered.

"Yes?"

"She's awake, sir. She left the hospital but I've got eyes on her."

"Good. Follow her."

17

Tuesday November 18, 1997 Noon
Offshore Hawaii

'Slice of Heaven' had been anchored off the southern coast of Maui ever since the previous evening. The gentle movement of the ocean barely affected the large vessel. It'd been a few days since they'd successfully escaped and had become another anonymous high end yacht that cruised around the Hawaiian Islands. The service that Captain Bob, Ginger and Felicia provided had been nothing short of spectacular. Dinner the night before had consisted of a selection of fresh seafood that had been caught that morning by the Captain himself.

Laura relaxed in one of the lounge chairs. She had decided, after a few days, that she particularly enjoyed the serenity that the rear second deck offered. It was smaller and somewhat private, but it also allowed her to check in on the children from time to time by merely getting up and looking over the side. The kids, if they weren't inside, tended to congregate on the lower deck together. Laura took a moment and did just that. All five were interacting in the sunken hot tub, splashing and laughing. Kim and Julie sat nearby sunning themselves while the five SANDBOX personnel drifted around the boat constantly on guard yet trying to relax at the same time.

Laura smiled as she watched them play. *It's amazing how much they've bounced back in just a few days. They've been through such a traumatic event….just like my kids.* Laura left the railing and sat back down. She picked up the journal she'd started since they'd been aboard and began to write.

It's been four days since the attack. I think all of us are coping in our own ways, but I worry the most about the children. What lifetime scars will this leave on them?

Will they be inundated with nightmares and flashbacks as they grow older? Will they need therapy in the future? I don't know. What I do know is that I wish my husband was here so I could talk to him. I miss him so much. I can only hope that both he and my daughter are alive and are together, wherever they are. If they aren't I'll hunt down and kill whoever took and hurt them.

Laura paused for a bit. *Fuck me. I'm the one that needs therapy right now.*

But I can't dwell on their absence. I have to stay positive about the future. We're all safe for the time being.

For the time being? Why would I write that?

I don't know what else to do and I don't know how long we can stay out here on this yacht. I don't even know if anyone is after us anymore. I don't know a Goddamn thing and that's the most frustrating part about all of this. I don't have any answers and I don't have any control. I just want to reach out and strangle the person who tried to kill us.

Easy there Laura. No. Keep writing.

Killing. I killed someone.

I didn't have a choice but I'd do it again to protect my family.

I didn't enjoy killing that man. When I close my eyes at night I can sometimes see his face. Other times I relive the moment in slow motion, just like a movie. I exit the Suburban after Gavin. It's loud. Explosion. There's fire everywhere. And then the man with the large rifle appears around the corner. That look. That look in his eyes. It's like time has stopped. It's pure hate. Why does he hate me? I've never seen him before. He shifts his weapon towards where I am. My arm extends and I don't know if I'm screaming or not as my finger continually pulls the trigger over and over and over again. The man's eyes change. The hatred has been replaced by surprise. His body falls back and his eyes go out of view. And then I wake up.

Shit.

I don't know if I should feel sorry or not. No, that's a copout. I don't feel sorry at all. Is it weird that I don't? Have I been changed because I took a man's life?

Yes.

"Laura?"

Laura jumped and looked up to see Kim standing over her.

"Sorry. I didn't mean to startle you. May I join you?"

Laura quickly closed her journal. "Sure. And it's okay. I was someplace else entirely and didn't hear you."

Kim sat down. "What's that?" she said as she pointed at the book in Laura's hand.

Laura paused and then answered. "To be honest….it's a journal. It helps me cope with all the shit running rampant in my head."

"Oh. Does it help?"

"It doesn't hurt. Sometimes it's good to get what I'm thinking out on paper. When I was seeing patients, or clients, I would recommend it to them. Sometimes the entries can be very revealing."

"That's right. You used to be a psychiatrist. I'd forgotten about it over the years. You never really seemed to want to talk about it."

"I kind of forgot about it too somewhat," Laura replied. "My life changed when I met Thomas. I don't know how to exactly describe it. The things he was going through….they were like nothing I'd experienced before."

"How so, that is if you don't mind me asking?"

"I don't mind but you already know the story. Thomas, Sam and Bill were on this one bully's radar."

Kim nodded. "Nigel."

"And then, as it turns out, his twin brother Albert was the one that's causing Thomas so much pain." Laura stopped and looked around before she continued. "But it was more than Thomas' pain now that I think about it. It was the journey he and I went through together to piece his mind back together." She stopped and just stared at Kim.

"What? What are you looking at?"

"Hypnosis."

"Hypnosis?"

"It's the process I used to help Thomas find himself again."

Kim shrugged her shoulders. "I'm not following."

"What if, and this is a big what if, but what if I tried the same thing on Julie? It might break through her amnesia and help her remember what she's forgotten."

"Seriously?"

Laura nodded. "What do you think?"

The smile on Kim's face was enormous. "Oh hell yes!"

Laura put her hand up. "There's no guarantee with this. It might work or it might not."

"I don't care. It has to work. I miss my sister. I know she's alive but she's not the same person. The kids know it too and it's starting to scare them. And, no offense, but I miss talking to her."

"None taken. I understand. She's here but not here. It's frustrating." Her excitement level dropped. "I miss talking to Thomas."

"It'll be okay Laura."

It was Laura's turn to shrug. "Maybe. Sometimes it's tough to stay positive."

"Listen. I know I've been a basket case since the attack. What I haven't made time for is to thank you. We're on this boat and safe because you had the mindset to make it happen. I was a wreck."

"Thanks. Although I think the SANDBOX crew definitely gets the thanks. Without them we'd all be dead right now."

"True. I'll concede that. But it was you that made this happen. Anyway, what I'm saying is that it's okay if you take the time to lose your mind. Write in your journal or whatever you need to do."

Laura nodded.

"And I know this world is one fucked up place. However, the one thing I can count on is my husband Bill. Whatever the hell is going on right now, wherever he is, I know in my heart he's trying his damndest to get back to me and the kids. Laura, listen to me. With all the shit you've been through with Thomas I know he's trying to do the exact same thing. You have to believe in that. You have to."

"...I know."

The tone that indicated mealtime rang throughout the ship. They could hear the kids scramble out of the hot tub two decks below.

"Listen," said Kim. "You've been there for me, tough love and everything. I might not have appreciated it at the time but you pulled me up by my bootstraps. Let's go have some lunch and then come back here and revisit this, okay? Everything's going to work out."

They stood up. "Thanks Kim. Let's go enjoy some lunch."

* * *

Laura checked in with Gavin after they were done eating. He told her he was having a good time. With that she let him know where she could be found if he needed anything.

"I know. You know it's okay to be sad," he told his mother.

From the mouths of babes. "Why do you think I'm sad sweetie?"

"Because daddy and Em aren't here. I'm sad too."

123

Laura pulled her son close. "You're right. I miss them terribly."

"It's going to be okay."

Laura held back her tears. "Go on and play sweetheart."

"Okay mommy. I love you."

Like a dagger in my heart. "I love you too."

Laura started to head upstairs when a sudden commotion, followed by screaming and crying, interrupted her. She rushed towards the hot tub area to see Sarah, Kim's daughter, holding her right big toe with both hands. Blood was gushing out from between her fingers. Apparently she had been running and caught her foot on something. The other kids didn't know what to do and just stood around. Julie was nowhere to be seen. *Oh crap, this isn't good.*

"Ithurtsithurtsithurtsithurts!"

"I know baby," Kim said as she tried to soothe her daughter. "Let me see it."

"NO!"

"Honey, take your hand away."

"No! It hurts too much!"

Laura was about to jump in to help Kim when Gavin walked right up to Sarah. Tears rolled down her face uncontrollably.

"Gavin," said Kim, "you need to get out of the way so I can see please."

He ignored her and looked right at Sarah. "If you open your hand I'll let you play with Stir."

"Gavin, please move," Kim insisted.

"O…O…okay," she said between sobs and slowly began to open her hands.

"Don't be scared," he whispered to her.

Sarah finished opening her hands and the torn toe became visible. A huge gash ran down the side of her foot that began at the top of her big toe.

"Don't be scared," he said again.

Before anyone could do anything else Gavin grabbed her foot with both hands. Sarah started to scream and then stopped as suddenly as she'd started. She also stopped crying.

"What the hell are you doing?" Kim said as she raised her voice.

The screams had attracted the SANDBOX personnel and they came rushing.

"What's going on? Is everything alright?"

Oh shit. Laura moved to her son's side and knelt down.

Gavin removed his hands and Sarah's blood dripped from them and added to the puddle that was already on the wood deck.

"What the hell, Laura?" said Kim.

"We're fine everyone," Laura insisted. "We're fine. Just a little stubbed toe is all." She stared at Kim. "Would you please hand me that bottle of water that's behind you?"

Kim reluctantly retrieved the water and handed it over. Laura unscrewed the top and looked at Sarah.

"Does it hurt?"

Sarah shook her head no.

"I'm going to clean this off by pouring some water on your foot, okay?"

Sarah nodded this time and Laura began to pour the water over her toe. At first all that washed off was blood. Then, as she continued to pour, the majority of the blood rinsed off. The large gash was gone.

"Are you okay?" Kim asked her daughter.

Kim looked up at Laura who only smiled. Sarah closely inspected her own foot and was very happy.

"Thank you!" She gave Gavin a hug. "Can I still see Stir now?"

Laura spoke up. "Why don't you all go play inside, okay Gav?"

"K." He stood up and all the kids headed inside together.

Laura turned to Delta. "Sorry. False alarm. Just a stubbed toe."

"If you say so." The five member team dispersed which left Kim and Laura alone.

"Sorry."

"Don't be," Laura replied. "I'm still getting used to it myself."

"That's one hell of ability. You could make some serious money if you took him on the road." Kim smiled and Laura returned it.

"Don't tempt me. Too bad we're stuck on this boat."

Kim laughed. "Yeah, no shit. We're good, right?"

"Yeah, we're good."

A new ring emanated from two decks up and repeated itself. They both looked up.

"What's that?" Kim asked.

"That must be the satellite phone. Any new news will be good news. Let's go."

They raced up the stairs and Laura grabbed the phone that she'd left next to her journal.

"Hello?"

"Laura. It's Roberta."

"Ask her if she's heard from Sam and Bill?" Kim whispered.

"It's good to hear your voice. We haven't spoken since the hospital. Is everything okay?"

"How are you all doing?"

"You really set us up well Roberta. Thank you. To answer your question, we're all safe."

"Good. I'm really glad to hear that. I called because Rebecca got in touch with me earlier today."

"Rebecca's out of her coma?"

"Apparently. I don't know anything else. I didn't want to talk over the phone. What I do know is that she's on her way back to the office as we speak."

"That's great news."

Roberta paused. "I haven't heard from anyone else."

Laura's face dropped. "I see." She turned to Kim and shook her head.

"It's unusual I'll admit. The boys typically keep me in the loop. The fact that they haven't checked in yet could mean just about anything."

Laura let out a deep breath.

"Listen," said Roberta. "We don't know much yet. Just keep your heads low and keep moving. If and when I find out anything new I'll call you."

"Thank you. Thank you for everything."

"Okay. One other thing, and this is just me being paranoid."

"What?"

"I want you to turn off your satellite phone."

"I don't understand."

"I want you to minimize your signal. Just turn it off for now and turn it on twice a day at specific times." Roberta told her the exact times to turn the phone on. "If it's off it can't be used to locate you. You get it?"

Laura nodded. "That makes sense. Thanks for the heads up. You're the best, you know that?"

"I do what I can. Hang in there. I'll be in touch."

Shadows of the Heart

128

18

Tuesday November 18, 1997 Late Afternoon
San Francisco

Roberta was able to secure a last minute flight, out of Oahu to San Francisco International, for Rebecca who barely arrived at Honolulu International Airport twenty minutes before it left the ground. Her plane landed at SFO in the late afternoon.

She located a public phone and dialed. "I'm here."

"I'll be waiting."

Rebecca hung up the phone, immediately grabbed a taxi and braved the 101 commuter traffic north through the city, across the Golden Gate Bridge, and into Marin. The taxi pulled into the SANDBOX parking lot and Rebecca paid with what little cash she had left and walked inside. Roberta was waiting and gave her a huge hug.

"I'm so glad you're okay."

"Me too," Rebecca replied.

Roberta pulled back. "Let me have a look at you. Other than that bandage on your face you don't appear to be too hurt."

"It could have been worse."

"Well, it's great to see you alive and well dear. Before we continue," she said as she began to lead Rebecca away, "why don't we continue our conversation in the SCIF."

Roberta walked to one of the few nondescript doors that were located immediately adjacent to the lobby. Within that room there contained a second set of doors that opened into the Sensitive Compartmented Information Facility, or SCIF. This room was specifically designed for one purpose and one purpose only, to nullify anyone or any type of device from listening in on the conversation. Many of the military contracts that SANDBOX took on had been negotiated and finalized in this room without fear of someone, outside of Sam or Bill, knowing what or where the job would be. Roberta closed the doors behind them and they both took a seat in the very bland and beige room.

"Can I get you something to eat?"

Rebecca shook her head. "No, but thank you. I grabbed something when I called you. Thanks for having the plane ticket ready for me. I barely made it to the airport in time."

"I'm just glad you're okay. Now, let me tell you what I know. I learned about the attack from Laura before I began to follow it on CNN. She told me, as I'm sure you know, that Thomas called her and said that you were about to be attacked."

"Yes. Laura yelled for me and I got the families moving asap. We were all on the road shortly thereafter. Four vans came at our three Suburban's. Two rushed by us and blocked our rear while the other two prevented us from continuing north. Right after that we began to take small arms fire, AK's by the sound, and we were pinned down." She paused. "It all happened so fast."

"Take your time."

Rebecca took a deep breath. "We reorganized over the radios and began a counter attack that drove the attackers back behind their vans. We seemed to be making some headway until a grenade went off. That's when we....I lost Whiskey."

"It's not your fault."

"You don't understand. He was under my command. Then next thing I remember was another grenade landing between the vehicles. I had no place to go and it exploded. After that I woke up in the hospital this morning."

Roberta nodded. "The CNN coverage of the story says that all ten attackers were killed with the help of the Marines. One of the bad guys was found headless and no one knows why."

"What? I have no idea how that would happen." *Stir. It must have been Stir.*

"It doesn't matter. What does matter is that other than Whiskey everyone survived."

Rebecca was relieved. "No one other than me was injured?"

"Apparently Julie has amnesia and doesn't know who she is. Other than that no one else is physically injured."

"How'd you get them out?"

Roberta smiled. "Smart. Laura called me from the hospital. I scrambled to put together an extraction package for them as quickly as I could."

"And?"

"They're currently onboard a luxury yacht called 'Slice of Heaven' that's been sailing around the Hawaiian Islands. They're laying low."

"So they got out clean? No one followed them?"

"Clean as could be. In fact, I talked with Laura not too long ago for the first time. I made sure she had a satellite phone available to her. They're trying to recuperate but currently there aren't any issues. It seems they're in the clear."

"Good."

"I told her to turn off the phone and only turn it on twice a day at very specific times."

"Good thinking. That'll minimize any additional tracking in case whoever was after them is still looking for them. Okay, so what about Sam, Bill and that team?"

Roberta shook her head. "Not a word and I don't like it. Something's not right."

"I tend to agree. That doesn't sound like them at all. Weren't they at some CIA location in D.C. along with Thomas and Emily?"

"For all we know. Whether they're there now or not is a different story."

"Well, I can't stay around here. I have to do something."

"You just came out of an induced coma. You're sure you're up for it?"

"You know I was a medic. So trust me when I tell you that I'll be fine." Rebecca took that moment to peel off the bandage that covered her right eye and cheek. There was a noticeable scar that run from just above her right eyebrow and continued below her eye halfway down her cheek.

Roberta was shocked. "I thought it was going to be a fresh cut. How…how did it already become a scar?"

Rebecca touched her face and pulled her hand away. It didn't hurt and there wasn't any blood. She touched the scar and traced it up and down.

"I have no idea but that's the least of my worries right now. We need to find our people."

A red light blinked on and off on the wall and Roberta stood up. "Be right back." She left the SCIF and closed the door behind her. Rebecca kept tracing her scar until Roberta came back.

"What's up?" Rebecca asked.

"Security has informed me that you were followed."

Rebecca stood up. "Goddammit."

"He says they look like feds. Standard government type."

"Great. Just great. What the hell do they want I wonder?"

"Still want to head out to D.C.?"

"Nothing's going to stop me from finding them. They're family to me, just like you are."

Roberta smiled. "Good. Let's get you cleaned up first and we'll go from there."

19
Tuesday November 18, 1997 Late Evening
Miami

The door to the holding area swung open and four armed men entered. Sam, Bill and the other five operators looked towards the door, temporarily distracted from whatever they were doing to pass the time.

"It's time," one of the large guards said. "Let's go." He pointed at Sam and Bill.

"Here we go," Sam whispered.

"Easy brother, easy."

They stepped forward and made sure to look in to each of the other five operator's eyes that were with them. Quiet nods were exchanged as Sam and Bill exited the holding room without incident. The door closed and was locked behind them.

"This way," the same guard said as he led the way. Three others took up the rear.

At the end of the long corridor Sam and Bill found themselves at another door. Dark hoods were pulled out and tossed to each of them.

"Put them on."

Sam and Bill complied. A guard from behind stepped up and grasped each of their upper arms. A card key was produced, swiped and the outer door clicked open. A refreshing breeze washed over them as they were led outside.

"Walk forward. I'll tell you when to stop."

As they stepped outside they both breathed the fresh air in deeply, from beneath their hoods. They had begun to miss the little things in life during the past few days. The smell and feel of freedom was now all around them, but still very far from their reach.

"Stop," the guard said one hundred feet later. "Step up into the truck."

Sam and Bill reached out blindly, felt the back of the military truck and pulled themselves up into it.

"Take a seat and no talking."

They each used their hands to locate the outside benches and planted their butts. Two guards jumped in after them while the other two entered the truck's cab and started it up. The large truck rumbled to life, spewed a large cloud of diesel exhaust in to the air and jolted forward towards its destination.

* * *

The truck entered Homestead Air Force Base and was directed to one of the hangers. It pulled up, stopped and cut its engine.

"Take off your hoods and get out."

Sam and Bill removed the dark hoods and left them on the seats. They climbed out and looked around.

"Head in to the hanger and get on board."

They both adjusted their attention towards the small executive plane that was parked underneath the hanger. Two additional guards stood outside the extended staircase that led up in to the plane. Sam led the way and Bill followed right behind. They both paused for a second before they walked up the steps and entered the plane. Inside there were a number of large leather seats that were spaced out around tables. This executive plane was clearly planned out around comfort as well as the ability to collaborate on work while in the air. In one of the rear seats sat Victor Bannon, across from his bodyguard.

"Do come in."

Sam's eyes flared. "Give me one good reason why I shouldn't kill you where you sit."

The bodyguard reached for his holstered sidearm but the DCI waved for him to stand down.

"You and I both know I could give you more than one reason, now don't we?"

Sam didn't like it but he knew he had to bury those feelings for the time being. *The cost is just too high.* Sam ended up just staring at Victor instead.

"Good. Now have a seat," he said as he pulled out a file folder and tossed it on the other table. "We need to go over your mission in the next two hours before we land in New Jersey."

"Jersey?" asked Bill as he and Sam took seats across the table from each other.

The stairs retracted as one of the two pilots worked to secure the outer door for takeoff. As soon as that was completed the plane began to taxi out of the hanger and on to the runway.

The DCI continued. "I'll get right to the point. The Middle East has and always will be a time bomb."

Sam and Bill shared a glance. They'd spent some time in that particular overseas sandbox.

"Terrorism lives and breeds in that region of the world and we enjoy taking the armchair quarterback role until the issues directly affect us. Case in point is the United States involvement in the Gulf War. We were content to sit back until the control of the oil was at stake. Our economy, hell, our very way of life depends on making sure that oil keeps flowing."

"I'm not following," said Sam.

"Bear with me. Insurgents have begun to rise up and the stability of the entire Middle East area is at risk. Terrorism is rising. The days of seeing high-jacked planes all over the news are over. Afghanistan is now on the top of my shit list." Victor paused. "Funny how everything comes full circle. During the Cold War we supplied the Afghan rebels with training, small arm and Stinger missiles to thwart the Russian invasion. Now, a generation later, our help may have ultimately destabilized the area."

The plane accelerated and took off heading north towards New Jersey.

"Get to the point. What's the mission?"

"There's a civil war occurring in Afghanistan. It started last year when the Taliban took over the Kabul capital and established the Islamic Emirate of Afghanistan. It quickly gained recognition from Saudi Arabia, Pakistan and the United Arab Emirates. In opposition to the Taliban the defense minister created the United Front which included all Afghan ethnicities. It fought for a republic and national consolidation to achieve lasting peace."

"And how's that working out for them?" Bill sarcastically asked.

"The intelligence shows that they're losing. A group called al-Qaeda, and Islamic terrorist organization led by Osama bin Laden, has also joined in the fight with the Taliban. Suicide bombings are one of his favorite methods to encite terror."

Sam and Bill both shook their heads.

"Anyway, the mission is relatively simple but it takes place on American soil where I can't technically operate, hence this is where the two of you come in."

"Like we have a choice."

"And well, there's that too," Victor said as he smiled. "Intelligence continues to track down money wire transfers originating from the Middle East to the United States. The majority of them are legitimate. However, there are a few that have raised red flags."

"Get to the point," said Sam.

136

"A young man, by the name of Abdul Khaksar Turabi, has been receiving monthly transfers for over a year. Recently that activity has increased along with the size of the deposits. Intelligence has determined that Abdul managed to gain access to the US by means of a student visa. They've also discovered that the money he's been receiving has been traced and originates from a known terrorist used bank account."

Sam and Bill exchanged another glance.

"What are you asking us to do?"

"There is a potential terrorist on US soil. You will retrieve him so he can be questioned about his activities. All the information you need is in the folder; his location, neighborhood, credit card statements, etc. It needs to be done quickly, quietly and silently."

"And then what?" Sam asked. "I don't see you letting us go. Who says you even have our families at all."

"A fair question," Victor replied. "However, it's laborious. Shall we go through this all over again? The fact is your family is relying on you to get this done. If you want to go on believing that they're safe and sound then that's your opinion."

Sam bristled and Bill involuntarily clenched his fists.

"You need to understand one thing and one thing only. I own both of you. You will do exactly what I tell you to do. If you deter from the mission; if you attempt to contact anyone; or if you just plainly piss me off, I will not hesitate to show you pieces of your children."

"You sonofabit…"

"Are we clear?"

Sam and Bill didn't respond.

"Really? You want me to repeat myself? Fine, I'll give you this one pass, but that's it. Are we clear?"

"Yes," said Sam.

"Yes," said Bill.

"Yes what?" Victor was enjoying himself.

"Yes sir," they said together.

<u>20</u>
Tuesday November 18, 1997 Late Evening
D.C.

Thomas tried to roll over and discovered that he couldn't. He tried again but in his half asleep state he was still denied. *Dammit.* Thomas slowly opened his eyes, blinked a number of times and then tried to sit up. *I can't move my arms. What the hell?* He lifted his head and then realized he was strapped down.

"Where am I?"

"Oh good, you're awake. I was beginning to get worried."

Someone's head came into view and Thomas refocused. The man was Japanese.

"Who are you? Why am I here?"

The man smiled. "You already know me Mr. Clark. I'm afraid the drugs I used on you have a side effect. You've lost your short term memory, but it'll come back in a few minutes."

"I…I know you?"

The man nodded. "I am Yamato Takuma Matsushita and…"

"You're holding me prisoner."

Yamato smiled. "It would appear that your memory has returned as quickly as I was able to access it."

Thomas struggled on the table but to no avail. "What did you do to me? How long was I out?"

"So many questions Mr. Clark. The good news, at least for me, is that I now know the truth about you." He leaned in close to Thomas' face. "I know you. You no longer have any secrets from me."

Thomas didn't like that. "Fuck you. You don't know shit."

"Quite the contrary. I know everything from your mother dying, to your bully problems, to your father and so much more.

139

It's been one heck of a ride. But it would appear that what we've run in to here, with your daughter and son, really began with you."

"Go to hell," Thomas replied as he continued to struggle.

"Pumped full of mind controlling drugs. Word triggers. Overcoming those immense obstacles and still landing sane on your feet, mostly thanks to your wife Laura. But then your story becomes even more interesting. You have your first child, little Emily."

"Don't you dare talk about my daughter."

Yamato continued to ignore Thomas during his monologue. "Everything's normal during the birth except for a two second window where the doctor captured a third heartbeat. She dismissed it as a machine error. I mean, why wouldn't she? But two years later when your son Gavin was born the same error happened again."

"You couldn't possibly know that."

"Trust me, I know everything about you now. But back to my story. I talked to Dr. Anna Harper."

Thomas' eyes widened.

"Yes Mr. Clark, the same one who brought your children into the world. I managed to convince her that both of your children were showing abnormalities in their blood. She remembered exactly who you were because she never found an answer to the heartbeat mystery. She was more than happy to 'help' me fill in the blanks. Apparently when your children were born they both had the same two second window where a third heartbeat appeared. Strangest thing I've ever heard. The other thing Dr. Harper found odd was the antigen particles she found in Laura's amniotic fluid, during her pregnancy, for both Emily and Gavin. That continued to bother her as well."

"No. Stop all this."

"So what do you make of those third heartbeats Thomas? It baffles my mind."

"Please. Please leave my family alone."

"You know we're well past that now Mr. Clark. Your daughter Emily," he said as he motioned across the room, "is very special. I'm sure we'll come up with something for your daughter to do for us."

"Stay away from her. She's only six years old you sick asshole."

Yamato changed tactics. "Tell me where your wife and son are?"

Thomas' eyes narrowed. "You said you know everything. If I knew where they were then you'd know."

"Very perceptive. But you know what Mr. Clark, we now know what your children are capable of. You must also know that you're never going to get out of here. Chalk it up to a matter of national security and what not."

"I don't know what you think you're doing but this is wrong. You have to know this is completely wrong!"

Yamato leaned over Thomas' face again. "I need to let you in on a little secret. I now have samples of your blood and your semen. The work I can now do is unlimited."

"You'll never get away with this. I'll kill you first."

"Brave words Mr. Clark, but it's too late for any bravado, it's just too late."

21
Tuesday November 18, 1997
Afterlife

"Very perceptive. But you know what Mr. Clark. We now know what your children are capable of. You must also know that you're never going to get out of here. It's a matter of national security and what not."

"I don't know what you think you're doing but this is wrong. You have to know this is completely wrong!"

Yamato leaned over Thomas' face again. "I need to let you in on a little secret. I now have samples of your blood and your semen. The work I can now do is unlimited."

"You'll never get away with this. I'll kill you first."

"Brave words Mr. Clark, but it's too late for any bravado, it's just too late."

Betsy couldn't bear to watch her son tied up on that table anymore. She appeared next to Michael.

"We have to do something! I won't stand idly by and watch them both continue to be experimented on."

Michael tried to console his wife. "You need to think about what you're saying."

"Don't try to downplay this. This is our son and grandchildren we're talking about." Betsy took a different tact. "You owe me."

Michael didn't like that. "There's no need to bring that up."

"Too bad. I wouldn't have been killed in that car crash, leaving our five year old boy without a mother, if it wasn't for you and your job at the CIA. Thomas might have clawed his way back over the years but do you seriously want him to lose his entire family after everything he's been through? As much as I love you, you still owe me and you owe him."

Michael frowned and turned away. "Dammit. It's not that easy."

Betsy pressed on. "It's an easy decision for me, but apparently not for you. I wonder what that really says about you…"

<u>22</u>

Tuesday November 18, 1997 Early Evening
Marin

Rebecca gave Roberta a huge hug and then exited through the front doors of SANDBOX. She headed directly to the motor pool; unlocked one of the black Suburban's, tossed her new backpack inside and climbed in. After her talk with Roberta she took the opportunity to shower and change clothes. Currently she wore jeans, a black SANDBOX polo shirt, a white hoodie and running shoes. The backpack Roberta had prepped for her contained food, twenty thousand in cash, a change of clothes, a Glock 17 with three magazines and one hundred rounds of 9mm ammunition. However, the most important item Roberta made sure Rebecca had was a satellite phone. Roberta had made her memorize various phone numbers so nothing was written down.

Rebecca closed the car door behind her and started up the vehicle. She adjusted the rear view mirror to her liking and then stopped. She slowly tilted it back towards her so she could see herself. Rebecca stared at the scar that ran from above her right eye and down her cheek. She took her left hand and watched herself trace it from top to bottom.

It looks kind of bad ass. She smiled. *Nothing like having a visible story etched down my face. Could have been worse.*

Rebecca readjusted the rearview mirror, put the Suburban in gear and pulled out of the motor pool. Now it's time to go and track down the people I give a shit about.

The Suburban exited out the main gates of SANDBOX and began its journey back towards the Golden Gate Bridge. Rebecca checked her rearview and picked up the tail almost immediately.

*　*　*

"What's your status?"

"Rebecca Cross left Hawaii and arrived in San Francisco. We followed her to SANDBOX and waited for her to leave. We're on her as we speak sir."

Victor Bannon held the cell phone to his ear from inside a plane on the other side of country. "Stay on her and figure out what she's up to."

"Yes sir."

*　*　*

Victor hung up the phone just as Sam and Bill joined him onboard the aircraft.

"Do come in."

<u>23</u>

Tuesday November 18, 1997 Late Evening
D.C.

Yamato Takuma Matsushita hovered over Emily with great anticipation. Her blood work had been closely analyzed, alongside her father's, and his results were very promising.

This will lead us into a new human era of evolution and I'll take the role of the ultimate creator.

Yamato motioned to one of his two assistants. "Stop her drip."

"Right away."

"What are you doing to my daughter?" Thomas said with as much strength as he could muster from the other side of the lab. "Why can't you just leave us alone?"

Yamato pulled himself away from Emily's innocent face and walked over to Thomas who was still strapped down.

"I might as well converse with you while I wait for the anesthesia to wear off."

Thomas struggled against his bonds. "I said…what are you going to do to my daughter?"

A small smile spread across Yamato's lips. "It's show and tell time Mr. Clark. I have what I NEED from you, now it's your daughter's turn."

"Leave…her…alone."

"Or what? You'll kill me? Look around Mr. Clark. You're in an undisclosed facility. No one's coming to save you."

"I'm warning you."

"Idle threats from a desperate man is all I hear. But let's get real for a minute." Yamato pulled up a stool. "What happened to you, and the trickle-down effect to your children, is downright amazing. I mean, I can't even begin to fathom what you must have done, and been through, to keep these powers a secret from everybody. Your children are so young and crave your attention right now. I imagine they'd do anything you'd ask to make sure their powers remained a secret." Thomas only glared at Yamato. "But, let's think about this scenario for a second. If you weren't here, right now, as an unwilling participant your kids would grow older. And, like any normal progression, would begin to question, act out and start to rebel. What then? Would they have the control, or the insight, not to show off what they can do to their friends? Maybe. Maybe not."

"Fuck you."

"Language Mr. Clark. Your daughter is waking up and we wouldn't want her to hear you."

"What do you want? What could you possibly hope to accomplish?"

"I'm glad you asked actually. You've known how special your children are. Now, I do too, as do others. You have to realize that we're standing on the precipice of an evolutional change of power. It's incredibly exciting."

"What do you mean?"

"Oh, come now Mr. Clark. Don't play dumb with me. Within your DNA are the building blocks for human change. My guess is that we've only seen the tip of the iceberg. Just think about the possibilities; mind probing, invisibility, invulnerability or even flying."

"You're insane."

"Hardly. All I see is potential. Most likely the biggest potential the world will ever see."

"Wait. What?"

Yamato smiled. "You're going to be a father again Mr. Clark, a father to a whole new breed of humans. I plan on isolating the specific RNA anomalies in your DNA by comparing them to a

148

regular individual, most likely mine. In doing so I should be able to synthesize a concoction that will hopefully produce a random effect in whatever subject I inject it with."

Thomas' keys widened. *What the fuck?*

"Now you see the depth of my vision. Granted, creating test tube babies, cultivating and growing them will take years. In doing so my hope will be to manipulate their DNA so specific traits appear rather than the random powers your children received."

"You're not just any doctor are you?"

Yamato looked over at Emily and then stood up. "We all have our specialties Mr. Clark." He looked up and grinned. "It would appear your daughter has come out of her induced stupor. It's time for me to walk over and say hello."

"Don't you dare touch her."

"Nice attempt at playing Brer Rabbit. Of course I don't plan on touching her; that'd be exactly what you'd want me to do."

Thomas watched Yamato back away from this table, turn around and head over to his daughter's. *Goddammit! I have to get us out of here.*

Emily's eyes fluttered as she stirred back to consciousness. She finally opened them and the first thing she saw was Yamato staring down at her.

"I want to go home."

"Maybe at some point."

"You're a liar."

Yamato smiled. "You're pretty smart Emily. I have a little game I want to play with you."

"No. I want to go home."

"I want you to show me what you can do. Your father told us all about your powers. Now I want you to show me."

"Em," Thomas said from across the room, "don't do anything he says."

"Daddy!"

"I'm right here Em. Are you okay?"

"I just want to go home. I don't like it here."

"I know sweetie. Everything's going to be okay."

"Touching. Very touching," said Yamato. "Now, Emily, will you show me?"

She shook her head. "No."

"I see. Very well, you leave me no choice but to hurt your father." He motioned for one of his assistants. The man lifted a scalpel off a tray and walked over to Thomas. "That man has a very sharp knife Emily. If you don't want him to cut your daddy then just tell me you'll show me your powers. It's as simple as that."

Emily's eyes betrayed her. "Daddy!"

"I'm here Em. I'm okay."

"Tell me you'll show me or I'll hurt your father."

Emily didn't respond.

Yamato turned and nodded to his assistant. The man methodically placed the scalpel down above Thomas' left nipple, pressed down and slowly drew it across the skin.

"FUCKTHATHURTSOHMYGODSTOPIT!!" Tears rolled down Thomas' cheeks

"DON'T HURT MY DADDY!!"

Yamato raised his hand and the man stopped cutting into Thomas.

"Do you want to show me Emily, or shall I have your daddy hurt again?"

She nodded.

"Very well. Knock him out and then stitch him up. I don't want him interfering."

The assistant nodded and went to pick up a syringe off a nearby tray.

"You...you sonofabitch," Thomas muttered between labored breaths. "You're...an...animal."

"I don't envy your position Mr. Clark, but I do envy what you have to offer us."

The needle found its way into Thomas' neck and he passed out before he could respond. The assistant began to work on stitching up his scalpel handywork.

Yamato sighed. "Shall we begin then?"

"You're mean," Emily said defiantly.

"It's just business young lady. Now, stop stalling and let's begin the demonstration."

Emily didn't like it. "Let me touch you."

"We both know that's not going to happen. Why don't we wheel your father over here instead." Yamato motioned for the assistant to bring Thomas over. "You can finish up your stitching over here."

In no time Thomas' table was next to Emily's. The assistant continued his work on her father's chest. Yamato loosed the strap holding her right hand and stepped back. "Do it. Show me."

Emily slowly reached out and touched her father's unconscious hand. An instant later Michael Clark appeared in the lab next to Emily and Thomas' tables. Yamato and the two assistants jumped. Three guards immediately entered the room and pointed their weapons at him.

"Hi grandpa."

"Hi sweetie. Your grandmother and I are very happy to see that you're feeling better."

Yamato composed himself. "Wow. Just amazing. You must be Michael."

Michael finally looked up. "And you're Yamato. You should have listened to my son when he warned you to leave his family alone. You have no idea who or what you're messing with."

"Interesting," Yamato replied visibly unimpressed. "Then why don't you explain it to me?"

Michael began to move towards him and Yamato's smile faltered for a second.

"Don't move!" yelled one of the guards.

Michael stopped. "You don't understand anything that's going on here. You can't unleash this type of power into the world, it's not ready for it."

"Oh, but I can. And what, you, a ghost are going to stop me?"

Michael nodded. "Maybe."

"Well then. Let's try an experiment of sorts." Yamato turned to the closest counter and began to remove another syringe off a tray.

Michael took that opportunity to lean down and whisper in Emily's ear. "We're going to get you out of here. You need to be strong."

Yamato turned around and caught Michael whispering. "What did you just tell her?"

"Wouldn't you like to know," he responded smugly.

Yamato frowned for the first time. "Very well." He quickly advanced on Emily, with the syringe ready, and injected it into the meat of her thigh. Emily's eyes began to roll back.

"You bastar..." Michael disappeared.

"Just as I thought. Experiment over." The guards lowered their weapons and looked over at him for instructions. "Out. We're fine."

They nodded and left the lab.

"And finish stitching him up," Yamato said. "I need time to think."

24

Tuesday November 18, 1997 Late Evening
Offshore Hawaii

Laura looked up as Kim joined the two of them out on the deck. "How're the kids?"

"They're finally down. Gavin really healed up Sarah's toe. It's pretty amazing." Kim sat down next to her sister.

"Yeah. Still getting used to it myself," Laura replied. "Thanks for putting Gavin in bed for me."

"No problem. So how're things here? Any progress?"

"It's funny you should bring that up. Julie and I were just having a conversation about that."

Kim looked at her sister. "So what'ya think?"

Julie shrugged. "I don't know. Hypnosis could be scary. The only person I know is me. This person that you keep referring to seems like a stranger."

"But it's who you really are. Right now you're just an empty shell and…"

Laura cut Kim off. "I tell you what. Why don't Julie and I continue our conversation, alone, okay?"

Kim didn't like to be rebuked but held her tongue. "I'm pushing, aren't I?"

"It's okay. It just means you care. But this decision is up to Julie."

"You're right." Kim stood up. "Sorry sis. I'll catch up with you both in the morning. Goodnight." She turned and walked off.

"Night," said her sister.

"Goodnight Kim," Laura added.

Julie watched her sister head back inside and then turned back to Laura. "This has to be so frustrating for her. The fact that I'm here but I'm not here."

Laura nodded. "She's not the only one I'm afraid. You're like a stranger to me too. And not to be too heavy handed, but you have your children to think about as well. They're confused."

Julie sighed. "I don't know what to say. I hear them call me 'mommy' but nothing registers. I'm trying, but I don't feel like their mother, and that saddens me."

Laura nodded. "Let me ask you this then. What goes through your mind on a daily basis? What do you think about?"

"The only memories I have are from the moment I woke up on that street until right now."

"Is that confusing or frustrating?"

Julie thought about that for a bit. "Yes and no. I'm curious about the person I was but I'm also afraid that I won't like who that person is."

"Julie, the person you are is very likable. You have a fantastic husband and two adoring children. We have quite the unit and bond between all three of our families. There's nothing to be afraid of."

"Not even Gavin?"

That caught Laura off guard. "Well, you're right about that. I'm still getting used to what my son can do. His powers are amazing, frightening, wonderful and scary all at the same time. But he's young and needs everyone's support and nurturing. He needs your support Julie. He's the one who brought you back to life. Remember, you were shot twice in the chest. One of those bullets went through your heart. Your sister held your lifeless body in her arms." Laura paused. "I didn't want to believe you were gone either, but neither of us had any time to mourn because

Gavin did his thing and suddenly there you were again, alive and breathing."

"That must have been weird for the two of you."

"You say that so matter-of-factly, but I get it. You hear me talking about some other Julie, and not who you are right now. But yes, to answer your question, it was extremely weird. It all happened so quickly amidst all the chaos that surrounded us. But you know what sticks in my head?"

Julie shook her head. "No. What?"

"I saw your eyes change." She paused. "They were brown and right in front of me they turned to black. It was…"

"Creepy?"

"Yeah, a little bit."

"Soooo…you want to hypnotize me to try and cure me of my amnesia?"

"That's part of it, but there's no guarantee that will work. Your amnesia may fade over time and you'll regain your memories, or maybe it won't. Aside from that you've been on a journey, whether you know it or not, and potentially uncovering what that might be is extremely interesting to me."

"I see." Julie mulled it over. "Will it hurt?"

"Physically, no. Mentally, well, I can keep you calm but I don't know what barriers I'll discover along the way."

Julie stood up and leaned on the railing. The moon filled the sky and allowed her to watch the vast ocean. *Is this something I want? Do I want to be the person I know nothing about? Will that person replace who I am?* She shifted her gaze and watched some seagulls flying in the distance together. *But I feel all alone and I don't want that. I want to be part of something larger. I want my life back.*

Julie sat back down. Laura had watched her deliberate and had remained silent.

"I'm nervous, but let's see where this takes me."

"You're sure?"

Julie nodded.

Laura smiled. "Okay. Why don't you sit back and relax to start with. Get comfortable."

A warm, light breeze flowed over the deck and helped to calm Julie's nerves as she got settled.

"Now," Laura said lightly as she softened her voice. "Close your eyes and try to clear your mind. With your mind free of cluttered thoughts your body begins to float. My voice is the only thing you'll hear as your body gently begins to drift away. You are weightless and have not a care in the world. In the distance you see a bright light and you are drawn to it. The light is warm and inviting. Your body slowly drifts towards it. The light embraces you and everything fades away."

Laura watched as Julie's body relaxed. *Well, that was a lot easier than I remember.*

"Julie, can you hear me?"

"Am I Julie?" she responded dreamily.

Oh wow. Interesting. "Yes, your name is Julie."

"Okay. Yes, I can hear you."

"Are you relaxed?"

"Yes, very relaxed."

"Good. Do you feel safe?"

"Yes."

"I'm happy to hear that. Do you know where you are right now?"

"On a ship. Trying to stay ahead of whoever attacked us."

"That's right. I would like you to travel backwards in time. Today is Tuesday. Let's rewind time two days and make it Sunday. Can you do that for me?"

"Yes. I'm there."

156

"What do you see?"

"We're on the boat. Everyone is settling in and adjusting."

"Good. Now I'd like you to rewind a bit further. It's now Saturday afternoon. What do you see?"

"We're escaping from the hospital out the back. Our guards want us to move quickly and quietly so we don't get caught."

"Fantastic. You're doing great Julie. Can you take me back to that morning?"

"It looks like a hospital. There are armed guards watching over us. Kim is huddled with the children in the waiting area. I'm being led off to get checked out by Doctor Goodman. She's nice but is confused why there is so much blood on my clothes and how I don't have any injuries."

"Does she say anything else?"

"She's trying to talk privately with the nurse but I could hear them. She's angry that we took over part of the hospital. She also doesn't know why I can't remember who I am. She concludes its psychological trauma and heads off to look at Rebecca."

Okay, here we go. "Can you rewind the time again to earlier that morning? What's the first thing you remember?"

Julie's face stiffened. "I...I..."

Shit. "It's okay Julie. You're safe. Nothing can hurt you."

Julie relaxed.

"What's the first thing you remember from Saturday morning?"

"I'm cold."

"What do you mean?"

"I...I don't know. I'm just cold."

"What do you see?"

"The sky. I see the sky. People around me. Fires. Shouting. Crying. I sit up and there are so many strangers around me. Who are these people?" Julie started to shake.

"You're okay Julie. You're safe. No one is going to hurt you. Listen to the sound of my voice. You're relaxed and safe."

She stopped shaking.

This is actually going pretty well. Certainly nothing like Thomas' regressions. Holy shit those were bad. "Now Julie, I'd like you to take me back to before you woke up. Can you do that for me?"

Julie's face scrunched up. "I can't. I just can't. I don't remember."

"That's okay. Can you take me back earlier that morning? Do you remember waking up?"

"I don't know. Everything's black."

"Try Julie. I know you can do it."

"Yelling."

"Yelling? What do you mean?"

"Someone's yelling at me."

"What are they yelling?"

"They're telling me to get up. Get up and get ready. We have to leave."

Laura smiled. *Progress.* "What happens then?"

"I get out of bed and get dressed. I make sure I have my gun with me before I leave my room. I...I check on the kids."

"Whose kids are they?"

"They're...they're my kids. Amanda and Craig. They're sleepy and slow to get up. I grab them. We leave the house and get in a Suburban."

"That's right Julie. What happens next?"

"Lots of gunfire." She shuddered. "I don't like this."

"You're safe. Nothing can hurt you. What happens?"

"Bullets are thumping against the side of the car and cracking the windows. The kids are screaming." Her chest began to rise

158

faster and faster and her breathing increased. "Explosions. My ears hurt. It won't stop!"

"They can't hurt you. You're safe."

"No, I'm not. I need it to stop so I bolt out of the car."

"Listen to me. You're not there anymore. There are no explosions. There are no bad guys."

Julie wasn't listening to Laura's commands. "I'm out of the car now." Her breathing was ragged.

Oh shit. Laura got out of her chair, leaned over Julie and grabbed one of her hands. "You're not there anymore. Come back to me."

"I'm out of the car. I'm pissed off. I have to get them to stop. A man with a rifle appears out of the smoke."

"Come back Julie. You need to listen to me."

"The training from the kill house….I was so angry. I lifted my gun and fired. The man dropped to the ground."

I don't know what else to do. She can't hear me. This isn't good.

"Then…then nothing." Julie relaxed immediately.

What the hell?

"Julie? Julie can you hear me?"

"Yes, I can hear you."

Oh thank God. "You're safe."

"Safe…but nowhere."

"Nowhere?"

"Nowhere…drifting…"

"What do you see?"

"…drifting. People. There are so many people here."

"Where are you? Look around and describe it."

Julie twisted her neck to the left and then the right as she lay in her lounge chair. "Lots of people. It's like a stadium for a football game. So many people."

"I don't understand. Why are they there?"

"So many people…waiting…just waiting…just waiting…"

That's more than enough for now. "Julie, can you hear me?"

"Yes."

"I'm going to count backwards from three. After I do you will be wide awake and remember what happened. Do you understand?"

"Yes."

"Good. Three. The bright light is fading in the distance."

"Two. Your body is becoming heavier."

"One. You are relaxed and awake."

Julie blinked a few times and sat up. She looked right at Laura. "What the hell was all that?"

"I don't know. You were fine until I took you back to the time of the attack. Are you okay?"

"I think so. That was so weird. It was like I saw it all from someone else's eyes but then I realized I was only looking at myself through my own eyes."

"I'm sorry. I meant to keep you safe the entire time." Laura got up and sat back in her own chair.

"Actually, it's okay." Julie smiled. "I think I remember some things; bits and pieces of who I was. I want to know more. When can we do this again?"

"Seriously?"

Julie nodded. "I don't know what the hell I was describing to you but I have to know what it was. Whatever you did Laura has me very excited about the person I used to be. I have a whole life to recover in my head. You have to help me."

"Are you sure? You want to go through all of that again?"

Julie nodded. "It's worth it. You started me on this trip. You have to help me finish it. I have questions now that I didn't have before. I need those answers. I need to know who I am. Please."

Laura nodded. "Okay. Tomorrow then. We'll find some time." She paused. "Do you know what any of that meant? The stadium? The people?"

Julie shook her head. "Not yet anyway."

Shadows of the Heart

25

Wednesday November 19, 1997 Middle of the Night D.C.

The Director of Central Intelligence's private phone chirped. He immediately awoke, rolled over in his bed and answered it without any hesitation.

"What is it?"

"Sorry to bother you at this hour sir but you asked to be interrupted with any updates."

"I'm well aware of my standing orders."

"Of course sir. My apologies. Dr. Matsushita is ahead of schedule and has completed phase one of his initial tests. He wanted to pass on that his results show quite of bit of promise."

Victor smiled in the darkness that enveloped him within his bedroom. "Excellent. My plan is moving forward as intended. However, just in case things move too quickly, see to it that Calvin and Hobbes plant the evidence first thing in the morning."

"Yes sir."

"That is all."

Victor hung up the phone and climbed out of bed. He pulled his robe on and sauntered out of his bedroom in to his office. He turned on the desk lamp and settled down into his large leather chair. He pulled open one of his desk drawers that contained a safe. He dialed the combination and then cranked open the handle. From within he removed a few file folders and placed them on the desk in front of him. Victor opened one of the files, grabbed a pen and began to make notes in it. He stopped to collect his thoughts.

Project Zelda is a proper cover name to call this endeavor. With Emily's abilities analyzed and contained, along with her father's DNA at my disposal, the balance of power will forever remain with the United States. The potential that could come from this is unparalleled. In time I'll be positioned to acquire in-depth knowledge of anyone in the world. I'll know their weaknesses, their desires, and their secrets. Victor devilishly smiled. *I'll own everyone.*

26
Wednesday November 19, 1997 Middle of the Night New Jersey

The private jet Sam and Bill were on had landed at Newark Liberty International Airport just after midnight, after a quick stop in D.C. to drop Victor off. It taxied to a private hanger where a car was waiting. They disembarked to a chilly twenty eight degree temperature, opened the empty car doors and climbed inside. Sam turned over the ignition and manipulated the console to bathe them in heat. Bill looked in the back seat and immediately located a package that he was told was supposed to be there. He pulled it to the front seat and placed it on his lap.

"It's fucking cold," Bill said as he rubbed his bare hands together in front of the warming air vents.

"I'm too angry to be cold," Sam replied.

Bill looked over at this best friend and colleague. "You and me both brother. I don't like this situation we're in…"

"Situation?" interrupted Sam. "This situation is completely unacceptable. We're being manipulated by the head of the CIA for fuck's sake. He's using our families and our men against us. He was talking about sending pieces of our children to us. It doesn't get any worse than this."

"I don't like it any more than you do. But what are we supposed to do about it right now, at this moment? We're in a no win situation. Losing our minds isn't going to help out or save our families. Just relax and take it easy. We'll figure something out. In the meantime, we have a terrorist to take down so let's go over the plan again, okay?"

Sam typically was the one who calmed his friend down during stressful moments. *How ironic that Bill is attempting to talk me down. But he's not the one who lost his wife. Sam clenched his jaw. What am I going to do without Julie? She was my everything.* He collected himself over the next few seconds. *What I'm not going to allow is for Bill to go through the same damn thing.* Sam relaxed his jaw, relented and looked over at Bill.

"Let's do this thing and then figure a way out of this mess."

"Good. Drive while I walk us through the plan again."

"Roger that."

Sam made his way out of the airport and headed east on I-78 towards Jersey City.

* * *

Sam cut the lights and rolled to a quiet stop a block away from their target's address. They had passed by the location once and then pulled back around the block to park. From out of the package that Bill had retrieved he pulled two Night Vision Goggles, two silenced Beretta nine millimeter handguns with extra magazines, two black hoods, a roll of duct tape, a set of lock-picking tools, two sets of gloves and a digital camera. *Fantastic, no Kevlar vests. What the fuck.*

While Bill was organizing the equipment Sam took the time to quickly scan the area for any threats. Once he didn't discern any he then began to take his time and really concentrate on their immediate surroundings. The neighborhood they were in appeared lower class. A couple of vehicles were in various states of disassembly; one had all four tires missing and the other was missing both the hood and the engine.

Sam continued to scan the darkened street looking for any signs of trouble, security and anything out of the ordinary. During their initial drive by neither one of them had spotted any telltale signs that this location was anything other than what it really was, an abandoned house surrounded by a chain-link fence.

"Let me take another look at this guy's photo."

Bill handed the file over to Sam who opened it and took a long look at Abdul Khaksar Turabi, the supposed target who entered the United States under a student visa but had been receiving money for the past year through a known terrorist bank account. The DCI wanted him captured so he could be questioned. *Tortured more like it.*

Sam closed the file and placed it on the floorboard. Without saying another word Bill handed one of the Berettas over. Sam ejected the full magazine and then reinserted it. He quickly pulled back on the slide and let it ride forward. He thumbed the safety on and laid the weapon on his lap. Bill then handed over the extra magazines, gloves, a black hood and a pair of NVGs. He kept the camera, lock-picks and duct tape for himself.

"Ready to do this?" Bill asked.

"Let's get this over with. We have a plane to catch."

Bill smiled and pulled the hood partly over the top of his head to look like a knit hat. Sam did the same. The NVG's they hung around their necks for the time being. The both hoped that at this late hour no one would be up and watching the street, especially in this neighborhood. As they exited the vehicle they quietly closed their doors and kept their silenced Berettas against their legs to mask the weapon's profile. Their setup was far from ideal but they hadn't been given a choice on how to prepare.

The abandoned house was a hundred feet away. The sidewalk between their vehicle and the house was relatively unlit so Sam and Bill had little problem negotiating the distance and soon found themselves in a small alley directly next to the property. The chain-link fence that surrounded the house had numerous and obvious breaches in it. Sam and Bill silently picked their way through one of these holes, stopped, pulled down their hoods and placed their NVGs over their eyes. The surrounding darkness was suddenly replaced with an eerie green. The abandoned house in front of them now jumped out at them.

Using hand signals Sam slowly led the way around to the back of the house. The large backyard was full of discarded appliances from stoves, old refrigerators and the like. Bill guarded their ingress route behind them while Sam scanned the territory and yard in front of them. When Sam was satisfied that they hadn't been seen and that there weren't any threats he tapped Bill on the shoulder and together they slowly continued to proceed towards the backdoor.

As they neared it Sam abruptly stopped in his tracks and held up his left fist which meant stop. Bill immediately stopped moving and scanned the area. Sam pointed at the back porch and Bill saw why Sam had stopped. A thin beam crisscrossed the porch at waist high. It would have been invisible to the naked eye but with their Night Vision Goggles the beam was as prevalent as ever. They didn't know whether the beam, if tripped, would have sounded an alarm or triggered an explosion. At this point it didn't matter as they each squatted under the obstacle and stacked up on the backdoor. *At least we know we're in the right location.*

Sam tested the doorknob with his left hand and to his surprise it turned in his hand. He gently applied pressure to the door and eased it open ever so slightly. He carefully scanned the crack he'd made and didn't locate any wires or booby-traps. Finding nothing he pushed the door open further, just enough for his body to fit, raised his Beretta to eye height and entered weapon first. Bill was right on his heels. Sam took the right side of the room while Bill turned left. The room they had entered was the kitchen and it was clear of any immediate threats.

Bill motioned to Sam who then regrouped behind Bill as he made his way through the dining room and around to the living room. The living room contained a couch and arm chair with a coffee table that was in the middle and a television against the wall. The coffee table had remnants of past meals due to the variety of discarded pizza, fast food and other boxes that had yet to be cleaned up. Three separate plates were on the table along with three soft drink containers.

Bill made a three with his left hand and Sam nodded in agreement. *What the hell have we walked in on?*

The front door was at the edge of the living room along with a staircase that led to the second floor. Bill motioned that he'd cover the stairs. Sam continued past him and cleared the family room area that led to the kitchen. With that room clear he moved back to join Bill at the bottom of the stairs.

Bill once again took the lead and carefully took his time on each step as he kept his weapon pointed towards the top of the stairs. Sam crept behind him with his own weapon pointed over Bill's right shoulder. Sixteen agonizing steps later Bill reached the top of the landing. There were two doors in front of him, another door at the end of the right hall and a fourth to the far left at the end of that hall.

Snores could be heard from behind the closed door immediately in front of Bill. *Shit.* Sam joined him on the landing a second later. They both paused to take in the new environment and Sam heard the snoring right away. Sam signaled to Bill that he was taking the doorway at the end of the right hallway and for him to cover the door definitively occupied by someone in front of them. Bill nodded and Sam began to creep down the right hallway, weapon up and ready as Bill kept his at the ready to cover both the occupied room and the rest of the left hallway.

Sam was two feet away from the closed door when the floorboard he stepped on let out a loud groan. He froze. The snoring stopped immediately.

Fuck!

Sam heard someone scurry from behind the door in front of him.

Bill knew the element of surprise was lost and decided to take the offensive. He stood up and kicked the door in front of him as hard as he could.

Sam took one more step towards the door before he heard the familiar sound of an AK-47 being chambered.

Bill's door kick connected with an unknown entity with such force that it sent the individual flying back across the room.

The door at the far left of the hallway opened and a man holding a pistol appeared and turned on the hallway lights.

Bill followed through with his kick and used the momentum to jump on the man. He struck him in the throat just as the lights turned on behind him. He began to tear off his NVGs when gunfire filled the hallway.

Sam was already diving to the floor when the sudden light amplified through his NVGs and temporarily blinded him. Milliseconds later a burst of automatic gunfire erupted from the bedroom in front of him, punching holes in the door, and sailing through the air where he'd just previously stood.

The bearded man who'd flipped on the lights immediately, at the opposite end of the hallway, took two AK rounds in his chest and was dead before he hit the floor.

Sam, albeit somewhat blinded, instinctively began to fire his silenced Beretta as fast as he could pull the trigger at the door in front of him.

Bill took a quick look at the unconscious man at his feet before he rushed back to the doorway, stuck his right arm and part of his face out into potential oncoming fire and joined Sam in blanketing the door with rounds. The automatic weapon fire abruptly stopped during their barrage.

Both Sam and Bill proceeded to empty their weapons, ejected and then inserted fresh magazines in a blink of an eye. Bill glanced towards the other end of the hallway and saw another man down and a pistol on the floor near the body. *That makes three.*

"Sam!"

"I'm good. Blind, but good."

"Roger that. Stay down. Coming to you."

Sam continued to blink his eyes repeatedly as his vision started to return. Bill stepped over him and opened what remained of the door as he entered the room. He was back in a few seconds and helped Sam to his feet.

"You good brother?"

"Yeah. Damn floor turned this mission into shit in a hurry. I think I fucked us."

Bill shook his head in disagreement. "I've still got a live one."

Sam's face brightened up. "Good. Give me the camera and get him prepped ASAP. This might be a shitty neighborhood but the cops will show up eventually. We're out of here in two minutes. No traces."

Bill nodded, pulled the digital camera from his back pocket and handed it over. He turned and went back to the middle room to take care of the man he'd knocked unconscious.

Sam entered the room and quickly took pictures of the perforated man's face and the room. He then ran down the length of the hallway, turned the dead man's body on its side and captured that man's face. He entered the bedroom and stopped cold.

Bill had returned to the middle bedroom and secured the prisoner with duct tape to prep him for transport. Bill was about to lift the man off the floor and carry him when Sam called his name.

"Bill. Get in here."

Bill left the tied up man and quickly joined Sam in the third bedroom. As he entered he stopped short as well.

"Holy shit. You have got to be kidding me."

On a table in the bedroom lay three vests wired with explosives and ball-bearings. Components of the manufacturing process were stashed on a smaller table next to the larger one.

Sam began to take as many pictures as he could and as fast as he could. Bill turned and ran back down the hallway. With little time left he picked up all the nine millimeter shell casings the two of them had expended, shoved them in his pocket and went to pick up his prisoner.

In the distance the sounds of police sirens could be heard. Sam suddenly appeared.

"We good?"

"Clean. Are we going to leave all that?"

"We don't have a choice."

Bill knew the answer already and started down the steps with the unconscious man over his shoulder. They exited out the back door and avoided the laser beam for the second time. They rushed to the break in the chain-link fence, headed down the alley to the street, took a right and just made it to the car when the first police officer drove up and parked in front of the house.

In the dark Sam opened the trunk and Bill dumped their cargo inside. Without any words they got in the car, removed their hoods and started it up. The two officers had just stepped out of their vehicle and were waiting for backup when they heard the car start up down the street. Sam flipped a one-eighty in the middle of the street and then turned on the lights as he sped away. The

172

officers looked at each other but didn't react. They weren't happy they had to respond to a report of automatic weapons in this part of the neighborhood as it was. That car that sped away could have been anything. No use getting killed over it.

Sam turned a few corners and then bee-lined back to I-78. Traffic was light at this early hour. Bill finally spoke up.

"What did we walk in to? Did we just break up some terror plot?"

"You saw what I saw. The information we were given and the evidence we saw do connect the dots. Let's just get the sonofabitch in the trunk on the plane. Speaking of, do you think we got lucky enough and it's Abdul tied up back there," Sam said motioning with his thumb towards the trunk.

Bill shrugged. "It could be him. With the beard and all the blood on him…shit, I don't know. The door took quite a beating when it connected with his face."

Sam finally cracked a smile for the first time in a long time. Shortly thereafter it was gone again.

"Good job tonight Bill."

"Could have been me hitting the bad luck board, but instead it was you."

"Seems to be a pattern of mine."

Bill flinched. "Oh shit, you know I didn't mean…"

"Forget it. I know you didn't mean it. Let's just get this asshole to the plane and go from there."

The two of them remained silent until they pulled back in to the airport, received clearance to enter and drove back to the airplane hangar. As they exited their vehicles four men appeared with weapons drawn from inside the plane.

"Put your hands on the hood of the vehicle! Do it!"

Sam and Bill complied. The tools they had utilized that evening were taken from them. After they were searched they were led on to the aircraft.

"I need you to debrief me," said the man in charge.

Sam and Bill walked the man through the entire mission without being interrupted. At the end the man asked his questions.

"So you have a potential terrorist in the trunk of the car?"

"That's correct," Sam replied.

"And you don't know if it's Abdul Khaksar Turabi or not?"

"There wasn't time to verify his identity after everything went to hell."

Bill spoke up. "What the hell do you want from us? We did the job and got a live one for you to talk to. What's your problem?"

The man ignored the question and asked one of his own instead.

"At any point did you try and make contact with anyone else?"

Bill and Sam looked at each other and then back at the man.

"Do you have family you son of a bitch?" Sam demanded. "How dare you ask such a question when you have us bent so far over a barrel already you fucking prick!"

Bill placed his hand on Sam's arm.

"I'll ask one last time," the man persisted. "Did you, at any point, try and make contact with anyone else?"

Sam about lost it but Bill squeezed his arm and answered for them.

"No."

"Good. Keep it that way. He backed out of the airplane and left Sam and Bill alone.

"This sucks."

"Tell me something I don't already know," replied Sam as he tried to close his eyes and get some sleep.

The plane immediately taxied down the runway and took off in to the New Jersey night. They had no idea what lay in store for them at the next stop.

27

Wednesday November 19, 1997 Late Evening
San Francisco

Rebecca Cross was extremely busy after she had left SANDBOX. She knew she had a tail and her first priority was to lose it. She drove across the Golden Gate Bridge towards downtown San Francisco. After fighting through the evening traffic she eventually parked the black Suburban in a lot off the Embarcadero, as instructed by Roberta, left the keys in a hidden spot and then took off on foot. It wasn't long until she spotted the two men who pulled up alongside the curb, get out and follow her.

They're pretty obvious but I'm also not a spy. Rebecca smiled. *Well then, I'll have to update my resume after this is all said and done with this new experience.*

Rebecca continued south along the Embarcadero. She cut through Justin Herman Plaza to Market Street and made a pit stop at the Hyatt Regency to procure a map of the area which she tucked in to her pocket. She exited the hotel and caught the two men in her peripheral as she continued down Market a couple blocks to the Embarcadero B.A.R.T. Station, or Bay Area Rapid Transit. She entered the subway, figured out how to purchase a ticket and entered the crowded commuter platform. The overhead display informed her that a Concord train would arrive in three minutes.

Rebecca didn't need to look around to know that the two men were still close by. She knew she had plenty of time before her final destination and losing her tail was just the start of her adventure.

A gust of heated wind blew over everyone on the platform as the Concord train approached. It was standing room only as everyone packed into the train. The doors barely were able to close throughout the ten car train before it pulled out of the station and began its trip underneath the San Francisco Bay towards Oakland. Rebecca held on to a pole as the train rumbled down the track. Her mind drifted back to the attack on the families and those events played out in her head over and over. With her free hand she traced the scar that ran down her right cheek once again.

I let them down. When they needed me the most I let them down.

Rebecca knew she was being overly hard on herself and final admitted that the grenade that exploded could have easily killed her rather than have just broken her ribs and scared her face.

She willed her thoughts toward her mission at hand. *Where the hell is Sam, Bill and the rest of the team they were with? They were headed to Cuba and then nothing. No radio contact whatsoever. Nothing adds up. Is the family still in danger? I hope they're okay out there on the boat. I can't wait to touch base with them once I'm in the clear.*

The train pulled in to West Oakland station and enough people disembarked to give Rebecca a little more standing room. At Rockridge station she was finally able to locate an open seat. She pulled out the map of San Francisco she'd acquired and began to take a closer look at the area she was interested in. Out of the corner of her eye she caught the two men in the next car down eyeballing her. She paid them no attention.

The next stop was Orinda. Rebecca got up, walked off the train and headed to the opposite platform to wait for a returning train. The electric display indicated she had seven more minutes. The two men attempted to casually do the same. She sat down and waited for the train as she mentally walked through her plan of attack.

Seven minutes later she stood up, boarded the train and immediately found a seat. She covertly watched the two men split up and take seats in the train cars both in front and behind her. The doors closed and the train lurched ahead.

Forty minutes later Rebecca stood up as the train approached Montgomery Street station, one stop past Embarcadero. She moved with the crowd, used her ticket and then took the north exit. The men were behind her about seventy feet and that's all the distance she needed. At the top of the stairs she turned to her right and dropped out of her pursuer's view. The stop light at Market was on her side so she immediately ran south across the street and around the corner on to New Montgomery Street. She didn't have time to look back and see if they had seen where she'd gone so Rebecca sprinted three blocks to Mission Street, took a left and hailed the first taxi she saw, practically stepping off the curb in its way to get the cabby to stop.

The taxi blared his horn. "Hey, what's your problem!?"

Rebecca opened the door and quickly climbed in. "Go!"

"Where to?"

"Just drive!"

The driver rolled his eyes and pulled back in to traffic. Rebecca caught a quick glimpse of the two men as she peeked out the back window. One of them pointed at her taxi while the other brought a phone up to his ear.

"Where to miss?" the cabby insisted.

They saw the taxi number. "Take a right on First and pull over."

"Whatever." Twenty seconds later and he did as he'd been instructed.

Rebecca tossed a twenty dollar bill his way and was out the door before he could say another word. She knew she had only a small margin of time and she made the best of it. She crossed First

Street, against the light, headed down a small alley and ended up on Freemont Street. She entered the first café she saw and took a seat towards the rear so she could watch the entrance.

"I think that did it," she said quietly under her breath.

A large waitress appeared at her table with a pleasant smile on her face. "Hi. My name's Rosa and I'll be your server this evening. Can I get you started with some coffee or tea?"

* * *

"Goddammit. Make the call."

"Fuck that. You make the call."

"What? You a pussy or something?"

"Whatever. You know this is on both of us." The man pulled out his cell phone and dialed. "Sir. I'm afraid we've lost her." The man pulled the phone away from his face and put it back in his pocket.

"Well, what the hell did he say?"

"He said to pack it in and come back."

"That was it?"

"Yeah."

"Damn. That can't be a good sign."

* * *

Rebecca took her time eating, left a sizeable tip and eventually left the café towards her final destination. It was only a few blocks away and she pulled her hoodie over her head while she meandered towards it. She stopped across the street and checked her watch. She had thirty minutes to wait and the timing was right to make the call. She stood in an alcove, pulled the satellite phone out of her backpack, and dialed a number from memory. It was answered almost right away

"Roberta?"

"Laura. It's Rebecca."

"Oh my God, Rebecca, I'm so glad to hear your voice. I'm so sorry we had to leave you at the hospital. I feel absolutely terrible about that. Are you okay?"

"I'm fine. My ribs hurt a bit. How's everyone?"

"Apparently we're on the run, but we're all fine. Thanks for asking."

Rebecca nodded in the alcove to herself. "Roberta filled me in on a lot of the details but I need to know what happened to me."

Laura paused and lowered her voice. "It was a nightmare. I don't know what you remember from the attack but I thought you were dead. Julie lost her mind and left the vehicle. When Gavin saw you go down he got out and ran to you. I had to protect him."

"I understand."

"No, no you don't. I had to shoot a man to stop him from hurting my family."

"Damn. Laura, I'm sorry. You should have never been put in that position."

"You don't understand. I'm not complaining about that. I'm sure I'll have to deal with those emotions at some point but, to tell you the truth, I would do it again if I had to."

"Okay." Rebecca was confused. "What part am I just not understanding?"

"Julie died."

"Wait. What did you just say?"

"Julie was shot through the heart and died at the scene. The part that you need to understand is that Gavin brought her back to life."

"He did what?"

Laura continued. "You know about Stir. Hell, you know that both my kids are special."

"Sure, but…"

"Ask yourself this Rebecca. How are you up and around if you had a broken rib, a concussion and were in an induced coma?"

"I…I…"

"Gavin must have healed you." Laura paused. "He loves you. You know that, right?"

Rebecca was trying to wrap her mind around everything. "I'm..I'm pretty fond of the little bugger myself."

"He had to have done something to you, it's the only thing that makes sense. Anyway, Julie's recovering. She lost her memory but I'm working on that. The kids are dealing with this drastic change for the time being. We just don't know if we're still being hunted."

"I think it's best that you're exactly where you are right now until we can regroup. How's the rest of my team?"

"You heard about Whiskey?"

Rebecca lowered her head. "Yeah. Roberta told me. Pisses me off."

"Me too. I just hope Sam and Bill took care of business. You haven't heard from them, or perhaps even Thomas or Emily by any chance, have you?"

"I'm sorry Laura. I'm on my way to D.C. now to dig up what I can. I need to know what's going on as badly as you do."

Rebecca could hear Laura begin to softly cry. "It's…it's going to be okay Laura."

"That's easy for you to say. I'm supposed to be the strong one and I feel like I'm losing my mind. I just don't know what's happened to my husband and daughter. It's driving me crazy thinking about it."

"Do you trust me?"

"Wh..what?" Laura replied between tears.

"I'm asking you if you trust me."

"Yes, yes of course I do."

"Then I'm going to make you a promise. I promise to find Thomas and Emily and bring you all back together. Your family has been nothing but good to me and I'm not about to quit on you now. You're not the only one who wants payback." Rebecca touched her scar again.

"Thank you Rebecca. Hold on for a second."

Rebecca heard Gavin in the background before Laura got back on the phone. "Gavin wants to say hello."

"Becca?"

"Hey Gavin. How're you doing squirt?"

"Are you better?"

"Yes. Do I have you to thank for that?"

"Mayyyyybbbbbe."

"Well good. Thank you Gavin. I have to go now but could you do me a favor?"

"What?"

"Could you take care of your mother for me? She needs a few hugs."

"Okay. Bye Becca, love you."

"I love you too Gavin." She heard the phone being handed over.

"Rebecca, you still there?" Laura asked as she took back the phone.

"Your son is the cutest."

"Rebecca, I just wanted to say thank you for everything."

"I tell you what. Let's make a deal. You take care of yourself and everyone with you, and I'll be your eyes and ears on the outside. I'm going to find them Laura, I swear it."

"Thank you. You have no idea what that means to me."

183

"So, deal?"

"Deal," Laura replied. "But you have to do me a favor."

"Name it."

"Stay mobile, watch your back and don't take any chances. We thought we lost you once already."

"Everything's going to be alright. I've got to go. Stay strong."

"Thanks. You too. Bye." The line went dead.

Rebecca looked down at the phone in her hand and thumbed the power off. *What the fuck did I just promise? No pressure at all.*

* * *

At 10:30 she walked across the street to the Greyhound bus station and purchased a ticket using cash and a falsified name. There were a few seats left and she carefully looked around before she boarded the bus. She knew it would take a couple of days before she'd arrive in Washington D.C. but she was confident she would be a vital component to figuring out what the hell was going on. At 10:35 the bus pulled out and began its long trek eastward.

28

Wednesday November 19, 1997 Middle of the Night Offshore

It had only been four days since their escape from the roadside assault and the third full day onboard the luxurious boat. The gentle rocking of the ocean consistently helped everyone on 'Slice of Heaven' fall asleep very quickly. The constant Hawaiian breeze wafted through the yacht windows and lured them all in to a false sense of security. They hoped that here, on the open ocean, they could remain anonymous from whoever was after them. The truth was that their safety wasn't certain and that specific anxiety was constantly on the adult's minds. The children, on the other hand, had adapted to the change much more quickly than their parents, for the time being. But, the scars from the attack ran deep and would haunt each of them with nightmares for years to come.

Gavin tossed and turned in the bed next to his mother and Stickers. He'd had a hard time getting to sleep the night before as well, ever since he'd healed Sarah's gashed toe the day before. And ever since he talked to Rebecca on the phone he had been doubly amped up.

I'm growing stronger every day. I helped out that bird and I healed Stir.

Gavin smiled at the memory.

But then Aunt Julie got hurt. I didn't even know what I was doing. I made some doorway and I walked through it. Where did I go?

Gavin shifted his small body around some more to get comfortable. Laura gently stirred next to him but didn't wake up.

Where did I go? I remember seeing Grandma. But what happened?

Gavin's brow scrunched together in deep thought as he tried to recall the specifics.

I saw Grandma and she took me to Aunt Julie. But where was I? I don't know but I'm glad that Rebecca is better.

Gavin looked over at his mother and then quietly rolled out of bed. He adjusted his out of place pajamas, closed his eyes and concentrated. In the pale darkness, of their room, a small shimmering rift began to appear. A tear appeared in the middle of the air, right in front of Gavin, and continued to grow. Shimmering and dazzling light spilled out through the tear and brightened the small room.

Gavin opened his eyes and looked at what he'd created. With a quick glace over at his mother, to make sure she was still asleep, he stepped through the tear which immediately closed behind him. The room returned to darkness as Laura slowly rolled over in her sleep.

The four year old blinked a few times and tried to get his bearings.

Where am I?

He looked around at the absolute vastness that surrounded him. He was in a desert. It was flat and went on for as far as he could see. The tan sand sifted between his toes and Gavin bent down to touch it. The sand was warm and it seemed to call to him at the same time. A shadow suddenly loomed behind him. Gavin turned his head and looked up.

"You shouldn't be here sweetie."

Gavin recognized the voice immediately.

"Grandma!" He opened his arms and leaned in to for a hug which was immediately returned with such ferocity only a grandparent can provide.

"It's good to see you Gavin."

"I miss you Grandma."

Betsy smiled. "I miss you too sweetheart. What are you doing here? You're not supposed to be here." She loosened her hug and they both sat down on the warm sand together.

"I'm not?"

"No."

"Why not?"

Betsy sighed. "It's impossible to explain. But in the simplest of terms only the people that are dead are allowed here."

Gavin gave her a puzzled look. "But Auntie Julie isn't dead."

She shook her head slowly. "She was dead Gavin. She was until you brought her back."

"Oh," he replied. "Was…was I not supposed to do that?"

"There are rules in this place sweetie, rules that I don't always agree or believe in. And then there's you and your amazing gift." She saw that her grandson wasn't following her train of thought. "Let's just say that what you did should not happen again."

"Why?"

Kids. Questioning everything. Just like me. Betsy smiled. "Don't worry about it sweetheart. Let's just get you home." She stood up in the sand and Gavin followed suit.

"What if I want to stay and visit?"

Betsy took both his hands in hers. "There will be time for that in the future. Right now I need you to forget this ever happened."

"Why?"

"For your own safety." Betsy stopped herself and tried a different tact. "This has all been a dream. Dreams are the gateway to other realities. Time to leave and wake up from your dream. Go on. I'll watch you from here."

Gavin gave his grandmother another hug and then turned away. A portal appeared out of the ground, just high enough for the four year old, and he stepped through it. He appeared back in the same place he'd left. As the light faded from the receding rift he watched as his mother tossed and turned in the bed.

Maybe she's having bad dreams.

Gavin climbed back in to bed, got under the covers and curled up next to his mother just as Rebecca had asked him to do. She settled down almost immediately and fell in to a rhythm and Gavin fell asleep soon thereafter.

When Laura woke up in the morning she couldn't explain how so much sand had found its way in to their bed.

29
Wednesday November 19, 1997 Early Morning
D.C.

Calvin and Hobbes worked irregular hours due to the high demands the DCI placed on both of them. With multiple projects in play at one time, their downtime hours varied as did their sleeping patterns. Case in point, they had been up since three a.m. entrenched in video games. Calvin was playing Fallout on his PC, enduring the post-apocalyptic wasteland as he struggled to survive. Hobbes, on the other hand, was using the television to play Star Fox 64 on the Nintendo 64. The controller in his hands rattled from time to time due to the addition of the Rumble Pak. They were both clearly engaged with their games when one of their systems beeped at them.

"Check that out," said Calvin.

"Hell no. You're closer, you check it out," Hobbes shot back.

Calvin rolled his eyes. He paused his game and rolled his chair over to the system in question. He tapped a few keys and new information appeared on the screen.

"Interesting."

"What is?" Hobbes asked as he shot down another target.

"Our contact at the NSA tracked something down."

"Which is?"

"I was just getting to that part. Patience."

"Whatever."

"It appears that SANDBOX bought a large number of encrypted satellite phones at one point."

Hobbes shrugged as he blasted another ship out of existence. "Nothing odd about that."

"True," Calvin replied. "But since we've been tasked with locating the family since they disappeared from the hospital, it might behoove you to get your ass over here."

Hobbes paused the game. "Fuck. Fine." He walked over and sat down at his computer. He began typing and the new data appeared on his screen as well. He began to pour through it. A few minutes later he spoke up again. "There are quite a few phones from the list that are active. But this one is the most interesting."

"Which one?" Calvin asked.

"Look at number thirty-four. When you drill down in to its usage it's only synced with the satellite system twice a day. The logs show that the connections are between three and five minutes in length each time."

"Good catch. Let me launch the tracking program our NSA contact 'lent' us."

Calvin initiated a new program and plugged in the specific satellite phone's information it requested. He hit Enter and waited for the results.

"So how's Star Fox?"

Hobbes smiled and turned his chair towards Calvin. "It's awesome. The Ruble Pak really adds to the experience. You should try it."

"Maybe once I've finished Fallout. I have the feeling I have quite a number of mutants I still need to deal with."

"I bet."

The computer beeped and Calvin returned his gaze to it.

"Well well well. What do we have here?"

Hobbes got up, walked and peered over his cohort's shoulder. "That's a unique pattern."

"Definitely. The signal always originates from the Hawaiian islands, but just offshore and never in the same place."

Hobbes stood up straight. "Are you thinking what I'm thinking?"

Calvin nodded. "It makes sense. What other option is there?"

Hobbes went back to his chair and sat down. "I'll bring up a satellite and see what I can find."

"Good. While you're doing that I'm heading back to the wastelands."

Hobbes grinned. "Lucky bastard."

*   *   *

Two hours later Hobbes got exited. "Got em! I got'em!"

Calvin immediately stopped playing and came over. "What'ya got?"

"Take a look for yourself," Hobbes said very pleased with himself.

On the screen was a top down view of a large yacht. It was in motion around the north side of the Big Island. Dawn was approaching that part of the world and the sun was moments away from cresting the horizon.

"Zoom in," Hobbes said.

Calvin did just that. On the deck of the ship two men came into view. They both held assault weapons in their hands.

"This could be anyone. Why do you think it's them Hobbes?"

"I backtracked the satellite phone logs to where they indicated the phone was at the time of each connection. Based on that information I was able to put together a rough path the phone, or vessel in this case, had been taking. It felt that every twenty-four hours the signal would move to a new island. With that said, the last connection was late last night. They were still sailing around the Big Island at that time. I took that hypothesis and began a satellite search around the island taking in to account how many

191

people they had with them. I figured it needed to be a large boat. This one we're looking at is one of four that fits the parameters, but it's the only one that has armed men in plain view."

"Great fucking job Hobbes."

Hobbes smiled even more. "Tell me something I don't know."

"Yeah. Subtle. However, I don't mean to bust your bubble but this is hardly a confirmation."

"True," Hobbes replied. "But the day is still young. Go play your game and I'll watch the satellite feed."

"Well, you're not going to get an argument from me about that. Do you want a Coke or something?"

"What do you think?"

Calvin chuckled. "Coming right up."

* * *

Three hours, and two Cokes later, Hobbes called Calvin back over.

"Definitive?"

On the screen Calvin and Hobbes watched three women, a number of children, five armed men and what appeared to be a cat enjoying the morning sun aboard the large yacht.

"You, my friend, just hit the preverbal jackpot."

"Good. I'll make the call."

"Yes, I'm sure the Director will be very happy to hear what you have to say."

D.W. Neuman

30
Wednesday November 19, 1997 Late Morning
Offshore

It was another restless night for me. I woke up with Gavin curled up next to me. What I don't understand is why there was sand in the bed and on the floor. That was so weird. But overall that doesn't matter. I miss my daughter and my husband so damn much. I've been trying to be the strong one around here, the rock for everyone else, but this situation is taking its toll on me. Not knowing anything is killing me. Thomas' last words to me were to run and hide and that he was being held hostage by the DCI, the actual Director of Central Intelligence. What the hell is going on? We're attacked by Russian sleepers, we're on the run AND we have no idea when and if we'll see our families again. THIS IS SO FRUSTRATING!!

"Laura?"

Julie had startled her unintentionally. Laura quickly forced her face to relax.

Julie sat down. "I'm sorry to bother you. Are you alright? Your face looked pretty intense as I walked over."

Laura closed her journal, put it aside and took a deep breath. "My anxiety is at an all-time high. I'm worried about my daughter. I'm worried about my husband. I'm worried about Sam. I'm worried about Bill. I'm worried that we're completely fucked and there's little we can do about it. So no, I'm not alright."

Julie just sat there and took it all in.

Laura shook her head. "I do have a couple glimmers of hope. One is that Rebecca called last night and she's looking in to all of this. I trust her completely. Although I think she made a promise she won't be able to keep."

"And the second?"

"The second?"

193

"The second glimmer of hope you mentioned," said Julie.

"Right. The second glimmer is sitting right in front of me."

"Who? Me?"

Laura nodded. "You've come such a long way in such a short amount of time."

"I feel the same way. I want to remember more."

"And I want to help you do just that." She paused. "Listen, sorry about snapping at you."

Julie put her hand up to stop her friend. "Forget it. You've taken on one hell of a role because, let's face it, my sister and I were not up to the task."

"That's kind of you to say but…"

"Enough of the downplaying Laura, just own it. We're where we are right now because of you. And that's safe and out of harm's way. On top of that, you're juggling everything else. So of course you're stressed out. I can only begin to imagine what you're going through."

Laura didn't know how to respond.

"So, I figure if you help me remember what happened then maybe that will help us all out somehow."

Get it together. Your friend is asking for your help. Laura smiled. "Of course. Yesterday's regression was amazing. If you're up for it we should try it again. Why don't we head inside where we won't be disturbed?"

* * *

Within a few minutes Laura had brought Julie into another trance and had regressed her back to the time where she had been shot.

"Julie, can you hear me?"

"Yes," she replied sleepily.

194

"Good. Remember, you're safe. Look around. Where are you?"

"Nowhere."

Not this again. "What do you see?"

"There are people. People are everywhere."

"Where are all these people?"

"It...it looks like a stadium. So many people."

"What are you doing there Julie?"

"I'm waiting. I think I'm waiting. Waiting with everyone else."

"What are you waiting for?"

"I...I don't know. Something. Something important."

"What else do you see?"

Julie's body stiffened a bit. "Is that Gavin?"

"What do you mean?"

But Julie wasn't listening to Laura's voice any longer. "It is Gavin. Who's that older lady he's with?"

"Julie?"

"Where am I? Who are you?"

"Can you hear me?"

Julie extended her hand out to no one in particular. "Okay."

Laura gently took Julie by the shoulders and rocked her.

"We're flying."

"Julie, can you hear me?"

"Yes, I can hear you. We're flying."

"Who's flying?"

"Gavin, another lady, and me. We're leaving the stadium behind. All those people....they're still waiting."

At least she's acknowledging me now. "Where are you going?"

"Someplace else. Wait. What's that?"

Laura leaned forward. "What? What do you see?"

"It looks like a doorway. It doesn't look right. We're drifting downwards out of the sky towards it. We just landed next to it." Julie started to shiver.

"You're safe. Nothing can hurt you."

She shook her head. "No. No, you're wrong."

"What are you talking about? What's happening?"

"No. Don't. What do you mean it's the only way?" Her body tried to back pedal in the chair she was sitting in."

Laura took hold of Julie's arm to help reassure her but it wasn't working. "You're safe."

"I want to go home. No, please, you can't!"

I'm losing her!

Suddenly everything stopped. Julie slowly shook her head as if coming out of a dream.

Laura was beside herself. "Julie? Julie?"

Julie nodded. "I'm okay. Just give me a minute." She took her time and sat up in her chair. It was another twenty seconds before she looked over at Laura and spoke. "I know what happened. I remember everything. I know who I am."

Laura was speechless. Julie continued.

"The woman that was with Gavin was his grandmother. When she took us back to the portal she was distraught. Something wasn't right. Gavin wasn't supposed to be there and especially was never supposed to have come looking for me. She was upset."

"What did you mean when you said 'what do you mean it's the only way'?" Laura probed.

Julie closed her eyes and tears fell down her cheeks. "The only way I was allowed back was to wipe my mind. She told me there wasn't any time to think about it. Either I stayed where I was or I had to go back without knowing who I was."

"So...so you made the choice to come back?"

196

"No, that's the thing. She made some comment about 'they're coming'. Immediately she whispered in my ear that I'd be changed forever, placed her hands on either side of my head and pushed the two of us back through the portal before I could say anything."

"Holy shit."

"Yeah, no shit holy shit. I can only assume that somehow she was the one that changed my brown eyes to black as a constant reminder."

Laura slowly nodded her head. "It has to be. But what I don't understand is how easy it's been to have you remember what happened to you."

"Regression hypnosis doesn't go this smoothly?"

"Not by a long shot, well, it never did with Thomas. But this is an extraordinary event that you're recalling. Do you have any idea what impact this could have?"

"That's assuming anyone wanted to actually listen or believe my story. Right now, the less I know about where I was the better."

"Dammit Betsy," Laura muttered.

"Shit. Now I remember her. When Kim and I walked in on everyone talking she was there. Michael and Betsy Clark."

Laura nodded. "Yeah, one and the same. From what I've gathered talking to Thomas, Gavin, and even Betsy is that she's got a bit of a streak in her."

"A streak?"

"I think you got very, very lucky to be back here amongst us Julie."

"I have a strange suspicion that you're right on the money."

Laura leaned over as Julie leaned in. The fierce hug lasted a long time before they stopped.

"You scared the hell out of me," Laura said.

"Thank you Laura. Thank you so much. Words can't express what I'm feeling right now. I'm actually me again."

"Who's me again?" Kim asked as she stepped in the room.

Julie stood up. "Get over here."

"What'd I miss?" Kim said as she walked over to her sister.

Julie pulled her sister close and didn't let go. "I remember everything. I know who I am again. I love you so much."

Kim returned the embrace. Her words were filled with a tremendous amount of emotion. "It's about time dammit. I've missed you."

"I've missed you too."

Kim wiped away her tears as they parted and sat down next to Laura.

"I was looking after the kids. What the hell happened?"

"All the thanks go to Laura. She's been amazing."

Before the conversation could continue, all five children appeared at the doorway.

"I said I'd be right back," Kim reminded them.

Julie opened her arms. "Amanda. Craig."

Instinctually both of her children both knew and wanted to be in their mother's arms. They moved from the doorway and through the small room where Julie smothered them in hugs and kisses while everyone else watched on. It was a reunion that was long overdue. They finally had their mother back.

Amanda finally spoke up. "Mom. Where's dad?"

"Yeah," added Sarah, Kim's daughter. "Where's dad?"

The three adults all shared a quick glance before Laura spoke up. "They're out there trying to protect us."

"When are they coming home? Do we even have a home?" Amanda persisted.

"Sweetie," said Julie. "There are a lot of unknowns. Your father is doing what he needs to do right now. You have to be strong for me. We'll be a family again very soon."

"Are more bad people going to shoot at us?"

"Stir will protect us," Gavin said matter-of-factly.

"No," Laura replied. "We're not in danger anymore."

"Promise?" asked Sarah.

The adults shared another quick glance.

"Promise," Laura assured them.

"Come on, let's go play," said Craig as the rest of the children followed him back outside.

When they were gone Laura let out a deep sigh. "Shit."

Julie and Kim nodded in agreement. Laura suddenly noticed the time. "Oh shit."

"I thought we just went through that?" said Kim.

Laura shook her head. "No, it's time to turn on the satellite phone. I almost missed the window." Laura opened the bag that contained a book, her journal, a Glock 17 and the satellite phone. She pulled it out and turned it on. Fifteen seconds later it rang in her hand.

"Hello?"

"It's Roberta."

"Good to hear your voice. I heard from Rebecca last night."

"Fantastic. I was going to ask you about that. Are Julie and Kim close by?"

"They're right here with me. I'll put you on speaker phone." Laura made the adjustment. "Go ahead."

"I want to keep this short so I'll just get to the point. I haven't heard anything from Sam or Bill yet. I don't know where they are and I don't like the fact that they haven't checked in. No one from their team has checked in either. I'm sorry for the bad news."

"Thank you for being so straightforward," said Kim. "We know you're doing everything you can out there. Thank you so much for everything you've done for us."

"I agree," added Julie. "You've been absolutely amazing Roberta. Thank you."

"Julie? Is that you? You sound, well, yourself."

"You can thank Laura for that."

"Glad to hear it. You all take care out there. I'll hopefully have something more positive for you during the next window. Bye." The line clicked off.

"She has really put herself out there," Kim offered.

"Big time," said Laura.

The room was quiet for a few seconds as the news sunk in.

"I just hope our men are taking care of business and working their asses off to make it back to us."

"Yeah," said Kim. "This yacht is just horrible."

They all looked at each other as the tension broke. They began to chuckle.

"Okay, I needed that," said Laura.

"Me too," Julie added. "Why don't we go check in on the kids and do our best to keep a positive attitude."

"Agreed."

"Ditto."

<u>31</u>

Wednesday November 19, 1997 Evening
D.C.

After a quick flight from New Jersey to D.C., the private jet landed and taxied off to yet another private hangar. Under guard Sam and Bill were searched again and then moved from the plane and placed in the back of a moving truck. They rode in darkness until the truck eventually stopped.

The door opened upward. An enormous amount of fluorescent lights littered the ceiling as they stepped down out of the truck. They instantly decided they must be underground.

Bill whispered to Sam under his breath. "We're not in Kansas anymore."

"This way," one of the guards commanded.

They were led off to a nondescript door. The same guard produced a cardkey, swiped the reader and the door clicked. He pulled it open.

"Let's go. Inside." Sam and Bill hesitated. "I won't tell you again assholes."

The two relented and entered. Just before the door closed behind them the guard said, "Enjoy your stay."

They looked around the new room. There was a small kitchen, a bathroom, two beds and a sitting area with a couch. Against one of the walls was a large shelving unit filled with worn paperbacks. A mounted television sat on the wall behind a security screen.

"What the hell is this?" Bill spat out.

Sam walked further in to the open room and looked around. He immediately noticed the video surveillance cameras.

Lovely.

The television came to life suddenly and the image of the DCI appeared on the screen.

"Do come in you two. Have a seat and make yourselves comfortable."

"Go to hell," replied Sam.

"Come now; don't be like that. This is a reward."

"A reward?" Bill added as he stepped up next to Sam. "You've got to be shitting me."

Victor Bannon smiled from wherever he was. "You've done your country a great service. The initial reports indicate that you two stopped an impeding attack on U.S. soil. You should be very proud of yourselves. You have a bright future ahead of you."

"And yet here we are, under lock and key, in some out of the way location that no one knows about," said Sam.

"Touché. You're right, of course. Heroes should be treated with more respect. Perhaps you'd like your families to join you?"

Sam and Bill didn't respond.

"No? I tell you what Sam; you should learn to keep your mouth shut. What if I just start sending you pieces of your children, hmm? What about that? In no time at all what's left of your family will be right there with you."

"I'm going to find you and I'm going to…"

The DCI held up his hand. "I'd advise you to be careful with your next words."

Bill grabbed Sam's shoulder and forcefully turned him away. "What my friend means to say is thank you for your hospitality, sir. We appreciate your thoughtfulness behind it."

Victor's smile broadened. "Well, that's better. You're welcome Mr. Nicholson. Now, if there isn't going to be any more ugliness, please unwind and relax. It's going to be a day or so before I have use for you again."

"Mr. Bannon."

"Yes?"

Bill used as much control as he could muster. "I'd like to request the opportunity to talk with my family."

"I see. A valid request. I tell you what, you complete another mission for me and I'll allow it." The DCI leaned in just a little. "Fuck with me and I'll just have to prolong your wait." He sat back. "Deal?"

Bill nodded.

"I can't hear you Mr. Nicholson."

"Yes."

"Yes what?"

Fucker. "Yes, sir."

"Better. And what about you Mr. Paige? Have you had a change of heart?"

Sam turned back to face the television. *You're going to die very badly you smug sonofabitch. I will take the life from you with my own two hands.* Sam's poker face revealed none of his thoughts.

"Yes sir. You have a deal."

"Excellent. Very good to hear. While you wait please make yourselves at home. Take a shower, make some food, enjoy a good book and get some rest. I'll be in touch." The television blinked off.

"I fucking hate that guy," whispered Bill.

"Let's wash up," said Sam.

"What?"

Sam headed towards the bathroom. "We should wash up." Sam entered the bathroom and turned on the sink's water. He looked around the small room and saw that there weren't any surveillance cameras. Bill joined him a moment later.

"You okay?"

"Get in here and keep your voice down." Sam turned on the shower as well. "I don't know how much cover this will provide us."

Bill nodded and spoke softly. "We're pretty fucked brother."

"Agreed. At this point we have more than just ourselves to think about. We have our men being held in Florida. Thomas and Emily, from what we last heard, are being held against their will. And we have our families that are supposedly in the Director's control as well."

"My gut tells me he doesn't have them."

Sam nodded. "Me too. Why not use them against us now to keep us in line rather than dangle the idea that he has them. Something doesn't add up. Regardless, that's another huge unknown we have to deal with as well."

"Even if he does have them we have to come to terms with the fact that we're all liabilities. He's not going to let them or either of us roam free ever again."

Sam didn't like it but he already knew it was the truth. "No witnesses or loose ends."

"So, with all those positive thoughts running around in our heads, what the hell are we going to do about it?"

"We come up with a plan of attack so we can get out of this shit alive. I'm going to grab the first shower. Let's put our heads together later and see what we've come up with."

"Roger that."

32

Wednesday November 19, 1997 Late Evening D.C.

"Where're we at?"

"Sir," Calvin replied, "Your personnel are in the air and the ground assets are coming together. The operation should be live by tomorrow afternoon."

"Get me that leverage right away."

"I'm staying with this and will give you an update as soon as it's been handled."

"See that you do."

The DCI ended the call and immediately placed another. It was answered after the first ring.

"Dr. Matsushita. Give me an update."

"Yes sir. I've isolated the specific RNA strand based off a quick pattern comparison."

"In English, doctor."

"Yes, of course. Loosely translated I'll have a synthesized, but preliminary serum very soon to start my initial tests."

"And this preliminary testing phase, will it harbor the necessary results I hired you for?"

"It's too soon to tell. I can't make any promises at this time. However, I'm confident that it will definitely yield some results."

"That's not terribly reassuring."

"You have to understand, these tests take time. I've barely begun to scratch the surface."

"That sounds like excuses to me. But let me ask you this, will another test subject help your progress?"

Yamato smiled. "Yes, indeed."

"Very well. Continue with your work. You will have the boy in the next forty-eight hours."

Victor hung up the phone. *Arrogant prick. I don't trust him. I need to keep a very close watch over him.*

The private phone rang. The DCI sighed and answered it.

"Yes?"

"Sir, sorry to bother you."

"I'm busy. What is it Hobbes?"

"The evidence has been planted in SANDBOX's file servers as you requested."

"Very good. Thank you."

* * *

Hobbes hung up the phone a little confused. Calvin noticed.

"What?"

"I dunno. The Director just said thank you."

"Yeah, that's pretty odd. Maybe he's starting to realize just how much work we do around here for him."

Calvin just stared at Hobbes until they both started to crack up. Soon afterward they both returned to their work at hand.

33

Thursday November 20, 1997 Mid-Morning
Facility Thirteen

"I don't want to. You can't make me!" Emily screamed.

Dr. Matsushita ignored the young girl's pleas. She had been bound to a wheelchair. Her left arm was completely immobilized while her right arm had been secured in a moveable aperture. Her right hand could move around but without the ability to move her arm Emily currently could be classified as a puppet. On the table, next to her, lay the cold corpse of Nikolay Dmitriev.

The doctor continued. "You will touch him. I need to see what your powers can do when used on the dead."

Emily shook her head back and forth. "No! That's gross!" She was adamant.

"Enough!" the doctor yelled as he lost his composure. "You are nothing more than a guinea pig to me you little brat! If you do not do what I tell you to do then I have no choice but to hurt your father!"

"NOOO!"

"I will have you sit here and watch as I remove his fingers, one by one. Would you like to see that young lady, to see your father scream as I cut his fingers off? I think I would. Let's make that happen." Yamato walked over to the phone and placed it to his ear. "Bring Mr. Clark in here."

"No! Don't hurt my daddy!"

"Hold for a second." He turned to Emily. "Are you having second thoughts?"

Emily writhed madly in the bonds that held her to no avail. *I want my mommy. I don't like this place. I want to go home.*

"I'm waiting for an answer. I'll count to three."

Emily continued to struggle.

"One."

"I hate you!"

"That's nice dear. Two."

Emily, at that moment, began to cry and sob.

Yamato was unimpressed. "You're just delaying the inevitable. You'll do what I ask now or you'll end up doing it later. The difference is that your father will have five less fingers. Two and a half."

Emily continued to glare at the man holding her against her will.

"His loss. Thre…"

"Don't! I'll do it."

Dr. Matsushita smiled and spoke in to the phone again. "Mr. Clark's presence will not be necessary at this time." He hung up the receiver and walked back over to the table. The video cameras in the room continued to record everything from multiple angles.

"Good. I see you've come to your senses. You must love your father very much." He took hold of her immobile right arm and manipulated it towards the exposed, graying thigh of Nikolay.

Emily flinched as her exposed hand slapped against the dead skin. She instinctively tried to pull away but she couldn't move. The man's skin was deathly cold to the touch.

"Do your magic."

Ick! This is soooo gross.

"I'm waiting."

Emily stopped wincing. Nothing had happened. Nothing at all. No one appeared out of thin air.

Yamato put his hands on his hips with impatience. "Nothing's happening."

"I know. I'm trying."

"Don't lie."

"I'm not." She closed her eyes and pressed her hand deeper into Nikolay's cold thigh. Still nothing. "I...I don't know. It's not working."

"And why should I believe you?"

"Because I wish it did. Maybe whoever appeared would kill you and save me!" Emily spat back.

He smiled. "Fair enough."

Yamato then motioned to an assistant who came up behind Emily and quickly injected her. Emily became unconscious in seconds.

"Take her away. I have a very unpleasant phone call to make."

* * *

The door to Richard and Thomas' cell opened and three guards made their way inside.

"Where's my daughter? I demand to see her!"

"Same shit, different day," retorted one of the guards.

"Both of you, on your feet," said another guard.

"Where are you taking us?" Richard asked.

"You'll know soon enough. Until then, no more questions or you will be punished."

Fucking great. Here we go again. Won't this ever end? Thomas reluctantly got up, along with Richard, and headed to the hallway. They both knew where this was going; back to another round of interrogation. His chest hurt like a sonofabitch and he was sure that whatever was in store for him would certainly pop those stitches.

As the hallway split off in another direction one of the guards led Richard away while the other two opened a door for Thomas to enter. Thomas paused and watched his father's mentor being led away to another room before he was pushed from behind into his own.

*   *   *

"I'll ask you again old man, what do you know about the Clark family?"

When Richard didn't respond the man made a hand motion. The guard behind where Richard sat applied significant pressure to his shoulder. The same shoulder that had become extremely sore and bruised when he'd been tossed across his cell a few days earlier.

"FUUUUCCCCCCKKKKKKKTTTHHHHHATTTHUUURRT TSSS!!"

Sweat immediately appeared and trickled down his face.

"Let me begin again Mr. Moore. What do you know about the Clark family?"

Richard's breath was ragged. "This....this isn't the first...the first time I've been fucked over by my own government you prick. Eat shit." He managed a quick smile before his interrogator motioned to the guard again.

*   *   *

Thomas wasn't fairing any better down the hall. Before any questions had even been asked one guard had pulled Thomas' arms behind his back as the other worked him over. Blood ran down an open gash on his cheek and his ribs were now tender to the touch.

Thomas was forced to sit down and face a man he hadn't seen before.

"How does it work?"

"Wh..what are you talking about?" Thomas mumbled.

"Don't play dumb with me. How does your daughter so what she does?"

"Fuck you."

The guard behind Thomas quickly boxed his ears. Pain riddled through his head and he rolled over to one side. The guard pulled him back up so he was sitting straight.

"Asshole," Thomas breathed softly.

The guard went to hit him again but the man waved him off.

"You know, Mr. Clark, you can resist all you want. We know everything already but I do admire your resilience."

"Lucky me."

"Speaking of luck, I believe you just walked in to some."

Thomas didn't follow. "What are you talking about?"

"I've recently received news that your son will be joining us here at the facility very shortly."

Thomas' eyes abruptly widened and the interrogator smiled. "In fact, the good doctor tells me that he can't wait to dissect his brain once he's finished all his tests."

Thomas couldn't take it anymore. "I'LL FUCKING KILL YOU!"

He rose out of his chair with the intention of strangling the bastard in front of him. He never made it as the guard tasered him. Thomas collapsed on the table, with his outstretched hands, and then slid backwards onto the ground.

The interrogator stood up. "I guess we're done for today. Take him back to his cell."

<u>34</u>

Thursday November 20, 1997 Late Morning
Offshore

On the top aft deck Julie, Kim and Laura were laid out and let the sun do the rest of the work for them. The scenic shores of Maui filled the background along with other vessels that dotted the picturesque landscape. Laura had just turned off the satellite phone and returned it to her bag she always kept by her side.

"Anything?" Kim asked hopefully.

Laura shook her head. "I'm afraid not. No word on anything yet."

"Let's not go down this road again every day, okay?" Julie implored. "We can worry all we want but we have to try and remain positive, not only for ourselves but for our children as well."

"You're right," Kim replied. "I just miss my knuckle dragging sonofabitch husband."

Laura and Julie smiled in agreement and went back to letting the warm rays tan their bodies.

'Slice of Heaven' had anchored off the eastern shore of Maui and its crew diligently worked on lunch preparations for their guests. Captain Bob, Felicia and Ginger were professionals and knew not to ask any questions or engage their guests in idle chat, but that didn't stop them from privately talking amongst themselves.

"So what do either of you think their deal is?" Felicia asked.

"Our passengers are definitely a unique group," the captain replied. "Five armed men that reek ex-military along with five children and their three mothers."

"I think I know who they are," said Ginger.

Felicia stopped what she was doing. "What do you mean? Like they're famous people or something?"

"Kind of. I was listening to the radio last night and a news story came up about a family that had been attacked on the east side of Oahu."

"Attacked?" Captain Bob inquired.

Ginger nodded. "There were some casualties before the Marines showed up and ended it. Anyway, the report says that they were all at the hospital when suddenly...poof, they disappear."

"Wait. What are you saying?" Ginger asked. "That these are those people?"

"Yes. I believe they are. The timing is perfect."

Captain Bob spoke up. "If that's true then they need our protection, and our silence. We don't know what they've been through but they seem like really nice people. We're all being paid quite a bit of money for this job. Whether they are the same people that were attacked or not don't forget that we're here to make them feel comfortable and safe."

The trio continued to prepare lunch as their conversation drifted to other topics.

*   *   *

Gavin split off from the other children and made his way from the lower deck and up two floors to where his mother was sunbathing. Laura, and the others, opened their eyes when they heard someone stomp up the stairwell towards them.

"Hi sweetie," said his mother. "What's going on?"

"I want to go see grandma again."

Laura immediately sat up. "What do you mean again? When was the last time you saw her?"

214

"I dunno. The other night."

"You saw grandma the other night?"

"Uh huh."

"Where?"

Gavin softly shrugged his shoulders. "Someplace sandy. It felt good between my toes."

Oh shit. "Gavin, sweetie, you can't just go off and do that, okay?"

"Why?"

Julie and Kim sat up at this point, suddenly very interested in the conversation. "It's not safe."

Gavin took a step back. "Yes it is. Grandma's nice."

Laura shook her head. "That's not what I'm talking about. It's about where you go whe…"

He interrupted her. "It's safe! I want to show you!"

In the small section of the third floor aft deck a rift began to appear out of thin air. Kim and Julie's eyes opened wide. The tear opened wider at an alarming pace.

"Gavin." Laura said with as much authority as she could muster. "Do not go through there. Come here this instant."

"No!" he replied with a defiance she hadn't heard from him before.

"Come here right n.."

But it was too late. Gavin stepped through the tear and disappeared.

* * *

Gavin stepped through and appeared on a very small deserted island in the middle of a vast ocean. The waves slapped gently against the shore while a single palm tree moved in the rhythm to the gentle wind he felt on his skin. He looked around and didn't see anyone.

"Grandma?"

Nothing.

"Grandma?"

"You shouldn't be here."

Gavin jumped at the man's voice that had come from behind. He turned around and then smiled.

"Grandpa!"

Michael bent down and received his grandson's huge hug.

"I missed you grandpa."

"I've missed you too squirt."

"Where's grandma?"

"She's gotten herself in a tad bit of trouble I'm afraid."

"Trouble?"

Michael looked around quickly and then became very serious. "Gavin, there's no time to talk about that. In fact, we have very little time as it is. I need you to listen to me very carefully. Can you do that?"

Gavin nodded slowly.

"Very good. I need you to tell your mother where your sister and father are."

Gavin's eyes opened wide. He began to ask a question when Michael cut him off.

"There isn't time for questions. You need to remember everything I'm about to tell you."

He closed his mouth and nodded his head vigorously. "Kay."

Michael began to describe where Facility Thirteen was located in plain detail including the street names where the building was located. He went over it twice and then had his grandson repeat it to him.

"Excellent Gavin. I'm very proud of you for being so brave. Go back and tell your mother right now."

"Can…can I come back later?"

"Maybe. Maybe after everyone's back together, okay?"

"Kay. I love you grandpa."

Michael softened. "I love you too kiddo. Now go."

Gavin waved goodbye and stepped back through the ripple he'd created in the fabric of the universe and time itself.

* * *

"Come here right n.."

Gavin disappeared into the tear and immediately reappeared a moment later.

"..ow."

The tear closed up behind him as Laura reached for him and then held him tight. Julie and Kim were startled but Kim had seen something similar happen before. This was Julie's first time.

Laura panicked. "You scared me. You scared me so much."

"I have to tell you something."

"Shhh my little man, whatever it is, it can wait. I'm just glad you're back safe."

Gavin pushed away. "No. I have to tell you something. Grandpa made me."

A puzzled look washed over her face. "What do you mean grandpa made you? Made you do what?"

"Remember something. I don't want to forget."

Laura didn't know whether to cry or start laughing. She was beside herself. "What is it? What don't you want to forget?"

"Grandpa told me where Daddy and Em are."

Laura immediately recognized the importance of what her son was trying to communicate to her. "Tell me everything he told you."

Gavin did just that as Laura wrote it all down in her journal.

When he was through Laura pulled him close again. "You're a brave, brave little boy. Thank you. Thank you. But I just want you to have a normal life, that's all I've wanted."

"But I'm special and so is Em," he stated matter-of-factly.

Laura smiled. "Yes. Yes you are. And most importantly you're my special little man. Now, before I start crying, why don't you head off and go wash up for lunch. I'll be down shortly."

"Kay."

Gavin walked past Kim and Julie who could only stare at the four year old with untold powers as he walked by and headed down the stairs. When he was gone they turned and looked right at Laura.

"Holy shit," said Julie.

"What my sister just said," Kim added.

"No wonder you guys freaked out when he did that and came for me," Julie added. "I was not prepared for whatever the hell just occured."

"No one is," said Laura as she reached in to her bag and removed the satellite phone. But she stopped. "Shit."

"What?" Kim asked.

"I already talked with Roberta this morning. I'm only supposed to turn the phone on a couple of times a day."

"This," said Julie, "might be one of those times you break the damn rules."

Laura was torn. "I know, I know. I don't know what to do. The next window is hours from now. I can't sit on this information until then."

218

"You don't have a choice," said Kim. "It sucks but you don't."

"What? Why would you tell me something like that?"

"Don't deviate from the plan Roberta setup for you. You need to protect your family even though it's going to be impossible for you to wait." Kim paused. "Their lives may depend on you not breaking the established protocol, that's all I'm saying."

Laura almost pushed the phone's power button but stopped herself.

"Let's go get some lunch and we can come back here and talk about it as much as you want until the window opens this evening. We're here for you Laura, just like you've been here for us."

Shadows of the Heart

35

Thursday November 20, 1997 Evening
Offshore

The remainder of the day slowly dragged on. Laura's patience was constantly tested as she struggled with her newly acquired information her son had provided her.

What amazing gifts my children possess. What incredibly scary and powerful abilities. But they're so young and have been through so much in the past six months. I'm worrying about my sanity when I really should be thinking about theirs.

Laura, along with Kim and Julie, made their way to the top of the yacht's upper deck where they had sunbathed earlier that day. She gripped the satellite phone tightly in her hand as the three women looked out over the horizon.

"I do love it here," Laura said.

"Do you mean the boat?" Kim asked.

"No, of course not. I mean Hawaii in general. Look how beautiful everything is." A few moments later her face grew sullen. "But that'll never be the same again. As much as I'd want to stay here I fear the memories of what happened to all of us will overshadow our ability to positively move forward."

Julie and Kim reluctantly nodded in agreement.

Laura put her thoughts on hold. "But first things first."

She looked at her watch, powered on the phone, and then they waited in silence. Thirty seconds later the phone chirped in Laura's hand and she answered it immediately.

"Roberta."

"Hi Laura. I'm afraid I don't have anything new to tell you."

"That's fine. I have something new to tell you though."

"Oh? Is everything okay?"

"We're fine. Listen closely. I know the location in D.C. where Thomas, Emily and Richard are being held."

"What! That's incredible! How do you…"

Laura cut her off. "There's no time to explain how I know. Write what I'm about to tell you down."

Laura took the next minute to describe the location of Facility Thirteen to Roberta who didn't interrupt Laura while she took copious notes.

"That's it. That's all I have."

"I don't know how you came across this information Laura but the detail is amazing. I'm going to call Rebecca immediately and pass all of this along to her."

Laura was relieved. "Thank you Roberta. We feel so isolated and helpless out here. I only hope this information will help uncover some news about Sam and Bill as well."

"I'll keep my fingers crossed on this end Laura. I need to go. Hang in there, all of you."

The call ended and Laura powered off the phone.

* * *

Rebecca Cross was roused from sleep when her pocket began to vibrate. She opened her eyes and remembered she was still on the Greyhound bus. It was the middle of the night and sounds of snoring drifted down the aisle from a few of the other passengers. She pulled the phone out and answered it.

"Yes?"

"Rebecca. It's Roberta. I'm sorry to disturb you at this hour but I have something very important to tell you."

Rebecca shook the remnants of sleep out of her head and instantly came awake.

"One second."

She opened her backpack and pulled out a small notebook and a pen she had acquired at one of the stops the bus had made.

"Go ahead."

A couple of minutes later Rebecca stopped writing as Roberta finished relaying the information to her.

"Wow, those are some pretty specific details." She checked her watch. "I should arrive in D.C. in five or six hours. I'll check out this location right away."

"Thank you Rebecca. Thank you so much."

"You hang in there too. It's late where you are as well. Get some rest."

"Oh, you know me," Roberta replied, "I can't help myself."

"Join the club. Good night."

"Good night."

* * *

Hobbes watched the yacht from five hundred feet in the air as it sat anchored off the north eastern shore of Maui. He could have zoomed in closer but the evening sun had long dipped under the horizon. Instead he watched the inhabitants interact using an infrared thermal filter.

One of their servers started to beep at them and Calvin pulled up the new message.

"Wow. My guy at the NSA is really good."

Hobbes was intrigued. "What've you got?"

"Oh nothing. Just a decrypted phone call that happened not fifteen minutes ago aboard the very ship you're spying on right now."

"He broke the encryption?"

"Yeah. We're in. He even supplied the call. I definitely owe him a couple of beer."

"Pull it up. Let's hear what they're talking about."

* * *

"I don't know how you came across this information Laura but the detail is amazing. I'm going to call Rebecca immediately and pass all of this along to her."

Laura was relieved. "Thank you Roberta. We feel so isolated and helpless out here. I only hope this information will help uncover some news about Sam and Bill as well."

"I'll keep my fingers crossed on this end Laura. I need to go. Hang in there, all of you."

The call ended.

"Fuck me," said Calvin. "How the hell did she know exactly where they're being held? That's impossible."

"Who knows? We've seen some weird shit that even we can't explain. We need to alert the Director."

Calvin shook his head. "It's the middle of the night. I'm not going to wake him up with something this trivial. I'll tell him when we have an update on the current operation." Calvin motioned for Hobbes to turn around. "Get back on that satellite feed. It's thirty minutes till go time."

* * *

Laura tucked Gavin in to bed. Stickers immediately jumped up and curled next to his head. He began to purr and she smiled. *This reminds me of simpler times. Better times.* She leaned over and kissed her son on the forehead.

"Goodnight sweetie. I'll be back in a bit. Love you."

"Love you too," he replied as he began to drift off.

She closed the door behind her and joined Kim and Julie on the forward deck. They had a glass of wine waiting for her when she sat down.

"How's Gavin?" Julie asked.

"Tired. I think he passed out before I even left the room."

Kim slowly shook her head in disbelief. "I was right there when he did it the first time. And then today, again. I don't know what to make of it. I'm having a hard time wrapping my head around it."

Laura nodded and took a sip of wine. "You and me both. What happened to Thomas seven years ago has really had quite the impact on everyone. I fell in love with a man who absolutely needed my help. Then we had seven fantastic years of marriage and two children. Well, seven this coming January." She took another sip. "Regardless, the abilities he passed on to them, as we've seen, only appear to be getting stronger."

Julie interjected. "I take it that worries you?"

Laura nodded. "Yes, absolutely. This isn't the first time someone in power has wanted my children for their own desires. What happens, if and when we somehow make it through all this unscathed? I'll tell you what happens. They grow older, more powerful, and turn into teenagers. What happens then? I can only imagine the fallout." Laura drank some more and refilled her glass.

Kim and Julie shared a glance.

Well," stated Julie, "I can tell from experience that both Emily and Gavin are in great hands. They're lucky to have you as their mother. When they grow up they'll be just fine."

Delta, one of the SANDBOX operatives, took that moment to interrupt their conversation.

"Ladies. I need all three of you inside." All of them recognized the urgency in his voice and stood up immediately.

"What's going on?" Laura asked as they began to move.

"The Captain just told me we have two boats directly approaching us, one from the west and another from the east. It could be anything but I'm not here to take that chance."

Kim couldn't help but think of the attacks from a week earlier. "Shit shit shit."

"Get to your children and bring them all down to the Galley," Delta ordered. "Arm yourselves and do not come up unless you hear from one of my team. Go."

* * *

"Team leader," said Hobbes back in D.C., "you are t-minus forty-five seconds from contact. How copy?"

"Good copy."

"Play by play in thirty seconds."

"Roger that," replied the team leader.

Both incoming boats contained six heavily armed men, plus a man who operated each craft itself, for a total of fourteen. Their orders were to secure three woman and five children. Everyone else had been deemed expendable.

Calvin and Hobbes watched the progress of the two boats through the satellite feed as the yacht was anchored and wasn't going anywhere. On screen they watched one man approach the three women. A few seconds later they were rushed inside and dropped out of view. Five heat signatures remained outside and quickly created a scattered defense around the ship.

"Team leader. You have five hostiles ready to repel your attack. Adjust your incoming vector by twenty degrees. Second team, come in straight and hard. I'm about to call out targets."

* * *

226

On the deck of 'Slice of Heaven' Delta, Foxtrot, Hotel, Oscar and Yankee gripped their MP5 submachine guns. They had each hunkered down behind something as they looked out over the water. The lights aboard the yacht shined brightly, illuminating them like a beacon.

The sounds of the engines were suddenly very loud.

"Here we go," Delta said in everyone's earpiece.

One boat throttled back hard and came to nearly a complete stop seventy feet off the port side of the ship. The other began to circle the yacht a hundred feet out like a shark.

* * *

"No movement," Hobbes said in the man's ear.

The team leader picked up a megaphone. "Slice of Heaven. Prepare to be boarded for customs inspection."

"We both know you're not here for a customs inspection," Delta yelled back from his secluded spot. "Try again!"

"Fine. Hand over the civilians and we can do this without any bloodshed."

"You damn well know I can't do that! I just called in the Coast Guard! They should be here momentarily!"

"Now who's lying? Your external communications have been jammed for the past five minutes. I'm losing my patience. You have ten seconds to lay down your weapons and surrender or..."

* * *

"You have ten seconds to lay down your weapons and surrender or..."

"Now!" Delta ordered.

Captain Bob, upon hearing the signal, turned off all the ship's external lights at once. Darkness washed over the ship as automatic weapon's fire began to light up the night.

* * *

"You have ten seconds to lay down your weapons and surrender or…"

The ship disappeared from his eyesight right before rounds began to pepper his boat. Two of his men were injured before the engine gunned and the boat took off parallel to the yacht at high speed. He dropped the megaphone on the floor and grabbed onto something for support.

Fuckers!

"Give me suppressing fire right the fuck now!" the team leader yelled in to his earpiece.

Automatic weapons fire opened up from the second boat as it continued to circle the yacht.

* * *

"I think we hit some of them but I can't be sure," Oscar said.

"Roger that," Delta replied.

Just then a barrage of rounds began a continuous pummeling to various parts of the ship.

Shit!

"Stay low and move inside. We'll be cut down or injured in no time if we stay out here."

* * *

Laura, Julie and Kim had quickly rushed back to their rooms, grabbed their children and headed below deck to the galley and storage area. Ginger and Felicia helped them as the children and women made their way down the steps to the bottom of the ship.

The five children were confused and looked to their parents for some explanation. Gavin held Stickers tightly in his arms.

"What's going on?" Sarah asked her mother.

Kim didn't want to answer her daughter's question so she sidestepped it. "We're coming down here to be safe sweetie."

Laura pulled out her satellite phone and turned it on. She dialed Roberta's number but nothing would connect. She tried again with the same result. In desperation she dialed nine-one-one and still nothing.

Dammit!

"What's happening?" Gavin asked her.

"I hope nothing at all," as she tried to reassure him and everyone else.

"I don't like it. I'm scared," said Craig.

Julie pulled her kids closer. "Shhh. It's going to be okay. This is probably just a drill, right?"

Kim nodded as she held her two. "Yup. Nothing to worry about."

Suddenly everyone heard the sounds of automatic weapons along with the impact of their rounds all over the exterior of the ship.

"Noooooo!"

"I want to go home!"

The kids began to cry, fuss and scream all at once. Kim tried to hold herself together but she began to cry as well.

Gavin left his mother's side and crawled underneath a desk with Stickers.

Laura pulled her Glock 17 out of the backpack. She dumped the useless phone in it and then positioned herself by the stairs they'd just come down. She turned off the light switch, which made the children cry even louder, and did the only thing she could do; wait.

* * *

"They're moving. Looks like they're heading inside to regroup," said Hobbes.

"Roger that. Team two, continue covering fire while we board." He turned to the driver. "Get us up there right now!"

The boat pulled a quick turn and within seconds was alongside the rear loading bay of the yacht. Four men, minus the two injured, exited the craft with weapons pointed forward. When they were clear the boat took off and began to circle a hundred feet out.

The four men moved quickly. Two carefully moved up the stairs to the main level and stopped while the other two covered the Landing Bay.

"Move in team two."

"You're clear," said Hobbes. "The five hostiles have retreated inside. There is no one on deck but your men."

"Copy that."

Twenty seconds later team two's boat pulled up to the same spot and unloaded their six men. The boat roared off and began to circle as well.

The noise level dropped off immediately and ten new bodies were now onboard the yacht.

The team leader whispered to everyone. "We're going from top to bottom. I want two men to fall back and secure each exit as we move up. Two stay here at the Landing Bay. The rest are on me."

Six men joined the team leader on the stairwell and, as a unit, they purposely moved up one level to the main deck. They covered multiple angles as they crept towards the next set of stairs that led to the upper decks. Two peeled off and placed their backs against the railing.

"Still clear. No movement," Hobbes said casually.

"Give me two more men at the opposite side of the main deck right away. It's too big to cover with just two on one side." *I needed all twelve men for this assault.*

Two operators silently diverged from the rear of the remaining six and slowly made their way around the port side towards the bow.

"Moving up to the second deck," the team leader breathed into his mike.

* * *

Captain Bob had tried raising the Coast Guard but immediately discovered his radio and cell phone were no longer working. After turning off the exterior lights he remained on the bridge. He opened up the First Aid kit that hung on the wall, and removed a six shot thirty-eight pistol which he now held in his right hand. He had stored it there in case of an emergency and he was pretty confident this definitely counted as one.

He had plastered himself to the floor when the automatic firing had begun. A number of holes had penetrated the glass surrounding the Bridge but had missed him entirely.

After a minute he peaked out the side of the bridge door, that was open, and vaguely made out multiple shapes making their way up to his position. *Not on my watch.* He pulled back from the doorway, got in to a crouch and extended his right arm out the door.

* * *

"Movement! Twelve o'clock! Looks like from the Bridge!"
BLAM! BLAM! BLAM!

Three shots quickly rang out in succession. Only one of them found its mark as the four operators were in the process of heading Hobbes' warning. One operator fell flat on his face and didn't get up.

The team lead saw his man fall and looked back from his concealed position. *Fuck.*

"All teams. We have a man down. Hold positions." He whispered to the two men with him. "Covering fire on the Bridge in three. Three. Two. One."

The remaining two operators aimed their weapons at the Bridge and began to rake it with automatic fire. The team lead pulled a M67 fragmentation grenade from his vest, pulled the pin and heaved it through the open door.

* * *

BLAM! BLAM! BLAM!
I got one!

Captain Bob smiled at his accomplishment just as multiple rounds forced him away from the doorway and back down on the floor.

A few seconds later he heard something bounce and skittle on the floor behind him. He turned and looked at the grenade.

Oh shi...

KABOOOOOM!

* * *

The yacht rocked as the explosion went off. Julie began to shake along with her sister. The rest of the lights aboard the ship suddenly blinked off. Laura felt her knees began to weaken. She took a deep breath and let it out. *What the fuck is going on up there?*

* * *

Delta and his team had initially sequestered themselves inside the main deck. They had quickly turned off the rest of the interior lights. The door that led down to the galley and storage area was their primary concern. There was only one way in and out and it was still their job not to let any harm come to the families.

From the darkness Delta caught a glimpse of eight men that emerged from the landing stairwell. He wished he had a better angle because it would have been a perfect opportunity to engage the enemy.

"Incoming. Rear stairwell."

Before he could move to a better shooting position the eight man team split up. Two remained and backed themselves up against the railing. Two more split off and headed towards the front of the ship. The remaining four took the next set of stairs upwards.

Shit.

Fifteen seconds later the five SANDBOX men heard three pistol shots followed closely by what they knew was a muffed grenade explosion.

"We're going to be flanked. Watch the front. If you get a chance then take the targets out. Otherwise, stand fast."

* * *

The team leader saw the windows of the Bridge blow outwards and knew whoever up there couldn't have survived. He motioned to one of the two remaining men with him.

"Check him."

One of them made his way to their fallen man and rolled him over. There was a hole in his head. "He's gone."

Shit. One dead and two wounded. We knew this wasn't going to be easy but this op has gone sideways from the beginning.

"I need the two at the Landing Bay to make their way up two decks to my location."

"On our way," came the reply.

* * *

Delta had scooted ever so slowly in to a better position when new movement caught his eye. Two men had just cleared the lower stairs and started to move to the right.

No time like the present. "I'm going hot, aft side."

Delta brought up his suppressed Heckler and Koch MP5, aimed down the iron sights and began to let out three round bursts as fast as he could pull the trigger.

* * *

The sounds of shattered glass pierced the night and both operators, who were on the move, were immediately hit by gunfire coming from within the ship. They crumpled to the ground.

"Man down! Man down! We're taking fire!"

Both teams of two, from the main deck aft and bow, opened up on the glass simultaneously. One hundred and twenty rounds from the invader's M4 assault rifles quickly penetrated the enclosed

234

space. All four men ejected their spent magazines and inserted fresh ones without taking their eyes off their target.

*   *   *

Delta knew he'd hit his intended targets right away. What he hadn't counted on was the enemy's overwhelming response. The glass ten feet in front of him blew inward at an alarming rate from two different angles. Before he could scramble back to better cover a round caught him under the neck and tossed him onto his back.

At the front of the boat the windows had exploded as well but there were no SANDBOX personnel that far forward.

The barrage stopped.

"Delta. Delta come in," said Oscar. "What's your status?"

Delta was unable to respond because he was already dead.

"Delta, come in. Fuck."

*   *   *

"Sit rep!" the team leader demanded after the gunfire stopped.

"Two more down."

"Goddammit! This is what I want everyone to do."

Ten seconds later the plan was put in motion.

*   *   *

"What's the plan?" Yankee asked.

"Hold your ground," Oscar replied. "Watch the two entrances and the stairs."

"Does anyone see anything?" Hotel asked over the comm.

The sound of metal clattering over the floor was suddenly heard from where Delta had been stationed. The same sound was heard from the front as well as another one that bounced down the circular stairs.

Three flashbang grenades detonated at once and temporarily blinded and deafened both Foxtrot and Yankee. Oscar and Hotel had ducked down in time but hadn't had a chance to cover their ears. The concussion deafened them but they both could still see.

Three more devices were tossed in after the first three, except these were fragmentation grenades. Not one SANDBOX operator heard or saw them due to the disorientation they were already enduring.

The M67 grenades exploded almost in unison in an enclosed space within the main common area.

Shrapnel penetrated and disfigured Foxtrot.

Yankee was unfortunate enough to be closer to one of the grenades and as it exploded he was propelled backwards through the window. His bloody body hit the ocean water and sank.

Oscar and Hotel had no time to react. The concurrent and powerful explosions shredded the room they were guarding. The heavy furniture they were behind was obliterated. They were both bleeding profusely, from numerous wounds all over their bodies, when the opposition entered the room.

* * *

"What the hell did you just do? My screen just lit up like Christmas."

* * *

"Go!"

The team leader followed the two men down the internal circular staircase while his remaining four men advanced from both sides. The devastation they had caused was above and beyond. Blood was everywhere. The entire area had been literally destroyed and the room had caught on fire.

"I've got a live one over here," said one of his men.

"No you don't," the team leader replied.

"Sir?"

"I said no you don't."

"Yes sir." The man removed his sidearm and put a final round in Hotel's head.

The team lead walked over to Oscar who was attempting to crawl towards his weapon that lay a few feet away. He kicked it out of reach and turned the man over with his foot.

"Secure the area and the fucking cargo," he barked to the others without taking his eyes off the man on the floor.

A few of the other men continue to scour the area for any threats while the remaining men stacked up on the doorway down to the Galley.

The team leader whispered in Oscar's ear. "You did well soldier, but we'll take it from here."

* * *

Blood oozed out of the corners of Oscar's mouth as his eyes locked on to the man above him. He tried to speak but he couldn't talk. He died with his eyes open.

* * *

Explosion after explosion detonated in the room above where they were hidden. Water pipes burst all over the Galley. Any undamaged sprinkler systems kicked on all over the ship showering the families with cold water.

The children were beside themselves with fear and the adults weren't in any better shape. Stickers didn't know where else to run to so he hid under Gavin's shirt and shivered uncontrollably.

Laura was half deaf and water poured down her face when the door at the top of the stairs opened. She saw a man she didn't recognize start to head down so she brought her Glock 17 up and began to empty rounds in to him.

* * *

One operator opened the door, took a quick peak and headed down. He wasn't expecting any opposition until he saw the pistol extend towards him. It was the last thing he ever saw. His dead body collapsed, slid down the rest of the stairs and came to a rest. The sound of crying from below became even louder.

"Get away from the damn door you idiots," the team leader cried out.

His team had been reduced to six. With two wounded and four dead the team leader spoke down the stairwell.

"Laura?"

"Who the fuck are you? How do you know my name?" came the reply from below.

"Listen. I'm going to make this quick. You know why we're here. Your protection detail is dead. We can do this the easy way or the hard way."

"Go to hell!"

He smiled. "I'll give you twenty seconds to drop any weapons you have and come out with your hands up."

* * *

"Go to hell!"

"I'll give you twenty seconds to drop any weapons you have and come out with your hands up."

Laura desperately looked around for a solution. Everyone one of her extended family was practically catatonic. Out of the corner of her eye she caught sight of her son under a desk. She rushed over to him and noticed Stickers was a huge lump under his shirt.

"Gav? Gav, are you okay? Are you hurt?"

His eyes barely met hers.

"Gav, I need Stir to save us. Can you do that for me?"

Laura quickly twisted her head around as she heard what sounded like an empty can of food bounce down the stairs and in to the Galley.

What the fuck is that?

At both ends of the can a very small pop occurred. Gas poured out and filled the small kitchen area within seconds.

Laura turned to talk to her son again but suddenly had a hard time thinking or moving. She fell over on her side.

Fuck, I failed again.

Her eyes closed as she continued to breathe in the gas.

Shadows of the Heart

37
Friday November 21, 1997 Morning
D.C.

The small jet plane taxied down the runway and took off as planned. During the past thirty-six hours Sam and Bill had had little choice but to sit on their asses and wait. They were extremely antsy to find a way out of their predicament, get revenge on the man who had twisted their lives up and reunite with their families. It was only hope, but they needed to hang on and believe in it.

A file folder sat on the table between them. Sam opened it up and began to pour through the contents.

"What are we looking at this time?" Bill asked.

Sam slid over two photos. They were of a man and a woman of Middle Eastern descent.

"Muhaajir Yassin and Nazeeha Ashraf."

"What'd they do? Are they in the same business as our guy in New Jersey?"

Sam sifted through the data in front of him.

"They came up during the interrogation. The two run a Television and VCR repair shop on the outskirts of Charleston."

"West Virigina. This will be a short flight."

Sam nodded. "The DCI wants us to 'investigate' the location."

"During the day? What's he thinking? This is a night operation."

"I don't like it either. But his intel on the New Jersey house was spot on. Maybe the guy we grabbed before gave up another cell. It looks like we're following up a lead."

"That's a lot of ifs," said Bill. "But more importantly, I don't like running unsanctioned errands for this sonofabitch, especially when he has us bent over a barrel."

Sam placed his finger over his lips and then pointed at the ceiling. *Bugs.*

Bill nodded and dropped it. "Anything else in the file?"

"A code phrase."

"A phrase? What's that supposed to get us?"

"Apparently it means we're on their side. The interrogators notes weren't terribly specific. It could mean anything."

"Great. Anything else in there that will help get us killed?"

"Nothing substantial."

"And what if we walk in on something that turns out to be substantial?"

"Then I guess he sent the right people for the job."

* * *

The plane landed at Yeager Airport, a small airfield, just north of Charleston. It taxied to a private hanger where, as before, a car was waiting for them. Bill drove this time while Sam looked through the 'supplies' that had been left in the backseat bag.

"Same shit?"

"Less this time. Just a couple of Glock 17's with silencers, some extra mags and a camera."

"That's a tad bit morbid. With that equipment it feels like we're in the assassination game."

"Maybe so," Sam began, "but if they're enemies of the United States then I'm okay with that."

"You are?"

"Listen Bill, what if the men in New Jersey woke up in the morning and dawned those vests packed with explosives and ball barring's? What if they had gone down to Time's Square, a crowded subway car or some indoor Mall? What then? I'll tell you what. We'd be seeing the same damn thing we saw on the news when Nikolay sent his sleepers to do his dirty work. Don't forget about the Sun Valley Mall in California, the Convention Center in Las Vegas, the Metro station in D.C., and the damn water park in Wisconsin."

"Listen Sam, I didn't mean..."

"I'm not saying we have to like it Bill, but putting people like this in the ground is one of the things we really do well. I don't like the circumstances we're under so we have little choice but to proceed."

"Sam..."

"I want you to see Kim and your kids again, okay. All this shit has to mean we're getting back to our families. I won't let that bastard continue to drag us around by a leash."

"You and me both brother, you and me both."

* * *

Bill drove past the TV Repair shop as Sam scoped it out.

"I didn't see any cameras on the outside. Turn around and pull into the rear parking lot."

A minute later Bill backtracked, took a left into the rear parking lot and turned off the car's engine. Sam scanned the area.

"Still not seeing any external cameras. You?"

Bill shook his head. "Nada. Back door looks locked."

"Good. You ready?"

"Yup. I'll just let you do all the talking."

"Fine with me."

Sam handed over one of the weapons and a spare magazine. They both managed to stuff them somewhat down the back of their

243

pants and pull their jackets over the rest. The spare mag went in each of their left jacket packets. Sam dropped the camera in his right jacket pocket. They exited the vehicle, took a moment to readjust themselves and then walked around the corner to the front entrance.

Ring ring. The bell over the front door chimed as the door opened. The customer side of the shop was very small as Sam and Bill walked in. Apparently most of the business took place in the back.

A young woman appeared from behind the curtain that separated the two sides. She made her way to the counter.

"May I help you?"

They closed the distance and stood on the opposite side of the counter from her.

"Nazeeha?" Sam inquired.

A puzzled looked crossed the woman's face. "Yes?"

"I need to speak with Muhaajir right away."

"May I ask what this is in regard to?"

Sam looked around first and then lowered his voice. "It has to do with our mutual friend, Abdul Khaksar Turabi. He sent us here."

"I'm afraid we don't know anyone by that name."

"That's strange," Sam replied, "because 'Omar sends his blessing'."

The code phrase rattled the young woman. She had definitely not expected two white men to be part of the operation.

"Of course. Please excuse me."

Nazeeha slowly turned as she watched the two men out of the corner of her eye. She disappeared and moments later they heard her arguing with someone else in the back. Twenty seconds later a man, in his early thirties, appeared from behind the curtain.

"You will leave my shop."

"Muhaajir, Abdul sent us."

His eyes never wavered from Sam's. "I have no idea what you're talking about. Leave."

Sam leaned in. "The house in New Jersey has been compromised. Abdul is in hiding. He needs more materials."

The man's eyes faltered for a split second.

"He is still committed to his martyrdom. Even more so since his comrades were killed right in front of him."

Muhaajir just stood there listening. Bill slowly reached behind his back and carefully removed his silenced weapon inch by inch using Sam's body to mask his intentions.

Sam continued. "I really don't care if you believe me or not. You're probably asking yourself how two apparent non-believers have anything to do with explosive vests and suicide bombings. Maybe you think we're full of shit or work for the government. In either case, my friend, your insignificant shop here would have already been swarmed by dozens of agents by now. But look around, it's just us. Now, do me a favor and cut the crap. We have a long drive ahead of us and would like to get back on the road as soon as possible if that's alright with you."

Muhaajir finally said something new. "Nazeeha, I'm going to go check outside. Please join us out front."

The man moved around the counter, past Sam and towards the front door. Bill kept his weapon shielded by his right side as the woman parted the curtain with a gun of her own pointed at them.

"If I'm not back in thirty seconds please dispose of our guests." Muhaajir exited the shop.

Sam turned back and stared down the barrel of the weapon she pointed at his head.

"Friendly neighborhood," he joked while willing himself to stay calm.

Ring ring. The door opened once again and Muhaajir appeared.

"There's nothing out there." He walked past Sam and motioned for Nazeeha to lower her weapon. "I don't like this but follow me. I want you out of here in less than a minute."

The two disappeared through the curtain with Sam and Bill on their tails. Bill still kept his weapon hidden against his right leg.

Muhaajir shoved a heavy table out of the way and pulled up a loose board in the floor. An additional section of floor rose with it. He reached in and began to pull on a heavy military box that had thick ropes on each side.

"Help me with this."

Sam moved to help the man while Bill kept an eye out. Together the two of them extracted the box and placed it on the table that had been moved out of the way. Muhaajir opened the box and inside was an excessive amount of C4 and other components needed to build the suicide vests they'd seen in New Jersey.

"Take it. Take it all and get out."

"It's not that easy," Sam said.

Alarm bells sounded in both Muhaajir and Nazeeha's heads as soon as Sam made that statement.

"I don't understand."

Bill quickly extended his right arm and pointed his weapon at Nazeeha. "Drop it."

Sam reached behind his back and produced his and pointed it at the man.

"Tell me if you understand this. I understand that you're waging war, or helping those to wage war, on my country. However, killing innocent civilians is nowhere near the same thing as engaging your enemy on the battlefield. There is no honor in what you've been doing here. No honor at all."

Nazeeha tried to bring the weapon to bear but Bill shot her twice in the chest.

"Go to hell you infidel," Muhaajir taunted as he reached beneath his robes for his own sidearm.

Sam shot the man twice as well. "You first."

* * *

They didn't talk on the ride back to the airport. As they entered Sam finally spoke up.

"We did what we had to do. It didn't mean I liked it."

"I get it."

Sam sighed. "It's go time brother. We're either in this together all the way or we let this play out."

Bill looked over at Sam. "I'm in. One way or another this shit ends our way."

<u>38</u>
Friday November 21, 1997 Morning
D.C.

Rebecca cautiously stepped out of the Greyhound Bus Terminal and surveyed her surroundings.

So far so good.

She walked towards the taxi stand, opened the back door of an available cab and got in.

"Where to?"

"Take me to the nearest used car lot please."

"You got it."

On the way she unfolded the map of D.C., she'd just acquired, and finally located her target.

* * *

Thirty minutes and twenty-five hundred dollars later Rebecca drove out of the dealership in a classic family owned station wagon. *This should blend in nicely.*

Rebecca's trip across country had been interesting and yet quite boring at the same time. There had been too much time to think about everything but part of her knew she had to come to grips with her own internal demons.

I should have never left their side. You did what you could.

I had a responsibility to protect them and I failed. It was an attack. Shit happens.

I should have done more. Look what you're doing right now. Cut yourself some slack.

Rebecca lifted her right hand off the steering wheel and once again traced the scar from the top of her right eye down to the middle of her cheek. Her face hardened just like her resolve.

These people are my family and nobody fucks with my family.

* * *

Facility Thirteen was located in an office park with three other buildings. Its outside appearance was just as boring as any other office building. The main difference, of course, was that the facility existed deep underground, well camouflaged and out of the public eye.

The buildings shared a huge parking lot. Rebecca pulled the station wagon in to a parking spot, towards the middle of the lot, and turned off the engine. She opened the door, got out and then slung her backpack over her shoulders. She closed the door, locked it and made her way towards the building she'd been told held both Thomas and Emily hostage.

* * *

The computer beeped next to Calvin. His ego was still bruised from the tongue lashing the Director had bestowed on him.

"Are you going to check on that?" Hobbes asked.

Calvin rolled his eyes. "I was just getting to it." He rolled over to the station and checked the message. "Wait, this can't be right."

That got Hobbes' attention. "What?"

"My guy at the NSA. He just sent me the real time tracking information on the satellite phone I believe Rebecca Cross is using."

"So? What's the big deal?"

Calvin looked over at Hobbes. "The signal is coming from directly outside Facility Thirteen."

"Holy shit! Get on the damn phone!"

Calvin grabbed the phone and dialed.

39
Friday November 21, 1997 Noon
Facility Thirteen

Dr. Matsushita, once off the phone with the Director, took his time to announce that they were to evacuate.

I have work to do. I don't have time for this nonsense.

He'd spent the entire night hard at work and had just completed synthesizing his first test batch. He was tired, but very pleased with himself as he picked up the phone.

"Get our guests prepared. We're leaving the facility."

"Sir?"

"Trust me; this is the last thing I ever wanted. This inconvenience will significantly impact my work and productivity." He sighed. "Just get it done."

"Yes sir. Right away."

* * *

Facility Thirteen's current staff level consisted of eight guards, two lab assistants and Dr. Matsushita himself. Once the order had been issued the preparations to leave got underway.

Two guards took the vehicle lift up, verified the underground garage was clear and exited the large elevator. They planned on bringing down two vans to help move equipment and their guests.

The two lab assistants began to tidy up the lab and prep Emily, who was still sedated, for transfer.

The Doctor was in his office making sure all of his handwritten notes were accounted for, as well as the data he'd collected. He stuffed all of it in his leather briefcase. Once he was satisfied he hadn't forgotten anything he made his way back to the lab. On his way out his phone rang. Dr. Matsushita smiled as he closed the door behind him and let the phone continue to ring.

Screw the DCI. Like I have any time to chat with him right now.

* * *

"He's not picking up," said Calvin.

* * *

Rebecca tried to appear inconspicuous as she walked through the parking lot towards the building.

Underground. Roberta said it was all underground. Some sort of hidden entrance.

In the distance she saw the pavement slope downwards. As she approached she knew it led to an underground garage.

If I wanted to hide a Black Site, something off the books and hidden, I wouldn't want anyone to see me coming and going. That eliminates some sort of public area or elevator. An entrance in an underground parking lot is the obvious choice.

Rebecca turned around and walked back to her station wagon. She unlocked the door and got in. She extracted the Glock from her backpack, chambered a round and rested it between her legs. She turned over the motor and pulled out of her parking spot. In no time she was at the underground entrance and slowly drove down the incline.

I'm coming you two. Just hang in there. I'm coming.

* * *

The two guards stopped what they were doing when they heard a car heading in their direction. A beat up station wagon appeared around the corner with a young woman behind the wheel.

"Send her on her way," one of them said to the other.

"I'm on it."

The second guard stood in the middle of the incline and put his hand up. The woman pulled to a stop. He approached the driver side as she rolled down the window. He immediately was drawn to the scar on her face.

"Ma'am, I'm going to have to ask you to turn around. This is a restricted area."

"Oh. It is? I'm sorry, I didn't see any signs. I'm late for my appointment."

I don't care. "Ma'am. Please turn around and leave."

"Well, there's no need for you to be so rude. What's your name? I think I'd like to talk to your supervisor."

Oh for Christ's sake. He moved his hand to the butt of his holstered sidearm. "Get the fuck out of here lady."

"Is...is that a real gun?"

"What the hell do you think."

"What's the problem here?" the first guard asked as he approached.

"She was just leaving, weren't you ma'am?"

The woman nodded.

"Good," the first guard replied as he relaxed and removed his hand from his weapon.

"I just have one more question," the woman asked.

Will this nightmare ever end? "What?"

"Can either of you tell me where I can find Thomas Clark?"

* * *

Rebecca, during the conversation, had moved her right hand from the steering wheel and placed it around her weapon. This question was either going to mean absolutely nothing or absolutely everything.

"Can either of you tell me where I can find Thomas Clark?"

Both of the guard's eyes, who were standing practically side by side, widened at the same time.

Both men immediately went for their holstered guns.

Rebecca raised her Glock from her lap to the open window before they could pull their weapons.

"Don't," Rebecca stated.

The first guard ignored her and began to withdraw his sidearm. Rebecca fired a single round that penetrated the man's right eye. She traversed her weapon to the second guard as the first man crumpled to the ground in a lifeless heap.

Seeing his cohort gunned down in front of him made the second man stop.

"You'll fucking pay for that bitch."

Rebecca continued to point her weapon at the remaining guard as she opened the car door with her left hand and stepped out.

"Keep talking if you want to get on my bad side."

The guard closed his mouth.

"With your left hand, slowly unbuckle your belt and let it fall to the ground."

The man did as he was told and all of his equipment ended up on the ground.

"Good. Now show me where he's being held."

"Go to hell."

"Show me."

"You're only one person. Whatever you're thinking won't work. Why don't you just give me the gun?"

Rebecca wasn't fazed. "You have no idea what I've been through and what mood I'm in. Show me the entrance to the facility or I'll kill you. It's really that simple."

Rebecca's words chipped away at the man's resolve.

"This way," he said as he turned and began to walk.

"Keep your hands up. Try anything and it'll be the last thing you ever do." Rebecca followed the man but kept a ten foot distance behind him as she did.

The guard made a direct line to the pillar that housed the keypad and stopped.

"Punch in the code," Rebecca demanded.

"I don't think so."

"Stop fucking around and do it."

"No."

Why is he stalling? Rebecca carefully looked around until she spied a camera focused on their area. *Shit! Stupid Becca, really stupid.*

The guard suddenly charged her out of the corner of her eye. Rebecca instinctively pulled the trigger twice. She barely caught the man's surprised expression as his momentum propelled him past where she stood. His body came to a rest on the cold garage floor.

How the hell am I going to get in there now?

A large portion of the wall opened in front of her as Rebecca locked eyes with three armed men.

* * *

"I'm about ready in here," said Dr. Matsushita to one of the guards. "Bring Thomas and Richard to me so I can prep them for transport."

"Right away, sir."

Three guards headed to the cell where Thomas and Richard were being held. They opened the door and stepped inside.

"What the hell could you want from us now?" Thomas stated in a tired voice. "Enough is enough."

"Get up. You're being moved to a new location."

Thomas and Richard glanced at each other.

"Why? What's changed?" asked Richard.

"Shut the fuck up and get on your feet," said one of the other guards.

One of the guard's radios crackled. "We have an issue topside. A lone female is holding one of our men at gunpoint. I need the two men not transferring the cargo to join me in the elevator."

"Roger that," came the reply from the radio.

"What the fuck?" said one of the guards.

"It doesn't matter. She'll be taken care of whoever she is." The guard focused his attention back on the two prisoners. "Now, are you going to come with us or do I have to make you?"

Thomas and Richard stood up and made their way to the doorway where their hands were secured with plastic wrist ties. One guard led the way while the other two followed behind.

"Take me to my daughter."

"Not that it matters but that's where we're going. Now shut up."

The five men entered the lab and Dr. Matsushita turned to greet them. Emily was strapped down and on a sedative drip in the corner. Thomas made a move towards her and was immediately restrained from behind.

"Now now Mr. Clark. I didn't have you brought here for a family reunion." He turned and produced a tray that held two syringes. "You're here because I can't have you and Richard here making any trouble for me when we move you."

"Why? What's going on?" Thomas demanded.

"Enough talk." The doctor motioned to the guards who then forced Thomas and Richard to sit down in separate wheelchairs.

* * *

Rebecca moved towards the pillar as she traversed her weapon towards the open elevator doors. She depressed the trigger as rapidly as she could which sent the remaining fourteen bullets in her Glock towards the armed adversaries. One guard dropped to the elevator floor when he saw her movement. The other two were perforated with bullets and died where they stood.

Rebecca barely made it behind cover before rounds began to impact the pillar she'd made it to. She pulled a fresh magazine from her back left pocket, thumbed the release, inserted it and used her left hand to manipulate the slide. She was back in action.

* * *

The guard didn't like being pinned down in the elevator. As he hit the ground he began to shoot in the woman's direction which forced her to take cover behind a pillar. The other two men that were with him hadn't reacted fast enough and he knew they died on their feet. He continued to keep the woman pinned as he got to his knees and then got his feet under him.

He knew he only had a few rounds left in his weapon so he bent down and picked up another handgun that was next to a body. As his weapon locked open, empty, he continued to shoot with the second one.

* * *

Round after round continued to tear chunks out of the concrete pillar Rebecca hid behind.

He doesn't have any cover in that elevator. It's only a matter of time. I just have to prevent him from flanking me.

She gripped her Glock and waited.

* * *

"Prep the girl. Once I'm done here we're on our way," he said as he motioned to the two lab assistants.

Dr. Matsushita then picked up a syringe and depressed the end until a bit of liquid squirted out.

"There we go. I'm ready. Hold him."

Two guards held Thomas' arms down as the doctor prepared to stick him.

The lab lights flickered a few times and everyone in the room couldn't help but look up at the ceiling. In that moment two new people appeared in the room behind Dr. Matsushita.

All three guard's mouths opened wide as they realized they weren't alone anymore.

The doctor sensed something was different and began to look behind him.

Thomas and Richard turned their heads.

The guards began to remove their side arms.

Dr. Matsushita's right arm was grabbed and the hand that held the syringe was forced forward before he could resist. The needle plunged in to the closest guard and the contents were injected in the blink of an eye.

The two remaining guards had their weapons out now and pointed them at the man, but he kept the doctor in front of him as a shield.

Richard was the first to speak. "Holy shit Michael."

260

Thomas spoke up a split second later. "Dad?"

The guard's voices boomed. "Freeze!"

Thomas shifted his gaze to the second individual who had just abruptly appeared. "Mom?"

Betsy and Michael Clark somehow had materialized in the room even though Emily was fully sedated.

The guard who had been stuck with the needle lost control of his weapon and it fell out of his hands. His body followed the weapon and he hit the floor hard.

"Don't move motherfucker!"

"I don't understand," Dr. Matsushita said. "How is this possible?"

Michael kept a firm grip on the doctor while the two guards pointed their weapons at him.

"Son. Fight!"

Thomas gritted his teeth, raised his legs and kicked out at the guard in front of him as hard as he could. When he connected the guard stumbled back, hit a table and accidentally fired a shot in to the ceiling. Sparks started to rain down from a destroyed light.

Richard couldn't believe what had just happened and sat paralyzed with fear.

Dr. Matsushita pushed back on Michael and then spun his left elbow around and caught Michael in the side of his head; who fell to his knees, stunned. Betsy charged the doctor with ferocity and managed to push him to the ground knocking a tray of syringes off the counter on his way down.

Thomas slid out of his wheelchair and picked up the unconscious guard's gun. He pointed it at the same guard he'd mule kicked.

The remaining guard, identifying a direct threat, pointed his gun at Thomas.

The first guard recovered from the kick and pointed his weapon at Thomas as well.

Thomas pulled the trigger.

Richard overcame his fear and stood up which instantly created a barrier just as the second guard pulled his trigger. Richard took the round in his chest and staggered backwards on his feet.

The first guard tumbled backwards from the bullet's impact and discharged another round, which connected with an oxygen tank in a corner of the room.

Dr. Matsushita swung widely and knocked Betsy backwards and off her feet. He then punched Michael, who was on the floor next to him, in the gut and managed to stand up.

The hole in the oxygen tank forcefully began to expel its contents until the sparks from the ceiling ignited the flammable gas.

The room was immediately engulfed in a large fireball and everything seemed to catch on fire.

The first guard's body flew through a lab window.

Thomas, Richard and the other guard were forcibly knocked over by the blast. Richard absorbed the majority of the blast that would have hit Thomas.

Dr. Matsushita was briefly stunned but recovered quickly.

Most everything in the lab was on fire.

The ceiling sprinkler system kicked on throughout the entire facility.

The two lab assistants left Emily strapped to the table and fled the laboratory through the broken window.

* * *

Richard sat up from the floor just as a guard pushed his body off of him. Richard stood up as he watched his body flip over on its side, lifeless and burned.

What's going on?

Honey?

Richard turned his attention away from his corpse and looked over towards the voice he'd just heard. Standing there was his wife Katie and their daughter Olivia. They'd been dead for decades, pulled away from him in that dreadful pileup.

Katie? Olivia? What's going on? Where am I?

His wife and daughter came over and they all embraced.

It's okay Richard. You did a very brave thing. Come with us, it's time to go home.

* * *

The remaining guard recovered. He pushed Richard's body off him.

Thomas shook his head and looked around. Everything was on fire.

Movement. Thomas looked to his right. The guard rolled Richard off him just as Thomas pointed his weapon at him.

The guard saw Thomas extend his arm in his direction before he could take any additional action. *Shit.*

Thomas pulled the trigger twice. *Die asshole.*

Thomas shifted his gaze to Richard whose eyes were opened wide and unfocused. *Goddammit. I'm sorry Richard.* Thomas slowly tried to stand up while avoiding the flames.

Betsy crawled along the floor towards Emily.

Dr. Matsushita reached for his burning briefcase on the table just as something on the lab table exploded. The burning contents clung to his right arm.

263

"EEEooooWWW!"

He recoiled from the flames. He pulled his lab coat off and smothered his burning arm. His right hand had third degree burns and he tried to cradle it.

Thomas saw his father on the floor and went to his side.

"Are you okay?"

Michael turned over. "I'm okay. Go get Em."

Betsy had successfully made her way over to Emily's gurney and stood up to check on her. Emily was unhurt but unconscious. Betsy began to remove the sedation equipment.

Thomas nodded, stood up and then helped his father to his feet. He watched the doctor hold his hand in pain six feet away.

"It's over you sick sonofabitch," Thomas hissed.

Dr. Matsushita turned away. "No! This is my legacy!"

"It ends here." Thomas took a step forward and raised his weapon. "Look at me."

Michael spoke up behind him. "Don't do it son. He's not worth it. Self-defense is one thing, but shooting him now would be in cold blood."

Thomas took another step closer and then another. He pressed the barrel against the doctor's head.

"You must have seen what he did to Emily! You must have seen what he did to me!"

Michael put a hand on his son's shoulder. "We saw everything. That's why we're here. It had to be stopped."

Thomas faltered for just a second.

Dr. Matsushita abruptly swiveled to his right, out of the way of Thomas' weapon. In his left hand he held a syringe. He stabbed Thomas in his right arm and injected a portion of the contents before Thomas pulled back.

"Sonfoa!" The gun fell from Thomas' hand and clattered to the floor as he pulled his injured arm to his chest. In doing so the needle snapped off and left a jagged tear down his arm.

Michael stepped past his son and walloped the doctor in his face who fell back on the floor and lay still. Flames licked at his briefcase as it hit the floor.

"Are you okay?" his father asked.

"Other than my arm fucking hurts; yeah, I'll live."

"Let's get out of here before this place comes down around us."

Thomas sat down all of a sudden a little cross-eyed. "I'm not feeling too good."

Michael picked up the gun off the floor and placed it in his waistband. He helped Thomas up off the floor. "There's no time for this. We have to go."

Thomas nodded a little groggily and shook his head to clear it. "I'll be alright."

Betsy made her way across the room with Emily safely in her arms.

"Let's move," said Michael.

The four of them made their way out of the burning lab and down the corridor towards the elevator. Halfway down the hallway Betsy just stopped.

"Oh no." She bent down and lay Emily on the floor.

Thomas didn't know what was going on. "Mom?"

Michael moved to her side. "It's time, isn't it?"

Betsy could only nod. She looked at her son.

"Mom? Dad? What's going on?" Thomas knelt down and picked up his daughter.

"Goodbye my son. You've made me very proud. I will always love you." And with that Betsy Clark disappeared.

Thomas looked at his father in disbelief. "Wha...?"

Michael interrupted. "I'm sorry, there's no time. Take this." His father pressed a folded piece of paper in to his son's hand. "I can't explain what's happening but I don't think your mother and I will ever be able to see you again."

Thomas' puzzled look spoke for itself.

"Your mother and I love you very much. I wish your childhood could have been better my son. Take care of your family; it's all you have in this world."

"Dad, what are you sayin…"

Michael Clark disappeared. The handgun fell from three feet in the air and skittered along the floor until it hit Thomas' foot.

What in the fuck just happened? The lab was ablaze. *Just go Thomas, just get out!*

He looked down at his unconscious daughter and then at the gun. He bent over, picked up the weapon and headed back to the laboratory. The fire had spread to other areas of the facility but the sprinkler system was doing a good job of keeping it at bay.

Thomas stepped back in to the burning lab and stopped.

Sonofabitch. Are you fucking kidding me?

Dr. Matsushita was no longer sprawled on the floor. He was nowhere to be seen.

Thomas spun around expecting an attack from behind but no one was there. *Fuck this.* He turned and ran towards the elevator.

When he entered the large room he raced to the button and pressed it. As he waited he noticed a door that read 'Service Area'. He walked to the door and opened it up. Inside he found the sprinkler controls and turned them to the off position. All across the facility the water stopped and the fires began to regain control.

Thomas exited and stood in front of the large elevator door as it opened. In one hand he held his weapon while in the other he held tightly to his daughter.

266

* * *

Rebecca remained protected behind the pillar as the remaining guard continued to shoot at her protected location.

She heard a new sound; the sound of the large elevator door closing.

Rebecca poked her head out in time to watch her adversary protect himself as the elevator began to descend back underground.

Fuck! Back to square one.

* * *

The elevator door opened. Thomas saw two bodies on the floor. Another guard still stood and held a pistol by his side.

The guard's face showed surprise as he saw Thomas standing there holding his little girl and not the other guards.

Thomas didn't hesitate. He hadn't come this far to stop now. He raised his weapon and shot the guard four times showing zero emotion on his face. Thomas knew he had a new mission now; and that mission was to get his daughter to safety and then to locate his family.

* * *

The large hidden wall panel opened up once again. Rebecca stood to the left of the entrance this time and waited. She heard someone in there. Before she could pounce the individual walked out and right in to her trap.

"Drop it," she said.

The man slowly turned towards her. It was Thomas with what appeared to be a death grip on little Emily.

267

"Oh my God!" She lowered her weapon.

It took Thomas a couple of seconds. "Rebecca?"

"I need to get you both out of here right now." She saw the large gash on his right arm. "Are you okay?"

"I'll live. Your face. What happened to your face?"

"I'll tell you later. Right now we have to get out of here."

"Okay."

Shit, he seems a little dopey. "Do you want me to carry Em?"

"No!"

"Okay. No problem."

"Is it just you two? What about Richard?"

Thomas gave her a faraway look. "He….he didn't make it."

"Oh."

"I think he took a bullet for me."

Rebecca herded him towards the station wagon and put them in the front passenger seat. She got in the driver's seat, turned around and drove out of the underground garage towards an unknown destination.

"My family!" Thomas yelled out of the blue.

Yeah, he's out of it a bit. "They're okay. They're safe."

"Really? Are you sure?"

"Yes. Open the backpack on the floor there and pull out the phone."

Thomas put the gun on the floorboard and did as he was told. He dialed the number Rebecca gave him with one hand while he held on to his precious little girl.

The phone rang and rang.

"No one's picking up. What's wrong?"

"Shit, I'm sorry. They're only supposed to have their phone turned on a couple of times a day. Let me call Roberta."

She took the phone from Thomas and dialed.

"Rebecca?"

.W. Neuman

"It's me Roberta. I have them."

"Listen to me very closely," Roberta insisted.

Alarm bells began to go off in Rebecca's head.

"We're compromised. You're on your own."

The line went dead in her hand.

What the hell?

"What happened? What did she say?"

"I don't know. I don't get it. She said that we're compromised."

"What does that mean?"

"I'm trying to figure that part out right now. Just let me drive and think."

Emily finally stirred in Thomas' arms.

"Dad..dy?"

Thomas started to cry. "Yes sweetie, it's daddy."

"Where…where are we?"

"Safe. I think we're safe."

"The bad man doesn't have us anymore?"

"No sweetie, not anymore."

"Good."

* * *

Fifteen minutes later Rebecca had them in a completely different part of Washington D.C.

"We're going to have to change vehicles. They have to know about this one by now. Too many cameras and I'm not willing to take the chance."

"So that's the plan?" Thomas asked.

"I don't know. I'm coming up with the rest as we go now that we're on our own."

Rebecca checked her rearview mirror again.

"Shit."

"What?"

"I just noticed that we picked up a tail."

40
Friday November 21, 1997
San Francisco

Roberta woke up early in one of the unused SANDBOX offices she'd converted in to her temporary sleeping quarters. She immediately checked the satellite phone for any messages. Finding none she quickly made her way to the locker room, brushed her teeth, took a shower and got ready for yet another day of consistent worrying.

Once she was done she walked back to the office, dropped off her used clothing and headed to the front desk. She sat down and tried to appear busy. Clients still called and operators were still being utilized all over the world. Business hadn't slowed down just because the owners were unaccounted for. As far as anyone knew Sam and Bill were still on a mission with five other men and had yet to check in.

This is all going to drive me so damn crazy. Roberta sighed. *Keep it together. They need you more than ever now. The families need to be protected. Get a grip; they need you to be strong right now. Besides, the window to talk to them will be open soon. Just relax.*

Roberta began to focus and dived in to her work.

* * *

A few hours later Roberta looked up from her desk in the main lobby as four vans quickly pulled to a stop in front of the building. Vehicle doors flew open and three dozen men and women emerged.

What the hell is this?

A speaker on Roberta's desk chirped to life. "Ma'am, we've got inbound."

"I'm looking at them right now."

"Orders ma'am?"

Roberta stood up and eyeballed the men and woman that were now entering the SANDBOX lobby. Their jackets matched and they all bore the initials FBI.

"Orders ma'am?"

"Stand down. It's the FBI."

"Yes ma'am, standing down." The speaker clicked off.

One man approached Roberta and spoke with authority. "My name is Special Agent Greg Packard and I head up the San Francisco FBI office. I have a warrant to search these premises." He produced the paperwork and handed it over.

"Is that so," Roberta replied. "We have an excellent rapport with all local and government law enforcement offices. Perhaps you should have called ahead and given me a heads up that you were on the way."

"And tip our hand? I don't think so."

"Actually, it was for your own safety." Roberta smiled. "This lobby would have been flooded with armed men pointing their weapons at you already."

Greg Packard's demeanor changed ever so slightly. "I suggest you cooperate fully. The allegations that have been made against this company are quite serious."

"By all means Mr. Packard, go ahead with your search. In the meantime I will be contacting our lawyers." She reached for the phone.

"You will be doing nothing of the sort." He leaned in closer. "Sit down before I have you handcuffed and placed in one of the vans."

Roberta stopped, considered her next move and then sat down. "What is this all about?"

"All in good time; all in good time." Packard turned around to the twenty-nine other agents behind him. "You know what to do. Get to work."

* * *

An hour later Roberta still sat in her chair. She watched the clock creep up on and then bypass the five minute window she had with Laura.

She didn't call. Maybe she was waiting for me to call? Crap. Damn these Feds and whatever the hell it is they're looking for. It's outrageous!

The satellite phone, on her belt, began to vibrate. Roberta looked around. Greg Packard was talking to two other agents in the distance, but other than that she was alone for the moment.

This can't be Laura.

She pulled the phone off her belt and answered it.

"Rebecca?"

"It's me Roberta. I have them."

Oh thank God. "Listen to me very closely. We're compromised. You're on your own." She ended the call.

"Hey!" Greg Packard cried out as he rushed over. "Who the hell are you talking to?"

Roberta didn't reply.

"Fine. We'll do it the hard way." He turned to one of the other agents. "Handcuff her."

"Yes, sir."

A minute later another agent entered the lobby and approached Agent Packard. Walter held a laptop in his hands. He was their top technical wizard and definitely knew his way around computer systems.

"Sir, do you have a moment?"

"Report Walter."

"I found it sir. The files were buried pretty deep and they were encrypted. It took longer than I thought, but they were there."

Agent Packard was pleased. "And their contents?"

"They're detailed, sir. Very incriminating," replied Walter.

Agent Packard smiled. "Excellent. Good work. Time to close this place down." He took his radio off his belt and spoke in to it. "Shut it down."

He walked back over to Roberta. "I'm placing you under arrest."

"What the hell are you talking about?"

"We've uncovered evidence that directly implicates SANDBOX with the planning and killing of one Nikolay Dmitriev, whose assassination took place in the country of Cuba with zero governmental authorization."

"That's preposterous."

"SANDBOX's days are over. Now, why don't you take a moment and think about the position you're in."

Roberta squirmed in her seat with her hands cuffed behind her back. "Go to hell. This isn't right."

Agent Packard kept at it. "Why don't you tell me where Sam Paige and Bill Nicholson are?"

Roberta stared at the man with defiance. "Even if I knew where they were I would never tell you."

"That's not going to bode well for you. Take her away."

A female agent walked up to Roberta, stood her up and began to walk her across the lobby when Roberta spoke up.

"Agent Packard."

He had watched her leave. "A change of heart? You have something to tell me?"

"How well are you going to sleep once you find out that you're being used as a pawn in a bigger game?"

His smile faltered.

"You're being used."

"I don't think so, but thank you for your consideration. Now, get her the hell out of here."

Shadows of the Heart

41
Friday November 21, 1997 Early Afternoon
D.C.

"Sir, there's been an incident. The lab burned down."

"What do you mean the Goddamn lab burned down!?" Victor was suddenly furious as he stood up from his desk. "What the hell are you talking about!?"

"We don't know sir. We arrived for the shift change to find all the men on duty dead. There were two bodies in the garage, more in the elevator and the rest in the lab. The place was ablaze when we arrived. I managed to turn on the sprinkler system and that will nullify the fire."

Sonofabitch! "What's left? Is anyone else dead? What about the doctor?"

"I don't know sir. We have to wait for the smoke and fumes to clear out. Everything is charred."

"So you have no idea whether my subjects are alive or dead?"

"Not at this time, sir. But the guard's bodies suggest a breakout of some kind."

Fucking hell. If they got out. Fuck. The DCI paced. "What's the fallout?"

"Sir, currently this situation is contained on site."

"Keep it that way."

"Yes, sir."

Victor slammed down the phone. *How did Thomas, Richard and Emily overpower that many armed men and escape? Did they escape? Are they dead? What about Dr. Matsushita? Without him my entire plan is now fucked. Hell, without Thomas and Emily I'm fucked. Wait. Maybe it's not entirely over. I do have the little boy in my possession.* He shook his head. *Forget that for now. I have to know what the hell happened.*

The DCI picked up his phone and dialed.

"Yes, sir," Calvin said.

"I need you to bring up Facility Thirteen's security cameras."

"Sure. Give me one second." He heard some typing. "Holy shit! It's on fire!"

Victor gritted his teeth. "So I've been told. Go back a few hours and watch it. I need to know what the hell happened."

"Of course, sir. Right away."

Victor hung up. *Of all the incompetence. These setbacks have become increasingly tiresome. If this project is potentially over then I'll have little choice but to tie up all the loose ends. No one survives.*

The phone rang. Victor looked down at it. *What now?* He picked it up.

"What?" He had a sharp edge in his tone.

"Someone left the lab. We're on them right now."

Victor got excited. "Can you see who's in the car?"

"Negative sir. Truth be told, we just got really lucky showing up and observing the station wagon exiting the facility when we did."

"Fine. Whatever. Stay on them. I want whoever's in that car taken down as soon as they stop. Whatever it takes, do you hear me?"

"Yes, sir. We're on it."

"Don't fail me."

The DCI hung up the phone and let a small smile escape. *Maybe it hasn't all gone to hell quite yet after all.*

<u>42</u>
Friday November 21, 1997 Early Afternoon
D.C.

Rebecca took a left at the next corner and kept her eye on the rearview mirror. The same car turned and continued to follow them.

"What are we going to do?" Thomas asked.

"Well, that's actually an easy answer. We either lose them or we get rid of them," she replied.

Thomas didn't hesitate. "After everything they did to Em, Richard and I...well...at this point we're too far down that rabbit hole already. They need to suffer from what we've been through."

Rebecca nodded as her scar stared back at her in the mirror. "Agreed. But right now we need to know what they know. We need actionable intelligence or we'll have little choice but to keep running."

Emily spoke up. "Becca, does it hurt?" She pointed at the scar.

"No sweetie, not anymore. Your brother helped me at the hospital."

Emily nodded. "Gavin's a good brother." She dozed off again.

Thomas cradled Emily firmly in his arms as Rebecca drove. His mind began to sift through a variety of flashbacks from the past two weeks.

Listening to my father's life story.

Discovering the microfilm in one of the legs of my childhood chair.

Going to Switzerland to transfer a billion dollars.

Bringing the microfilm to the attention of the CIA.

Freeing Richard Moore from federal custody.

Watching my dead father work relentlessly to locate Nikolay.

Being held hostage by Victor Bannon, the Director of Central Intelligence, once he knew my children contained powers he wanted for himself.

Being part of the excitement of taking down Nikolay Dmitriev.

Watching helplessly as armed men surrounded and began to attack my family in Hawaii.

Hearing Sam's voice crack when he heard Julie had been killed.

Not understanding what my son Gavin did when he created that portal and then watch as Julie come back to life.

My daughter taken away from me.

The days of torture, of questioning, of tests, of blood being drawn and never knowing if it'll ever end.

My parents appearing out of nowhere, without Emily's powers, to save us.

Richard taking that bullet meant for me.

Killing men to save my daughter.

Thomas' eyes refocused. *It's all been way too much and it needs to end.*

Rebecca spied a gas station, pulled in and up to an open pump. She turned off the engine.

"Hand me the backpack."

Thomas picked it up off the floor and gave it to her. Rebecca put her Glock in her waist.

"The plan is that we're going to get out and head around the corner to the bathrooms. Do it casually and don't look back over your shoulder, okay?"

"No problem."

They both opened their car doors and stepped out. Emily woke up again but was still tired. Rebecca slung the backpack over her shoulder, closed the door and the three of them began the trek towards the bathrooms.

The two men, who had followed them, pulled in and parked just as the three of them turned the corner and vanished from view.

"Let's call this in," said one of them.

"No. Not until we have them in custody. I'm not bothering the Director until then."

"Fine. I'm going to get one of the nerds on the line then."

"For what?" asked the first man. "You want satellite coverage on a gas station for one man, a woman and a child in an enclosed bathroom? I think we got this."

"Fine. Whatever. Let's go."

The two men got out, adjusted their hidden shoulder holsters and then quickly walked towards the corner of the gas station. At the corner they hesitated, took a quick peak and saw the alley was empty except for the two bathroom doors. They walked up to each of them and pulled out their side arms. With a nod to each other they each kicked in their own door.

*   *   *

The door to the men's room was abruptly kicked in and a man wielding a gun entered. He swiveled and pointed his weapon at Thomas, who held Emily in his arms by the sink. The man smiled slightly as he moved closer.

"I don't know how you got out, but consider yourself caught as of right now. Get your hands where I can see them."

"I don't think so," Thomas replied.

The man wasn't happy with the reply. "I'm not fucking around."

"And neither am I," Rebecca quietly said as she pressed the muzzle of her Glock against the back of the man's head. "Drop it or I'll drop you."

Shit. The man let the gun slip from his hands and fall to the floor. "IN HERE!" he yelled.

Rebecca stepped forward and clubbed the man in the back of the neck who then slumped to the dirty floor unconscious. She turned around as fast as she could just as the second man entered the bathroom with his weapon out.

"Drop it!" she demanded with her gun pointed at him.

The second man took the scene in. His partner was down and he'd lost the element of surprise. This wasn't how it was supposed to have gone down.

"I said drop it!"

"You'll never get out of here," he replied as he slowly placed his weapon on the bathroom floor.

"Kick it over here."

He reluctantly complied.

"On your knees."

"Seriously?"

"Shut up and do it already," Rebecca commanded.

The man got down on his knees while he kept his hands in the air.

"I work for the government. You have to know this isn't going to go well for you."

"What now?" Thomas asked.

"Collect both of their weapons."

"Em, I need to set you down for a bit. Can you stand up?"

Emily nodded and her father lowered her down. He then picked up the first man's gun and then the second one that had been kicked towards him. He put one in his belt and pointed the second one at the man on his knees.

"I've got him covered."

Rebecca put her gun away and began to frisk their prisoner. She found a wallet and a phone on him. She started to go through the wallet.

"Whatever you're planning, it won't work," he taunted.

Emily took a few steps forward towards him.

"Em. That's close enough," Thomas said.

The man was right at Emily's height and looked directly in her eyes. "I don't see what the big deal is with you kid. You're just a little girl."

"Don't talk to my daughter," Thomas said.

"Or what? What are you really going to do? We're in public. Anything you do is bound to draw attention. It's just a matter of time before it's all over."

Emily took two more steps and slapped the man right in the face.

"What the fuck!?" the man said in shock.

"You're a bad man," she said. "You hurt people."

"Get the fuck away from me you little brat."

Thomas moved in and gently pulled Emily back. "I told you not to talk to her."

Rebecca interrupted. "Stop. I have an idea."

"What?"

"This phone. These two must be in contact with either a support team or maybe even the DCI himself." Rebecca handed the phone to the man. "Take it. Call your support and tell them you have us in custody."

He laughed as he held the phone. "Like hell I will."

She pulled her gun from her belt and placed it against the side of his head. "Are you sure about that?"

The man was suddenly uncertain. "How the hell are those two nerds going to help you?"

Thomas perked up. "Nerds? You mean Calvin and Hobbes?"
The man immediately shut his mouth and didn't reply.

"That's it. If anyone knows what the hell's going on it'll be those two." Thomas backed up, knelt down and whispered in his daughter's ear. "Sweetie, are you up to making this bad man do what we want?"

* * *

"Hello?"

"Nerd...err...Calvin. Its Dan and Pete. We got them. Where do you want us to take them?"

"From the looks of it you're at some kind of gas station."

"Yeah. How do you know that?"

"The signal coming from the satellite phone."

"I see."

"Anyway, Facility Thirteen is out of commission now but Warehouse Forty-Two is prepped. Have you talked with the Director yet?"

"No, not yet. We wanted them secure before giving him the good news."

"That's a good call. How long will it take for you to get them there?"

"Thirty minutes or so."

"Hobbes and I will meet you there."

* * *

The man ended the call and handed the phone back to Rebecca who had watched the entire procedure with wide eyes. He had done everything that Emily had told him to do, immediately and without hesitation. Rebecca looked on as Emily still had the man's free hand gripped in her own.

"What the hell just happened?" Rebecca questioned.

"Do you now understand why the DCI wants my daughter?"

"I'm beginning to get the idea. Your son has…"

"Trust me, I know what he can do. Can we talk about this another time?"

Rebecca knew what was at stake. "Right. Of course. We need to get to Warehouse Forty-Two right away."

"Sounds like a plan to me. What should we do with these two?"

"We don't have much of a choice. We have to take them with us. Watch this one, although he doesn't seem to be a threat at this time, while I find their vehicle."

Thomas nodded. Rebecca hid her gun in her waist band, left the bathroom and walked out to the parking lot. It didn't take her long to locate the vehicle. Once she'd done that she walked back to the station wagon, got in and drove it around the corner where she abandoned it. Rebecca placed her satellite phone under the front seat, jogged back to the other car and performed a quick inventory. In the trunk she found duct tape and plastic zip ties. *Oh great, an abduction kit.* She placed those items in the front seat and then backed that car right up to the corner by the bathrooms. She popped the trunk on her way out.

Rebecca reappeared in the men's bathroom doorway. "Ready to go?"

He nodded. "Let's get him to the backseat, Em."

"Okay," his daughter replied. "Get up and come with me," she said matter-of-factly. The man did exactly what she asked as Emily followed Rebecca outside.

Thomas put his gun away and picked up the unconscious man. He ended up in the trunk, hogtied with tape over his mouth.

The second man sat in the back seat, next to Emily. Thomas got in beside her while Rebecca drove them out of the gas station lot and back in to the street.

"Where are we headed?"

Emily prompted the man to speak and he immediately gave up the location of Warehouse Forty-Two. Rebecca changed direction to follow suit and then spoke up from the front seat.

"I don't think we need him anymore."

Emily nodded and said, "Go to sleep."

The man closed his eyes and nodded off. Emily released her grip on him as Thomas reached across his daughter's lap to restrain the man with zip ties and duct tape. When he was done Thomas began to cough a little.

"Are you okay?"

"Maybe. I don't know. I got stuck with a needle back at the lab. I'm okay, I'm just feeling under the weather."

"Do you know what you were stuck with?"

Thomas nodded his head. "Yeah, the doctor had some damn syringes to knock us out with. I think what's bothering me is the gash on my arm. It's probably infected."

"Are you sure you're okay? Maybe you should let me take a look at it?"

"We don't have any time to spare right now."

Rebecca nodded. "Okay." She changed gears. "Hey Em, that was great work back there. Thank you."

Emily smiled. "Welcome."

"Do you need anything sweetie? Are you hungry? Thirsty?"

Emily nodded. "Both."

"We'll stop and get some food right after this, okay Em?"

"Kay."

"Hang in there."

"I will. I'm glad you're back Becca."

"Me too, Em, me too." She looked back over at Thomas in the rearview mirror. "Listen Thomas. We're playing this loose right now but it's all we have to go on."

He nodded. "I know. I'll do whatever has to be done."

"I'm not leaving you."

"Thanks Rebecca. Thanks for coming to get us."

"You're my family too, and the paycheck isn't so bad either."

Thomas caught her smiling and joined in.

D.W. Neuman

43
Friday November 21, 1997 Early Afternoon
D.C.

The private jet from Hawaii touched down and immediately taxied to a private hanger. Inside, along with two of the men that were part of the yacht's assault, were ten passengers. Five female adults, five children and one cat had been removed from the boat's galley, one by one. The gas grenade that had been tossed down the stairs had knocked them all unconscious. The men had been instructed to leave them in that state, for their own protection, and deliver them to a classified location in Washington D.C. The men didn't know what threat women and children would be to them, especially after the five man team guarding them had been eliminated, but they followed the directions they'd been given to the letter.

The 'cargo', which is how the men referred to them, had each been injected with chemicals that kept them docile and in a dream-like state. In addition a black hood had been placed over their heads, combined with secured wrist ties, to further illustrate all lack of control. All ten sat in their own seat on the plane and had not caused a lick of trouble the entire trip, not that they could have. The cat had surprised everyone, when he appeared from underneath the boy's shirt after the yacht had been sunk. The cat turned out to be the only passenger allowed to roam freely throughout the cabin during the flight.

The 'cargo' was transferred from the plane to awaiting vehicles for transportation to a holding facility.

44
Friday November 21, 1997 Late Afternoon
D.C.

Rebecca had chosen a spot to park down the street from the location designated as Warehouse Forty-Two. As they arrived the tied up man in the trunk had finally woken up and began thrashing about. Rebecca popped the trunk and used the butt of her weapon to knock him unconscious again. She closed the trunk and got back in the car.

"You know," said Thomas, "that Em could have just told him to go to sleep."

"Oh, I know. But it wouldn't have been nearly as satisfying."

Thomas paused for a second. "I see your point."

Rebecca pulled out the binoculars, they had quickly stopped to purchase on their way, and began to scan the area.

"It looks pretty quiet. There are a couple of people outside in plain clothes. Might be security." She kept looking. "I also see video cameras covering the entrance." She handed the binoculars over to Thomas who had climbed in to the front seat. "Maybe those are the two techs you were talking about?"

Thomas adjusted the focus and took a look at the area. He shook his head.

"Nope, that's not them." He lowered the binoculars.

"They're late then. Think they would have been more punctual to make sure you two were back in their custody."

"Gee, thanks."

"I'm just kidding of course." She checked the rearview mirror. "How ya doing back there squirt? You feeling any better?"

Emily had fully bounced back from the drugs that had kept her sedated. She and her father had been drinking water and eating beef jerky that Rebecca had also bought at the sporting goods store.

Emily nodded.

"Good to hear," replied Rebecca. "And thanks for your help back there in the bathroom. That's one heck of a gift you have young lady."

Emily smiled. "I know. You're welcome Becca."

"Em, I know it's going to be hard to talk about, but do you want to tell me what happened, or maybe what they did to you in that place?"

The little girl shook her head and slumped down in the back seat.

"What the hell?" Thomas stated.

"I'm sorry. I can't begin to even imagine what you've both been through."

"You're right, you can't. It was unimaginable." He took a moment and then softened up. "Listen. I know you mean well. It's... it's just that...well...that entire experience isn't over yet. Look at us. I killed men today to ensure Em and I could escape. And you; you have continued to risk your life for us. You have that scar because you risked your life to save my family. You have no idea how deeply thankful I am, but we're not there yet."

A new car pulled up and parked down the street.

"No problem," Rebecca replied. "It's my job and I consider you all to be my family as well. But right now it looks like we have company."

Thomas put the binoculars back up to his eyes. Calvin and Hobbes exited the vehicle and walked over to the two men that stood outside.

"That's them," he said. "Now what?"

"Now we throw a wrench in their plans." Rebecca turned around and looked at Emily. "Sorry about before. I love you and just want you to be safe."

Emily sat up. "I love you too, Becca. It's okay. I just don't want to talk about it."

"That's okay. Maybe someday. Anyway, I need your help. Would you mind helping this man make another phone call?" A slight smile formed on Rebecca's lips.

Emily smiled back. "Kay."

"Excellent."

* * *

Calvin and Hobbes parked, got out and headed over to the two guards watching the front entrance to Warehouse Forty-Two. One of those men spoke up first.

"What are you two doing here? I thought you two never ventured outside because you're stuck behind a computer?"

"Or that the sun burns your skin," said the other.

"Ha. Very funny," Hobbes replied.

"Yeah," Calvin added, "that shit never gets old. I guess we could leave and make sure any pension you thought you'd be receiving in the future ceases to exist."

The guard's face changed.

"Just fucking with you," said Calvin. "You know what's being delivered. Hobbes and I just need to make sure it's a done deal before we let 'him' know."

Calvin's mobile phone rang. He plucked it off his belt and answered it.

"Hello?"

"They're gone."

"Wait. What? I don't understand. You said you had them and were bringing them to the location."

"They escaped."

Calvin didn't like what he heard. "What the hell happened? You know what, it doesn't matter. You'd better find them. Count yourself lucky that you didn't tell 'him' you were on the way. He'd skin you alive right now."

"We're on it."

"No shit." Calvin hung up and turned to Hobbes. "Looks like we made a trip for nothing."

"Why? What's going on?"

"Somehow they escaped, again."

"How?"

"I didn't ask because I didn't want to know, okay? Let's just get the hell out of here and back behind our 'computers'."

* * *

Emily released her grip on the man called Dan while her father reapplied the duct tape over his mouth. Rebecca watched Calvin and Hobbes get back in their car and head off. She turned the car on and pulled out of her parking spot. Within a minute she was on their tail trailing at a safe distance.

"Maybe they're going back to the same place we stayed when we were tracking down Nikolay? Probably not though."

"I don't wanna go back there," Emily said.

Thomas turned around. "Don't worry Em, we're not."

"Let's just see where they take us," said Rebecca. "and we'll figure it out from there."

* * *

Twenty-five minutes later the car Calvin and Hobbes were in pulled in to a residential neighborhood. A couple of streets later the car paused in a driveway as the garage door rolled up. The car pulled in and the door went back down. Rebecca had stopped well back and was sure they hadn't been spotted.

"Home sweet home," she said softly.

Thomas turned and looked at her. "Why are you whispering?"

She chuckled. "I have no idea. Excited I suppose. From what you've told me these two have their hands in everything. This could really be the break we need."

"I need to potty," Em said from the back seat.

"How badly?" Thomas asked.

"Bad."

"Okay sweetie."

Rebecca opened the door and paused. "Can you hold it for two minutes?"

"Maybe."

Rebecca smiled at Em. "Thanks Em."

"Where do you think you're going?" he asked. "We just got here."

"I'm going to do a quick recon on their place. I'll be right back."

"Well hurry up; this is going to turn in to an emergency in no time at all."

"Will do."

Rebecca got out of the car and quickly walked down the street towards the house in question. The front entrance had a metal gate. She crossed the street and decided to chance it. She purposefully walked towards the gate, opened it as quietly as she could and stepped through. A large window spanned the distance from the outer wall to the front door. Rebecca hugged the wall and slowly peered in.

"Well that was a waste of time," she heard Calvin say through the window. "Now I'm hungry."

"Me too. Chinese?" Hobbes asked.

"Nah."

"What about Mexican?"

"We had Taco Bell the other night, and they don't deliver."

"Right. Burgers?"

"Come on Hobbes. Unless you're going out to pick it up we need something that gets delivered."

"Fine. Whatever. I'm going to go check the mail."

Oh shit! Rebecca had passed the mailbox on her way in through the gate. If he came outside there was nowhere for her to hide.

"You do that. I'm going to see if we missed anything while we were out."

Rebecca tried to back away but Hobbes immediately went for the front door. She plastered herself against the wall as he opened it. She held her breath.

Hobbes paused as he plucked something off the front door. "Yo, Calvin."

"What?"

"There's a new pizza place that opened up. They left a door hanger with the menu and some coupons."

"Sounds good," Calvin replied.

Hobbes turned back around, walked outside and headed to the mailbox that was right outside the open gate. Rebecca was gone.

* * *

Rebecca reappeared three minutes after she left and slipped back in the driver's seat.

"What took you so long?" Thomas asked.

"Well, other than the fact that I almost got caught I know what our next move is."

She turned the car on and handed Thomas a flyer.

He looked at it and turned it over. "Pizza?"

She nodded. "It's what they're going to have for dinner."

"Okay. But where did you get the menu?"

Rebecca smiled. "The next door neighbor's front door."

"I like your style."

"Anyway, I have an idea. Give their address and cross street and I'll explain on the way. Besides, we still have a situation in the backseat that needs taking care of and I know we all could use some food."

Shadows of the Heart

45

Friday November 21, 1997 Early Evening
D.C.

"We've been up here too damn long brother," Bill whispered.

"I know," replied Sam.

Sam and Bill had been stuck on the jet much longer than needed as it continued to meander outside D.C. airspace. They had completed their mission in Charleston, West Virginia, by effectively removing two additional players from the game board. The two didn't enjoy being used as puppets and were prepared to cut the strings as soon as the plane landed.

"This isn't right. We should have landed hours ago."

"Whatever the reason Bill, our goal hasn't changed. It's time to take back the control we've lost. As soon as we land its game on."

Bill nodded. "Fuck yeah it is."

Twenty minutes later the plane finally began to descend.

* * *

"Where the hell are we landing?"

Sam looked out one of the windows as well. "Someplace remote, that's for sure."

"This isn't a good sign."

"Yeah, no shit. Let's close all the window shades to make it difficult for anyone to see in."

"On it."

The plane landed and stopped in the middle of the deserted runway. A Land Rover came out of nowhere and pulled up outside. Four heavily armed men disembarked and took up positions that covered the plane's exit.

"This just went from bad to worse. Ideas?"

"We could try to gain entry to the cockpit. They probably have a sidearm," Bill said.

"I wish. It's locked with a reinforced door. We're not getting in there anytime soon."

The plane's exterior door automatically opened up. Two of the armed men cautiously approached the stairs while the other two watched the door using the Land Rover as cover.

A man's voice boomed from the outside. "Exit the plane right now!"

Sam and Bill looked at each other. "Perhaps it's time we indulge ourselves in some reading material," Bill stated.

"Agreed. Good idea."

"This is your last warning!"

* * *

"This is your last warning!"

The two men onboard the aircraft refused to appear in the doorway for the second time.

"Okay. Bring them out," the leader ordered the two men from behind the vehicle.

The two, who had approached the plane, slung their rifles and drew their side arms. They advanced up the few stairs, weapons out in front of them, and entered the plane.

* * *

Sam and Bill were both down on their knees in front of opposite aisle seats, with their hands behind their heads, as the two

armed men boarded the plane. The armed guards immediately
zeroed in on Sam and Bill. They never expected these two to
relent so easily.

The plane's aisle was comfortable enough to fit one person
walking down it at a time. With Sam and Bill on different sides of
the plane the first man down the aisle kept his weapon trained on
Sam, to the right, while the man behind him pointed his at Bill.

"Don't even think about moving," the primary guard said.

"Is there a problem?" Bill joked.

The first man began to shift his gaze towards Bill. At that
instant Sam whipped his right hand over his head and down on the
first man's extended arm with a rolled up magazine he'd been
concealing behind his head.

The man's weapon dropped from his numb hand.

The second guard turned his attention to Sam's actions just as
Bill quickly brought his right arm forward and threw his rolled up
magazine at the second guard. The magazine unfolded in
midflight and merely slapped the man in the side of the head.

The first man had no time to recover as Sam launched himself
off the balls of his feet, from the kneeling position, and barreled
head first in to the guard in front of him.

Bill dove for the fallen handgun.

The force of Sam's assault pushed the first man in to his
partner and all three tumbled to the carpeted floor.

Bill grasped the semi-automatic sidearm in his right hand.

The second guard still had possession of his weapon and
brought it up to bear.

Sam clawed his way up the first man's wriggling legs, balled
up his fist and punched the man as hard as he could in the groin.

Bill sat up and extended his right arm. His sight picture
aligned with the second guard's head and he depressed the trigger.

BLAM! The weapon discharged in such a small enclosure was absolutely deafening.

The second man's head snapped back from the bullet's impact.

The first man doubled up in pain as his testicles tore. Sam then took the opportunity to grab him around the neck, with the inside of his arm, and applied pressure.

Bill got on his knees and then in to a crouching position as he covered the plane's entrance.

Sam's grip couldn't be broken and the man passed out quickly from lack of oxygen.

"REPORT!" boomed a voice from outside. "WHAT THE HELL IS GOING ON?"

"You okay?" Bill asked.

"Yeah," Sam replied. "Two down and…"

"…two to go," finished Bill.

Without saying another word Sam began to strip the two men of their remaining gear. Bill continued to cover the entrance.

"REPORT GODDAMMIT!"

"We're out of time," said Bill. "They're either going to open up on this plane, call for backup, or both."

Sam handed a rifle to Bill. "I don't think they'll shoot at the plane, it's too damn expensive. However, if they called for backup that would really hamper our day."

"Well then, let's not let them take that opportunity. Let me help you stand this sonofabitch up."

"Exactly my thought. Try not to hit the transportation."

"No promises," replied Bill.

* * *

"REPORT GODDAMMIT!"

Nothing.

"Fuck. Call for backup," commanded the team leader. "And fuck the plane. If they show their heads I'm punching their tickets."

At that moment a member of their team appeared in the doorway.

What the fuck?

The man's eyes were closed.

The barrel of a rifle protruded from the side of the unconscious man's side.

"SHOOT!" the team leader screamed.

* * *

Sam propped the unconscious man's body up next to the doorway and then swung him out using his arm as a pivot. Bill knelt down and pushed the rifle out.

"SHOOT!"

Time seemed to slow down. Bill lined up his first shot just as rounds began to impact the man's body he was using as cover. Bill's first round hit the team leader in the shoulder and spun him around. His second shot entered the man's back, punctured his heart, and exited out the front of his chest. As the man fell Bill traversed to the last man standing. He depressed the rifle's trigger twice more and the incoming fire immediately ceased.

"Clear," Bill said.

Sam let go of the corpse and it tumbled down the short stairwell and onto the tarmac in a heap. He then picked up the second man's rifle he'd acquired and pointed it at the closed cockpit door.

"Pilots. You have ten seconds to exit the cockpit, unarmed and with your hands where I can see them. If you do not comply we will shred the compartment with automatic gunfire from the outside of the plane. It's your cal..."

The cockpit door immediately unlocked and the two pilots cautiously exited with their hands as high as they could go. Sam had them covered while Bill continued to watch the exterior.

"Please don't shoot us," one of them said as he eyeballed two dead men on the floor. We just fly the Company planes."

"Outside, right now," Sam ordered.

Bill took the queue, walked down the stairs and stepped over the body. He jogged over to the side of the Land Rover and began to check on the status of the other two men as the two pilots came outside and stood on the runway. Sam followed behind.

"What've we got?" Sam asked.

"We're clear. Two KIA."

"Good shooting."

"Let's just chalk it up to teamwork." Bill walked back over. "I figure we don't have a lot of time. We should get out of here right away."

"Yup."

"The immediate question now is what do we do with these two?"

One of the pilots started to visibly tremble. "Please...I...I have a family."

"Not all of us are that lucky anymore," Sam replied coldly.

"Easy brother."

"Fuck easy. Why shouldn't I waste them?"

Crap. "For more reasons than we have time to get in to right now. But for the sake of argument, you're not that person. These are unarmed noncombatants. If they had shot at us then hell yes we would have punched their tickets. But we don't have time. We have to leave. I say we disable their radio, load the bodies on the plane and have them get the fuck out of here. What'ya say?"

Sam mulled it over as he stared at both pilots with refueled hatred. "Fine. Get it done." He lowered his rifle.

Bill was relieved. "You heard the man. Load the bodies up. You touch a weapon and it'll be the last thing you ever do. Now move!"

* * *

Five minutes later the plane took off the deserted runway and up in to the sky. All that remained behind was a working Land Rover, a compliment of weapons, gear and their burning desire for revenge.

Bill got behind the wheel while Sam looked at a map to figure out where they were.

"Head southeast. That'll take us to D.C."

"Roger that." Bill paused. "Listen, I don't mean to be a pessimist, but once the DCI knows we're alive he's going to kill our families. Aren't we fucked? We don't have the first clue of where to find them. Not to mention our five operators that got left behind in Miami."

"Maybe. I don't know. But I did find a couple of phones with all the gear we collected. I'm going to call SANDBOX and let Roberta know we're alive and mobile. Just keep driving."

Sam dialed and the phone in his hand began to ring.

"Hello, this is SANDBOX. How may I direct your call?"

Sam's face turned to puzzlement. "This is Sam Paige. Who is this?"

"Please hold for a moment."

What the hell? "Bill, something's weird."

Bill turned his head. "Weird how?"

"Roberta didn't pick up."

"Maybe she's sick."

Before Sam could reply someone new came on the line. "Is this Sam Paige?"

"Yes. Who the fuck is this?"

"Mr. Paige. My name is Special Agent Packard of the FBI."

"Who? What?" Sam's mind started to spin.

"Tell me where you are Mr. Paige."

"I don't understand. What the hell is going on Agent Packard?"

"Don't make me laugh. You know exactly what's going on and you'll be better off turning yourself in rather than having us hunting you down."

"I...I'm lost."

"I wish you wouldn't take me for a fool. I don't believe for a second that you've been hiding under a rock. It's all over the news."

Realization dawned on Sam. *Shit, he's keeping me on the line.* "Whatever you think is going on Agent Packard, the fact is you're being played. It's been a common theme."

"Mr. Paig..."

Sam ended the call.

"What the hell is going on?" Bill asked.

"Yeah."

Sam turned on the radio and found an AM news station. Three minutes later they had their answer.

"In other news, the internationally known Private Military Company known as SANDBOX, based out of Marin, California, was raided earlier today by agents of the FBI. At a press conference all questions were denied. However, anonymous sources within the Bureau have leaked the fact that SANDBOX was involved with the killing of a Russian national by the name of Nikolay Dmitriev within the borders of Cuba. The sources also tell us that Sam Paige and Bill Nicholson, the founders of

SANDBOX, are wanted in connection to what is clearly being classified as an assassination. We'll have further details for you as this story unfolds."

"Are you kidding me?" Bill exclaimed. "No fucking way."

Sam shook his head. "The hammer is coming down hard."

"What the hell are we supposed to do? The two of us verses the government?"

"I don't know yet. Let's just get to D.C. while I try to think."

Sam was about to toss the phone out the window when it began to ring.

Shadows of the Heart

<u>46</u>

Friday November 21, 1997 Early Evening
D.C.

The doorbell rang.

"Sweet," said Hobbes as he stood up. "The pizza's here."

"You need any cash?" Calvin asked.

"Nah, I got it."

Hobbes opened the front door. He was immediately caught off guard by an attractive female figure.

Wow. You don't see this every day. "What's the total again?" he asked as he eyed her up and down. *I have to stop reading the Penthouse letters.* Her delivery cap was pulled down and obscured a portion of her face.

"Twenty-four fifty plus tip."

"Right." He thumbed through some bills. "Here's thirty," he said with a sly grin.

She removed the pizza from its carrying bag and exchanged it for the cash in his outstretched hand. With his hands now full she took her left hand, removed her cap and looked Hobbes straight in the face.

Oh my God. No way is this happening. He caught himself as his eyes were drawn to the scar that ran from the top of her right eye and ended halfway down her cheek. His smile faltered as something clicked in his mind. *Wait a minute.*

Rebecca dropped the cap and reached behind her back as Hobbes' brain tried to warn him. She pulled out her weapon and pointed it at him.

His hands were full and he didn't know what to do.

She shoved him back with her free hand. He caught his foot on the rug and fell back on the floor. "Oof!"

"What the hell is..." Calvin stopped short as his eyes focused on the gun in the woman's hand.

"Move away from the computers, right now," Rebecca commanded.

Before Calvin could react to her demands, two more people appeared in the doorway behind her. One of them had a gun in his hand as well. *Holy shit. That's Thomas.* Calvin quickly turned around and began to type on his keyboard. Rebecca rushed over and yanked him by the back of his shirt. His chair tipped over and Calvin spilled onto the floor. He raised his head and looked in to the business end of her weapon.

"Shall we try this again? We need to know what you know."

Thomas covered Hobbes whose hands clutched the pizza box so hard it had caved in on both sides.

"Go to hell," Calvin sneered. "I don't know how you found us, but you're well out of your depth." He found strength as he continued to taunt her. "You're all going to be hidden someplace so deep that you'll never see the light of day ever again."

Thomas spoke up as he closed the door behind him. Emily was right by his side. "The DCI, Victor Bannon, and your boss has his own agenda. When we brought him the microfilm that contained Cold War Russian sleeper agents, amongst other intelligence, I believe he wanted to act on that information in an effort to protect the United States. However, as we closed in on Nikolay Dmitriev, my family and I obviously became his new agenda. He knows, just as the two of you know, how special my daughter and my son are."

"That's for sure," Hobbes said under his breath.

"I have no other choice but to believe that he put his own needs, desires and ambitions ahead of anything else. He wanted my family for what we could give him; power. Whoever he left in his wake to obtain that goal was, and still is, inconsequential."

"Nice speech," said Calvin.

Emily walked across the room and looked down at him. "Can I touch him now?"

Calvin flinched and tried to retreat, but there was nowhere to go.

"Don't let her touch me."

"And why's that?" Thomas asked. "I tell you why. It's because you know what she can do. It's because you know what she's capable of. Why don't you take a long moment and look at her." Calvin refused. "I said look at her." He turned his head and finally looked at Emily. "That's right Calvin. She's my daughter and she means the world to me. Do you think for an instant that I won't do whatever's necessary to secure her freedom and safety? Did you see what went down where we were being held?"

Calvin slowly nodded.

"Good. Gentlemen, it's time to make a decision. Do you want to freely give up your boss or shall I have Emily just take the information from you, and then make you believe you're both mentally incompetent?"

"I'm...I'm afraid," Hobbes whined.

Thomas shifted his gaze back to Hobbes.

"I live in fear every day that if I don't do what he says I'll end up disappearing."

"Shut the fuck up Hobbes."

Rebecca kicked Calvin to silence him.

"It started out as a good job. I got to do anything I wanted and show off my tech skills. But then your family showed up and everything changed. The DCI changed. Boundaries that never would have been crossed before were now stepped over without hesitation. Before I knew it I was in over my head and there was no way out. The subtext was that I either perform anything asked of me or become a liability."

311

Hobbes paused as everything he'd been a part of came to the surface.

"I don't like what I've done. I'm so sorry. I know that doesn't change anything but I am truly sorry."

"You fucking pussy," Calvin chided.

Rebecca kicked him again.

"I appreciate that Hobbes," said Thomas. "You can start by helping us."

"Of..of course. Anything."

"You're a dead man Hobbes," Calvin warned.

"Em, sweetie. Why don't you put him to sleep for a bit?"

"Kay," she replied.

Emily quickly reached down and grabbed Calvin's exposed arm before he could react.

"Sleep now bad man."

Calvin's eyes glazed over and his head thumped on the floor as he passed out. Rebecca lowered her gun as Emily stood back up.

Thomas looked right at Hobbes. "Let me ask you a direct question. Are you planning on giving us any trouble?"

"Hell no," was his instant response. "Absolutely not."

"Fine. Glad to hear it." Thomas lowered his own weapon. "But, let me remind you Hobbes. If you do cause a problem I will not hesitate to shoot you right in the head and then obtain the same information you have out of Calvin. Deal?"

Hobbes vigorously nodded his head. "Whatever you want Mr. Clark. Anything at all. You definitely came to the right place. What do you want to know?"

"Why don't we start with you getting up off the floor."

"Good idea. Thanks."

Hobbes managed to stand up while still holding the pizza box in his hands.

"We have a lot of work to do. I tell you what, why don't you sit down at your station and have a slice of pizza."

"O...okay."

Hobbes slowly walked over to his main computer and sat down. He placed the box on a side table, opened it and removed a slice.

"Um, would you like some?" Hobbes offered.

"We just had some a little while ago as a matter of fact," Rebecca said.

"Oh. Okay."

Hobbes took a few bites, chewed and swallowed. He was nervous.

Thomas walked over, stood Calvin's chair up and sat down in it. "I'll start with an easy one. Where is my family?"

"They just landed in D.C."

"What do you mean? Why are they here? What happened?"

"Do you want the long or the short story?" Hobbes asked.

"Cliff note version."

"Right. Okay. After the attack on the three families that you watched with us at the TOC; they were all taken to Castle Medical Center. We had the place covered but somehow they slipped away. It took a number of days but, with the help of the NSA, we tracked down the satellite phones that were being used. The signal was tracked to various locations in the ocean."

"In the ocean? What does that mean?"

"A boat. All of them were on a boat. Well, a large yacht to be specific."

Thomas liked that. "That's smart. They kept moving."

Hobbes nodded. "I agree."

"But that didn't stop you apparently."

"Uh...um...no, sir."

"What happened?"

"The DCI ordered the vessel be hit with a team. The families were taken and the yacht was sunk."

Rebecca spoke up. "What about my team? What happened to my five guys?"

Hobbes shifted uncomfortably in his chair. "I'm sorry to say that the five man SANDBOX team that was protecting them was all killed."

"What!?" Rebecca's gun came up and she pointed it right at his head. He put his hands up and tried to sink in to his chair. "What the hell are you talking about!?"

"Your men did everything they could. We watched it live. They took out a number of the team the DCI sent."

Rebecca was furious. *I failed them.* She turned her attention back to Hobbes. "You just sat back and watched them get slaughtered like it was a Goddamn movie? You mother fucker!"

"Don't shoot me. Please don't shoot me. What else was I supposed to do? I'm just a geek."

"You're just as responsible as the DCI for all of this. Don't think your hands don't have any blood on them. I should shoot you right here and right now."

Rebecca moved in closer and pressed the barrel of her weapon against Hobbes' temple. She leaned in and whispered in his ear.

"This is your lucky day you fuck. That little girl has seen too much violence already. But I warn you, don't you dare hold back on us. Got it?"

Hobbes could only nod his head as sweat poured down his face. Rebecca backed off.

"We...I mean I...I have files. I have files on everything. We made and kept copies as insurance in case the DCI no longer required our services one day," Hobbes blurted out.

Thomas and Rebecca shared a glance. "It's a start," said Thomas. "We're going to want everything and anything on the DCI, the missions, the projects, the secret locations, etc."

"No problem," said Hobbes clearly happy to be doing something other than pleading for his life. "I'll start compiling the data for you."

"I'm going to go check the perimeter and make sure there aren't any surprises," she said.

"Okay," Thomas replied.

One of the computers beeped and Hobbes turned his attention to it.

"Um, you're going to want to hear this."

Rebecca stopped at the front door and turned around.

"What is it?" Thomas asked.

Our guy at the NSA just picked up on a real time conversation with the FBI.

"So?"

"So, the caller was Sam Paige."

"What!?" Thomas was exited. "But I don't understand. Why is Sam talking to the FBI?"

"He didn't know he was going to. He called the main line at SANDBOX."

Thomas was confused. "What the hell are you talking about?"

"Shit, right. Sorry. You obviously don't know. Earlier today the FBI raided SANDBOX. They found files in their servers that linked them to Nikolay's assassination in Cuba."

"Assassination? The DCI sent them there." Thomas paused. "Oh shit, I get it. He's covering his tracks. Our escape must have triggered his panic. Fuck. But that doesn't explain some bullshit files."

"I'm afraid that's my fault. That was me. I..I planted the false evidence for the FBI to find."

"Oh my God," Thomas exclaimed. "This shit never ends. It's one layer after another. Tell me this, can you prove that the evidence is false and was ordered by the DCI?"

Hobbes finally cracked a smile. "What do you think?"

"Good. So what were you saying about Sam then?"

Hobbes turned back around. "The call originated from a mobile phone outside D.C."

"He's here, in D.C.?"

"Yeah."

"Okay then. Tell me this. How do we call them back?"

47
Friday November 21, 1997 Early Evening
D.C.

Sam looked down at the phone that rang. He was about to toss it out the Land Rover's window.

"The FBI called back pretty quickly," Sam said.

"You might as well answer it," Bill suggested. "Maybe you could find out more information on what the hell is going on."

Sam answered the phone. "You traced this faster than I give you credit for."

"Sam?"

A puzzled look appeared on Sam's face.

"Thomas?"

"Yeah."

"I don't get it but it's good to hear your voice. Don't tell me the FBI has you in custody as well?"

"It's Thomas?" Bill asked.

"No, I'm good," Thomas replied. "Listen, don't ask me any more questions. We need to meet up as soon as possible."

"Hell yes. We're right outside D.C."

"We know."

"Wait. What?"

"Come to this address." Thomas gave him the directions.

"We're on our way," Sam assured him.

"You and Bill are together?"

"Like always."

Thomas smiled. "Fantastic. See you both soon."

"You got it."

Sam hung up and tossed the phone out the window.

"What the hell?" Bill asked.

"You and I both are wondering the exact same damn thing brother."

<u>48</u>

Friday November 21, 1997 Evening
D.C.

Rebecca opened the front door and popped her head in.

"I think they just pulled up."

She closed the door and headed towards the front of the house.

After Thomas spoke with Sam he had Hobbes continue to compile the evidence they needed to prove the innocence of SANDBOX, Sam and Bill's activities, as well as back the Director in to a corner even he couldn't squirm his way out of. Hobbes seemed to exhibit a new flair for life as he worked. The constant threat of the DCI, along with Calvin's constant reminders, he appeared to have temporarily forgotten about.

Thomas finally started to relax a little. Even Emily had perked up. Knowing that after all this time he'd see his best friends again, especially after everything everyone had been through, was going to be cathartic. He still felt a little under the weather but he forgot all about that when the two men he considered to be his brothers walked in.

Sam and Bill stopped as they entered the room. Thomas walked towards them and all three of them embraced in tremendous bear hugs. Rebecca, Emily and Hobbes all smiled.

"Damn it's good to see you brother," said Bill.

"You too. You have no idea," Thomas replied.

Emily walked up to the three men and Bill instantly picked her up in his arms.

"Uncle Sam and I missed you terribly little Miss Emily. How are you?"

Without missing a beat she replied, "I've had better days."

The tension in the room evaporated as everyone began to laugh.

Bill let Emily down. "Oh man, I needed that."

Sam stepped past the group and surveyed the room. Hobbes was in his chair while Calvin lay on the floor. "Quite the setup you two have here." He walked over and glared down at the tech. "I'm assuming this is your home, Hobbes?"

Hobbes could only nod.

"Why isn't he tied up?" Sam asked Thomas without taking his eyes of the prey in front of him.

"He's helping us," Thomas replied. "And he knows what we'll do to him if he doesn't."

"Is that so? Are you helping us now Hobbes? Because last time I checked you worked for that DCI. The same man who has constantly fucked us from the start."

"I'm...I've been compiling the evidence you need to take Victor down. It was our insurance policy."

"Smart man," Sam replied. "But why would you so eagerly hand that over to us?"

"Um...well....because I'm one of the good guys now?"

"I see. That remains to be seen. Don't fuck up."

"Yes, sir."

Sam looked back at the people he considered family.

"Okay. I have a shitload of questions," Sam stated. "But before we go down that path I think asking 'what the hell' is as good a place as any to start."

"I was thinking the same thing," Bill added. "How the hell did you guys end up here?"

"Story time then," said Thomas. "Why don't we all take a seat? There's cold pizza on the table and there's plenty to drink in the fridge."

"Maybe later," Sam replied.

"I'm good for now," Bill added.

They all settled down on the couches. Emily climbed on to her father's lap.

In the light Bill finally saw Rebecca's face. "Wow. Nice scar. You okay?"

"We'll get to that," she replied.

"Who wants to start?" Thomas asked.

"I have an interesting idea," Rebecca stated. "There's a common denominator between everywhere here."

"Which is?" Sam asked.

She pointed at Hobbes. "I have to assume he's had his hand in everything we've all experienced in one way or another."

"You're right," said Sam. "Good call. Hobbes."

Hobbes turned around in his chair. "Sup?"

Sam just glared at him.

"I mean, what can I do for you Mr. Paige?"

"Fill us in on what you've been privy too."

"I'm afraid I know it all. Thomas, Emily and Richard were taken to a black site called Facility Thirteen. Dr. Yamato Takuma Matsushita was brought in to head up the research and development. He was tasked with duplicating and then expanding upon the powers that Emily had."

"What does that mean?" Bill asked.

Thomas spoke up. "It means Em was poked and prodded. For the majority of the time we were 'guests' I heard she was kept sedated. I, on the other hand, was drugged and repeatedly interrogated and tortured. Richard endured the same treatment."

"Shit brother," Bill said with a long face, "I had no idea. But that explains your messed up face."

"The doctor took samples of just about everything from me. He seemed very excited with his initial results."

"But you obviously escaped?"

"Yeah," said Thomas. "That was weird. My parents appeared out of nowhere and caused a distraction. In the ensuing struggle, and gun battle, a fire broke out. I'm also sad to report that Richard took a bullet intended for me and is dead."

"Damn. I'm sorry to hear that," said Sam.

"I grabbed Emily and fought my way out only to run in to Rebecca fighting her way in."

"No f'ing way," Bill added.

"She was one hell of a sight for sore eyes. I thought we were going to be all alone until she showed up."

"And the fire? What happened with that?"

"I don't know."

Hobbes interrupted. "The video footage I ran through earlier shows that the entire lab was destroyed. You should also know Dr. Matsushita escaped through the back."

"What!" Thomas exclaimed. "I fricking knew it."

"Okay," said Sam. "You ran in to Rebecca." He turned to her. "How'd you get there?"

"We followed her from Hawaii to San Francisco," Hobbes said before anyone else could speak, "where she dropped by SANDBOX. From there she was followed and apparently lost her tail. The next time we picked her up was from her satellite phone. She was right outside the Facility."

"Hobbes is right. I ditched the men tailing me and jumped on a Greyhound out to D.C. Nearly two days later I arrived. When I talked with Roberta she told me she knew where Thomas and Emily were being held."

"How?" Thomas asked.

"All she knew was that Laura passed her the info. We didn't have a lot of time so I just took what she told me and went with it."

"Wait," said Sam. "How did Laura ever call Roberta? She and our families are being held by the DCI."

"Oh shit, I can't believe I forgot."

"What?" Sam asked.

"Sam. Julie's alive."

The room was completely quiet. No one said a word.

Sam leaned forward. His hands shook a little. "I know you would never lie to me Thomas so what the hell are you talking about? You said, hell everyone else said, that Julie had been shot and was dead."

"You're right Sam, she did die. But you cut off communication from your end."

"I don't understand. I shot Nikolay in the head right after I heard my wife was dead at the hands of his people. What the hell are you telling me?"

Thomas held up his hands. "I wasn't there. I can only tell you what I saw from the satellite feed and heard through the communication relay."

"Go on."

"My son opened what looked like a portal."

"A portal? What the fuck Thomas?"

"He's not lying, sir," said Hobbes. "I can pull up the video if you'd like to see."

"Do it Hobbes," said Thomas. "That'll be easier than trying to explain it."

"Okay."

Hobbes typed and fifteen seconds later the feed from the assault appeared on one of the computer screens. Sam, Bill and Rebecca all got up off the couch and began to watch the battle unfold. Rebecca had only witnessed part of it up until she was injured, while Sam and Bill had only heard it from what seemed like half a world away. Hobbes had the volume turned down low.

They all quietly watched everything unfold.

Rebecca exited the Suburban as a grenade detonated near her.

Gavin shot out of the car and went to her.

Julie and Laura exited behind him.

The sounds of bullets pinging off the exterior of the armored cars.

The children screaming.

The SANDBOX crew doing their jobs.

Julie shooting one of the attackers with her gun.

Laura took down one as well.

The satellite feed got to the moment where the last attacker fired his AK. Julie took two hits and fell to the ground. Sam flinched and his eyes instantly watered up. Bill put a reassuring hand on his shoulder as they continued to watch.

A small, but very fast, blur shot out from underneath a destroyed Suburban towards the last man. Before he could react the blur decapitated him.

"That had to have been Stir," said Rebecca.

"What's a Stir?" Hobbes asked. "What was that thing?"

"Not now," said Bill.

"Turn up the audio," Sam commanded and Hobbes immediately complied.

"What happened? Somebody fucking talk to me."

"Sam?"

"What happened Laura?"

"I...I...there was so much shooting..."

"What about Julie, Kim and the kids? Tell me they're okay?"

Laura grabbed Gavin by the hand and slowly stood up.

"Julie? Julie, where are you?"

Laura walked over to the other side of the burning Suburban just as a Marine stopped her.

"Ma'am. I don't think you want to come over here."

"Why? What...Get out of my way! Julie!"

"Oh my God Sam. Julie's down. She's...oh fuck...she's dead Sam."

Sam flinched again from the memory of that exact moment. A tear slid down his face as the playback continued.

"My men will be there momentarily to take you into custody. I recommend that you surrender upon their arrival."

"Thomas. Did I just hear that right? You're being arrested?"

"It's bigger than that now. The DCI's been holding us hostage."

"What?"

"He knows...or he thinks he knows something. He wants Emily and he's prepared to take her by force."

"Oh my God!"

"I had to shoot the man holding us just so I could talk to you. He was going to kill me. Laura...listen to me. You have to get everyone out of there. You're not safe. None of you are safe."

On the satellite feed they all watched as Kim, Bill's wife, approached. She clearly saw her sister lying on the ground.

"Julie?"

"Kim...I'm...I'm so sorry."

"No! I don't believe it!"

Kim rushed to her sister's side and fell to her knees.

"Julie's fine."

Kim began to shake her sister.

"Come on Jules...stop faking it. It's not funny anymore."

Laura tried to pull Kim away but she resisted.

"She's fine. You'll see. Come on Jules. Time to wake up."

"NOOOOO!"

Everyone jumped as Gavin screamed, both on the satellite feed and those watching the replay.

"Honey..."

"NOOOOO! Get away from her!"

They watched Kim back away from her sister's body while other personnel drew closer. Gavin knelt next to Julie's body.

Out of the ground rose a shimmering doorway right next to him and Julie.

Laura and Kim fell over in shock. Everyone else took a step back.

"What the hell?" said Sam and Bill at the same time.

Gavin stood up. Without even glancing at his mother he stepped through the portal and disappeared from the face of the Earth.

"Gavin!"

There was even more confusion and disbelief as Gavin reappeared. However, in his hand he held onto a corporeal form. Laura and Kim stared, mouths wide open as Julie, very translucent, stood over her unmoving body. The portal lowered into the ground and disappeared.

Gavin looked up at her. *"Here you go."*

"Oh. Is this for me?"

Gavin nodded and let go of her hand.

Julie's form lay down over her body and faded away.

Julie coughed and abruptly sat up.

Kim immediately moved forward and hugged her sister. *"Jules! I knew you were okay."*

Julie stopped coughing and opened her eyes.

Laura spoke up. *"Are...are you alright?"*

"I don't know."

Laura pulled Gavin to her. *"Do you know what your name is?"*

"What are you talking about," said Kim. *"Of course she knows what her name is."*

Julie looked at both of them. *"I have no idea. Who are you?"*

"Uh..Laura? Are you still there?" It was Thomas' voice on the recording.

"I'm here."

"What the hell is going on?"

"I literally have no fricking idea. I can't begin to describe what just happened."

"Neither can we. But you need to do me a favor. Run and hide. I'll find you. I love you Laura."

"I love you too."

Hobbes paused the video.

"It continues, but basically just shows them being taken to the hospital."

"I...I don't know what to say," said Sam. "She's alive?"

"Let's go sit back down brother," Bill offered.

"Yeah. Okay." Sam slowly made his way back to the couch and took a seat. He was in shock.

"Where are they? Please tell me they're safe?" Bill asked.

Thomas shook his head. "I wish I could. They were safe. Roberta chartered a yacht and they were able to sneak away from the hospital without being seen."

"And they left you behind Rebecca?"

"I was in an induced coma. Apparently Gavin worked his healing magic on me as well before he left. When I woke up they were gone but I had no idea where."

"Back to our families." Bill tried to remain calm. "You said they were on a yacht but they're not safe anymore. What happened?"

"Hobbes told us that they tracked the boat through the satellite phone. A team was dispatched."

Bill looked around and then focused back on Thomas. "But they had a protection detail with them."

"I'm sorry brother. They didn't survive the assault. Our families have been taken hostage."

"That sonofabitch!" Sam yelled. "I fucking knew he was playing us when he wouldn't show us proof of life. Motherfucker!"

"Forget that for now. Where are they right now?" Bill demanded.

"As far as I know," said Hobbes, "they're in transit and I still don't know their final destination yet."

"I don't want to hear that!" Sam roared as he suddenly stood up.

Hobbes cowered in his chair.

"Find our families right the fuck now!"

"I'm on it," Hobbes replied meekly.

"Easy brother, easy," Bill said.

Sam sat down. "I can't believe she's alive. My Julie. She's alive." Tears began to stream down his cheeks.

"Don't worry man, we'll find them." Bill turned back to the rest of the group. "Okay, so we have an idea of what happened to you. On our end it was a bit different." Bill paused for a few seconds to collect his thoughts. "Sam shot Nikolay and then we took off and met up with the rest of our team at the rendezvous. Once we were onboard we were taken in to custody. It's weird though. The sub didn't leave the Cuban coast right away for some reason."

"That's because a team of divers were sent out to recover Nikolay's body and bring it back," said Hobbes.

"Great."

"And his body burned up in the fire earlier today," Hobbes added.

"This story keeps getting better," Bill added. "Anyway, everyone was transferred to a holding facility until the DCI took Sam and I out and put us on our first mission."

"A mission?" asked Rebecca.

Bill nodded.

Hobbes spoke up again. "It was completely off book. The DCI is still a patriot and wants to protect our country, but he's also out there collecting power for himself. Right now he's very much in the President's favor."

"Well that's going to change soon," said Bill. "So we completed our first mission, which turned out bloody, and were sequestered away from our team in Miami and held in a new D.C location. Then we were sent on our second mission this morning."

"I actually have good news on that front," said Hobbes. "The DCI had your men transferred as well. My assumption, at this point until I get it confirmed, is that they're probably going to be held in the same location as your family members."

"And where do you think that will be?"

"At this point my money's on someplace close," Hobbes replied.

"That would definitely be a break for us," Thomas said. "Sam. How're you doing?"

Sam wiped his face off. "The best word I can come up with right now is relieved. After that the next on my list is revenge."

"That's my boy," Bill said. "He's back."

Sam stood up again and walked over to Hobbes. He placed his hand on one of Hobbes' shoulders.

"I'd really like to know where the DCI can be found as well as where our families are being held. Can you do that for me?"

"Sir, I can call the DCI. We're overdue for a check-in as it is and he doesn't like his schedule altered. Let me try and assure you. I work for you now. Whatever you want you've got it. I just want your protection." Hobbes paused. "I'm officially asking for asylum."

Sam thought about it. "You're beginning to grow on me Hobbes, but you still have a lot to answer for. But right now you know what I need. I need those files and evidence. I need to know where our families and men are. And I need to know where that smug sonofabitch is going to be this evening. It's time for a reckoning."

The phone began to ring and Hobbes turned to it. "Speak of the Devil. From the caller ID it's him."

<u>49</u>
Friday November 21, 1997 Evening
D.C.

Victor Bannon walked in to the holding area, with two armed men that flanked him, and peered down through the second story observation area. Five women, four children and one cat.

What I do in the name of science and progress.

He'd had Gavin placed in a separate room with orders that he remain doped and not a threat. Once he had a new research & development location ready he'd transfer the boy to it.

The setback at Facility Thirteen is upsetting. The good doctor hasn't checked back in yet, but at least he's not dead and can continue where he left off. I still need Thomas and Emily though. I need an update.

The DCI pulled his mobile phone out and handed it to one of his personal guards.

"Call the two computer freaks and demand an update."

"Yes sir. Right away."

The DCI walked over to the next holding zone and saw the five SANDBOX operators that had been transferred from Miami.

All my eggs in one basket. Once we have our 'subjects' back everyone else is just a liability. Too bad for them.

He turned, headed down the open stairwell, and then stopped in front of the door that was flanked by two guards.

"Open it."

They complied and the door slid open. The family members looked up as the DCI entered.

Laura handed Stickers to one of the children and stood up.

"Where's my son?" she demanded. "Where's Gavin?"

"The boy is unharmed. He is being held elsewhere."

"Why?"

"I don't have time to play this game so I'll cut to the chase. I know everything."

"What do you think you know?" she replied defiantly.

"Very well. Your daughter can bring the dead in to existence, and as if that wasn't enough, can command people by merely touching them."

Laura's eyes widened. *So, it was true. He does know.*

"Furthermore, your son possesses remarkable abilities as well. He made some sort of portal and brought your friend there," pointing Julie, "back to life. Don't ask me how because I really don't know. What I do know is that I need to harness your children's powers. We've had some interesting preliminary results based on the tests we've run on both your daughter and your husband."

"You monster!"

Laura quickly advanced towards Victor but stopped short as his bodyguard pushed her back.

"Remember Mrs. Clark, you are only valuable to me based on your level of cooperation."

"Go to hell. Where are our husbands? Where's my daughter, dammit!"

"I see this is going to turn in to a lesson of tough love. We'll chat later." Victor turned to his bodyguard as he exited the room. "The two other women are no longer needed."

He left the holding area and walked towards his other bodyguard who was on the phone. Behind him he heard intense screaming as two gunshots rang out. He didn't stop to watch as Felicia and Ginger's bodies were removed from the room.

<u>50</u>
Friday November 21, 1997 Evening
D.C.

The phone next to Hobbes rang a second time.

"What do I do?"

"Answer it and put it on speaker," said Sam. "Try and sound normal."

Hobbes pushed the answer button and activated the speaker. "Yes sir?"

"What the hell went down?" the DCI demanded.

"Sir?"

"Are you kidding me? With the removal of Sam and Bill of course. I was just informed that the jet they were on landed and the four man crew I sent was found onboard, dead. What do you know about that?"

Hobbes got visibly nervous. "Nothing. When the team didn't check-in I assumed they had talked to you instead."

"Goddammit Hobbes. I don't pay the two of you to think. I pay you two to do your fucking jobs. Right now Sam and Bill are in the wind with the FBI actively looking for them. If they are caught before they can be eliminated…"

Hobbes interjected. "Even if they're caught what could they possibly say? They think you have their families. They won't risk it."

The Director paused. "Yes, they'll go to ground rather than risk getting caught. Of course, now that I actually do have their families my rouse is now reality. Oh, and I have the boy now. Any new information on the father and daughter?"

"I'm afraid not. The teams got a hit on Rebecca's phone but it'd been ditched."

"And the doctor?"

"He hasn't checked in either sir."

"So you don't know a damn thing. It's all crumbling down. I'm going to have to continue tying up loose ends to cover this all up if this doesn't turn around."

"I'll...we'll work through the night sir."

"Damn right you will. Your top priority now is to locate all of them by whatever means necessary."

"Yes sir."

"Get it done." The line went dead.

"Nice guy," said Bill.

"Now we know he has our wives and kids," said Sam. "Do you know where they are?"

"I'm ahead of you on that. I just sent a ping to his mobile." Hobbes typed some more. "And here it comes." He pointed at a location on the screen. "The DCI is currently right there."

"Where's that?"

"Let me cross reference that. Give me a few seconds."

Sam turned away and looked at Thomas, Bill and Rebecca. "Time isn't on our side. We need to go extract them tonight."

"Got it," said Hobbes. "He's at a holding facility up north. And, it gets better."

"Better how?"

"The facility has cameras as well. Accessing them now."

On the screen a grid appeared with a different image in each. The group collectively leaned in for a closer look.

"I'm going to run through each camera one by one."

Hobbes pushed a few buttons and the grid was replaced with one video feed. It was from an outside angle.

A second exterior shot. A third. A fourth. A fifth. A sixth.

An inside camera popped up. The room that held their families appeared on the screen.

"Holy shit, that's them," said Bill.

On the screen were Laura, Julie and Kim and their four children. Laura held Stickers in her arms while all eight of them huddled close together on the floor.

Sam reached out and gently touched the screen where Julie and his kids were. "Oh, Jules. I thought I had lost you forever."

Thomas and Bill stared at the images of their loved ones on the screen as well.

"Wait," said Thomas. "Where's Gavin? I don't see him there."

Hobbes clicked to the next feed. Their families were replaced with a new room. In it were five unshaven men.

"Bingo," said Sam.

"Oh yeah," Bill added. "Our cavalry has arrived. Those are our guys."

"Keep going," Thomas prompted.

Hobbes went to the next feed and it was a hallway shot. The next was a reverse of the same hallway. Then the video feed of Gavin popped up on the screen. His tiny body was strapped down on a gurney with an IV stuck in his arm. The only thing that moved was the slight inclination of his chest as he breathed.

"Sonofabitch," Thomas hissed. "I'll fucking end this guy's life."

Sam moved away from Hobbes' station. "Here's the plan. We inventory what equipment and weaponry we have. After that Bill and I will assault the location while Thomas, Emily and Rebecca stay here and help us via the camera feeds."

"Bullshit," said Thomas. "I'm going." He then coughed.

"I'm going too," Rebecca added. "You need all the help you can get."

Sam shook his head. "I'm sorry Thomas, but this is out of your depth. I can't take the risk. Besides, it sounds like you're sick."

"I'm fine and this isn't your call to make Sam," Thomas rebutted. "It's my fault we're in this mess. It all started with me. But more importantly, he has my wife that's being held hostage as well. He has my son. I'm going with you and that's final."

Sam and Bill exchanged glances.

"The man's got a point," said Bill.

"That he does," Sam conceded. He looked at Rebecca. "I'd love to have you along but I need eyes and ears from here, not to mention Emily needs to be looked after."

"I can do that," Hobbes offered.

"If you think I'm going to leave my daughter alone with you you're insane," Thomas said.

"Thomas is right," said Sam. "You're on a very short leash and this new relationship has just begun. On top of that, there's Calvin to deal with."

"Oh crap," said Rebecca. "There are also two more guys in the trunk of the sedan I forgot about."

"We need you here to assist Hobbes and watch our own set of prisoners."

"I understand," she replied. "So why don't we stop talking about it and get this shit done."

* * *

Ten minutes later they were ready to go. The two men had been brought inside and placed on the couch. Calvin's hands and feet were secured in case he happened to wake up and he was also placed on the couch.

336

Thomas, Sam and Bill each carried a CAR-15 assault rifle and a sidearm. The remaining assault rifle was left with Rebecca. The three men donned earpieces and tested the radios to make sure they worked.

"We're good," said Sam. "We'll take the Land Rover."

"I'll finish putting together all the evidence while you're in route," said Hobbes.

"Thank you. Rebecca, make sure you get your hands on that when he's done."

"Anything else? Maybe a group hug?" Bill joked.

"Get the hell out of here and go get your families back," Rebecca said. "Good luck. We've got your back."

51
Friday November 21, 1997 Late Evening
D.C.

Bill turned off the Land Rover's lights and drifted to a stop on a small rise outside the exterior fence line that wrapped around the entire perimeter of the holding facility. He made sure the Rover couldn't be seen from the road when he killed the engine. The facility itself was a relatively small building that sat square in the middle of a dozen acres of open land. From the outside it looked relatively nondescript; just another rundown building located a short distance outside of the city.

Sam began to scan the area with Rebecca's binoculars.

"What's it look like?" Bill asked.

"A handful of vehicles are parked outside. Looks like two stationary guards outside the main entrance. I don't see any additional security walking around so my guess is they're relying on the cameras. No idea if there are sensors planted in the ground. It looks like a helicopter pad towards the back. There isn't a terrible amount of exterior lights on at the moment either."

"Better for us."

"What'ya think Bill? Options?"

"Sneak and peak as always brother. We don't have any suppressors for our weapons so we need to take this nice and slow. Right now our only option is that we have surprise on our side. Once we lose that we place our families in even more danger. Besides, we don't even know how many men are guarding that place yet."

"I can answer that," Rebecca replied in all of their ears. "We've been watching the camera feeds while you drove to the facility. Right now I believe a comfortable number onsite is nine. Six guards, the DCI and his two bodyguards."

"Copy that Rebecca," replied Sam. "Let us know if anything changes as we make our ingress."

"Wilco."

"How's Em doing?" Thomas asked.

"She's keeping to herself. Other than that she's doing just fine."

"Thanks Rebecca."

"No problem."

The three of them stepped out of the Land Rover and opened up the rear door. They pulled out the tactical vests they'd requisitioned and put them on. Each vest held extra magazines for their rifles and side arms, one flashbang and one M67 fragmentation grenade. They then slung their CAR-15's across their chests and let them hang loose.

"You up for this Thomas?" Sam probed. "I mean really up for this?"

"This isn't the first time I've been in this situation with you two. I know what I'm walking in to and you both know I can handle myself."

"That we do," Bill said in agreement.

"Then let's stop talking about it and go get it done," Thomas added. "Lock and load."

Bill smiled. "Did you teach him that line Sam?"

Sam quickly pulled the charging handle back and released it in one fluid motion. "Listen, it's time to get your game faces on boys."

Bill and Thomas loaded their rifles as well.

"Radio check," said Sam.

"Check," Bill replied.

"Check," added Thomas.

"You're all coming in loud and clear," Rebecca replied. "We're ready for you."

"I'm on point." Sam left the Land Rover and stalked off into the woods towards the fence line.

Here we go. Thomas followed Sam, and Bill promptly took up rear security.

* * *

The trio had bypassed the fence easily enough after it was quickly determined that it was neither electrified nor alarmed. Once they were through they paused and made another scan with the binoculars.

"Anything?" Bill asked.

"Nothing new. Only the two guards outside. I'm not sure if that's something I welcome or should be wary of. From here to the building is about a quarter of a mile. The entire way we'll be exposed. The only good news is that we have the darkness in our favor. Anything on camera Rebecca?"

"Nothing's changed. You haven't been detected, although the cameras don't extend terribly deep past the building's exterior," she replied.

"What about tasking a satellite?"

Hobbes spoke up. "No can do on that. That's definitely something I won't be able to cover my tracks on I'm afraid."

"Okay then. We're heading out. If anything changes you let us know immediately."

"Absolutely," Rebecca assured them.

Sam looked at Bill and then at Thomas. "Ready?" They both nodded. "Safeties off. Speak only if necessary. Give me fifty feet and then follow."

Sam pushed off from the fence line and began to jog across the field. He held his CAR-15 rifle across his chest in both hands and swiveled his head back and forth as he progressed. *My wife is alive. My kids are alive. I'm coming for you.*

Thomas waited until Sam was about fifty feet away before he followed. It was a cold night and the sweat that had begun to form all over his body was a combination of excursion and nervousness. He gripped his rifle tightly and tried to concentrate on his surroundings. *Check left. Check right. Don't fuck this up.* His breath felt ragged in his throat.

Bill followed Thomas across the field and continually checked his surroundings for any threats. The evening air seemed overtly quiet as if it was done on purpose to give them away. *This is crucial. Nothing will stand in my way. We're undermanned and outgunned, but that's nothing new.*

The two-story building grew larger by the second as the three men tracked across the open field. It sat on a small rise and the ground they were moving across began to angle upwards towards it. Sam came to a stop and hit the ground right below the incline where the field stopped and the pavement began. Thomas joined him a few seconds later followed by Bill.

"Perimeter check."

"Stand by," Rebecca said in their ears. "Nothing to report. Exterior cameras only show the two at the main entrance. Other than that there's been no overt movement. All nine tangos accounted for inside at this time."

"Roger that," Sam replied. "Once we come over this ridge they'll pick us up; both visually and on camera," he said to Bill and Thomas.

"Not necessarily," Hobbes interjected. "I can loop all the feeds for thirty seconds before they'll notice it. Course the drawback is if I do that they'll probably determine that someone's in their system."

"Thanks anyway Hobbes but without suppressors we're going to be compromised either way. Looping the video isn't going to trick them."

"Remember," said Rebecca, "that once you're inside your maneuverability is reduced. It's a small place. There are three holding cells downstairs, and two office rooms are upstairs as well as the security room. Your families are in the far left, our guys in the middle and Gavin is in the far right cell. The stairs are on your right as soon as you enter."

"Roger that Rebecca," said Sam. "You guys ready?" Bill and Thomas both nodded. "We're going in three, two..."

"HOLD!" Rebecca's voice boomed in their ears. "You have an inbound vehicle entering the property. Crap. It's about twenty seconds from your location."

"Is it a threat?" Bill asked as he looked to his right. He immediately saw headlights in the distance driving down the long entryway.

"Shit," she said. "Looks like six, I repeat six armed men inside. What do you want to do?"

"No time like the present," said Sam. "We're going."

Sam, Bill and Thomas scrambled onto the pavement, got to their feet and ran towards the front entrance.

* * *

"Sir, the extra security you requested just cleared the front gate."

The DCI nodded. "Excellent."

"What the hell?" the guard mumbled in front of the second floor security room video monitors.

"What?"

"Movement sir." He watched the video feeds intently for another few seconds. Gunfire erupted from outside. On the screen the two external guards toppled sideways as Sam's bullets struck them.

"Sonofabitch!" The DCI extracted a sidearm from beneath his coat and chambered a round. "Sound the alarm."

His two bodyguards pulled out their weapons as well.

* * *

"Two down," Rebecca informed them. "Two on the first floor and the rest are upstairs."

Sam, Bill and Thomas stacked up outside the entrance next to the two fallen men Sam had nullified on the run in.

"Bang'em." Sam ordered Thomas.

Bill turned the handle and pushed the door inward.

A shrill alarm suddenly began to emanate throughout the facility.

Sam and Thomas both underhanded their flashbangs through the open doorway, pulled back and covered their eyes and ears.

The flashbangs detonated.

Bill immediately entered with his eyes sighted down his rifle's optics. He double-tapped the first two dazed men he encountered and they fell backwards. He scanned for more threats before he headed for the stairs.

Sam followed Bill in, pivoted to the right and began to cautiously make his way up the stairwell.

"The truck's pulling up!" Thomas yelled.

"I'm a little busy here!" Bill countered. "Deal with it!"

Thomas positioned himself in the doorway, raised his rifle and began to unload on the truck full of men.

Bill started up the stairs.

The truck was instantly perforated with numerous bullet holes. Thomas let go of his rifle, pulled his fragmentation grenade off his chest and pulled the pin.

"Second floor ambush!" yelled Rebecca.

Sam was halfway up the stairs when two bullets suddenly impacted in the wall next to Sam's head. He turned to engage the targets just as another round punctured his upper left shoulder. Sam spun from the impact, lost his footing and tumbled down the stairs.

Bill saw Sam get hit but there was nowhere for him to go.

Thomas flung the grenade towards the vehicle as men began to exit it.

Sam's momentum carried him right in to Bill, which knocked him backwards.

The grenade bounced off the vehicle's window and skittered to the ground.

Thomas was violently pushed sideways and his head wacked the door jamb as Sam and Bill rolled in to him.

The grenade detonated and three of the closest men were instantly killed. The other three never made it out of the vehicle as it exploded.

"Oh shit!" Rebecca yelled in their ears. "The stairs! The stairs!"

Thomas was dazed and couldn't catch his breath from beneath the human pile.

Bill struggled and finally managed to free himself from the tangled mess. His face felt wet so he pawed at it and his hand came back bloody.

Sam was on top of Thomas and his left arm and shoulder were completely numb. He rolled off and pulled his side arm out of its holster with his right hand.

Victor Bannon stood at the top of the stairway as the remaining two guards, and his two bodyguards, advanced down the stairs with their weapons trained on them.

Sam and Bill began to turn towards the stairs and froze.

"Drop your weapons!"

The four armed men quickly took up superior firing positions.

"Drop your weapons! This is your last warning!"

The DCI slowly and methodically sauntered down the stairs with his weapon down by his side. "You should really think of complying. You just killed ten of their brothers and I'm guessing they're 'itching' for some payback. That's your call of course; it's not like your families are in the next room and are dying to see you."

"Drop them!" came the command again.

"We're fucked," Bill admitted as he tightened his grip on his lowered rifle.

Sam gritted his teeth, partly from the pain and partly from the situation they now found themselves in. *What the hell do we do now? All of this, every single piece of shit we've swallowed, we ate just to get our families back. Now it's all gone to hell.*

"Drop them!"

Sam relaxed the grip on his pistol and it slipped out of his fingers. Bill watched it hit the floor. Bill met Sam's eyes and pleaded with him but the light in Sam's eyes began to grow dim from his wound. Sam reached up with his right hand and unclipped the rifle release. It too fell to the floor.

The DCI smiled as he took a few more steps down towards them. "That's actually too bad Sam. The only one I really need out of the three of you is Mr. Clark. You should have gone out at least trying. So sad." He turned his attention to Bill. "But you Mr. Nicholson, you want to keep fighting, don't you? Why don't you see if you can turn that rifle on me before they obliterate you?"

Bill still grasped his rifle. There were four men, all with their weapons trained on him. He'd die where he stood. *My family. My family is right behind that door. I need to see them one last time.* Bill's face changed. The warrior in him took a back seat as he relaxed his grip and then let the rifle hang free. With his left hand he unclipped the release and let it fall to the floor. Then he slowly removed his side arm and dropped that as well.

"Smart. But for your bravery I'll let you visit with your loved ones one last time. It's the least I can do." He turned to the guards. "Restrain them."

With the two bodyguards covering them with their weapons, the remaining two guards pushed Sam and Bill away from their equipment, stripped their tactical vests off of them, yanked their ear pieces and then zip-tied their wrists behind their backs. Sam winced during the process as sweat ran down his face. His shoulder was in tremendous pain.

Thomas had made it to his hands and knees when one of the guards came over and kicked him in the gut. He then stripped Thomas of his gear, pulled him to his feet and secured his wrists as well.

The Director walked down the rest of the stairs and looked at all three of them. "I have finally regained control of this spiraling situation. And now I can finally close out this chapter by eliminating all nonessential personnel at once."

"Go fuck yourself," said Bill.

"Brave words indeed. Let's test that bravado in front of your wife and kids, shall we?"

The DCI walked over to the locked door, punched in a code, opened it and entered the room. The guards forced Sam, Bill and Thomas in afterwards.

The firefight had scared all the children and the women. They were all crying. But when the door opened and they all saw their restrained husbands and fathers getting pushed into the room they were beyond themselves. Sam's left shoulder was bleeding and it trailed down his arm leaving a trail behind him on the floor. Bill's face had a blood smear on it. Thomas' face was bruised and battered from the door jamb. They all looked haggard and beat down.

"Daddy! Daddy!"

"Oh my God."

"Daddy!"

The women wanted to rush to their sides but the guards pointed their weapons and shook their heads no. The children cried even harder. None of them knew what was going on and had been through too much already.

"Shut them up!" Victor demanded to the women. He pointed his gun at Sam's head. "Shut them up right now."

"It's going to be okay Kim," said Bill.

Julie and Kim did their best to quiet down their children until they were all whimpering instead of crying.

"Hey there beautiful," Sam managed to say to Julie through gritted teeth.

"Much better." The DCI lowered his weapon and then abruptly kicked Sam in the back of the legs. Sam fell to his knees.

"You sonofa…" Bill started to say before the DCI's barrel appeared in his face.

"Very touching. Anything you'd like to say to your wife, Thomas?"

"I love you," Thomas said to Laura.

"I love you too," she replied between tears.

"Enough of that," Victor said as he lowered his gun. "Join your friend Sam and get on your knees, both of you."

Bill gave the DCI a cold stare until one of the guards clubbed his legs. Bill fell to his knees. Thomas took his time and opened his mouth.

"So what's your plan Victor? What could you possibly hope to gain out of this?"

"Oh, that's quite simple actually. The balance of power in the world hasn't changed in decades. Sure, the Soviet Union collapsed and the Cold War ended, but they still had nukes, just like us. And now, the largest free nation in the world is fighting and spying over oil, new technologies and ideas. Don't get me wrong; we're still the big kids on the block using Democracy as our shield. But it's more of an excuse every time we flex our military muscles. In reality we're not helping other countries out of the goodness of our hearts. No, more often than naught we're doing it from the simple perspective of selfishness. Our country will do whatever it takes to sustain our way of life regardless of how and what we do to keep it."

"Like what you're doing to all of us," Thomas taunted.

"You're not wrong at all Mr. Clark. I see enormous potential when I look at you and your family. Potential you so desperately wanted to keep hidden and secret. But I know everything about you and what you've been through now, don't I?"

"Using torture and drugs. I'm very impressed."

The DCI smiled. "Yes, that's true. But the powers your children possess are extraordinary. I cannot let them fall in to the hands of another country. Whatever means I've taken has all been done to preserve our way of life."

"Don't kid yourself. This is about the power you want to control."

"That power is inevitable. I want it and our country needs it to take back the world's reigns. The absolute potential that could come from what your children have is limitless. Soldier augmentations, interrogation processes, new medicines and so much more. The sky's the limit on a new era I want to bring to the world."

"The world's not ready," Thomas pleaded. "Society isn't ready. Look at what you've done and the people you've killed. What you've done to me and my family has been barbaric."

"Your hands are hardly clean either, Mr. Clark."

"I've killed only in self-defense and to protect my family. You're the one that placed me in a situation where I've been left with no other choice."

"And yet here we are and you're my prisoner again. But I digress. The world may not be ready, I'll give you that. But that certainly doesn't mean a secret group cannot take advantage of what you and your children have to offer. The rules are about to change Mr. Clark. We have wars on multiple fronts now. We need an edge. No country is going to use nuclear weapons. Yes, the threat will always remain, but it's an outdated card that just can't be played. A fresh injection is needed; something new to change the balance of power but without anyone realizing it. Imagine a world meeting at the United Nations building. And we have people there that could read minds. Information is power. I have the ability to change the world as we know it!"

"Regardless of who you hurt in the process, isn't that right?"

"Don't be naïve Mr. Clark. You, Sam and Bill; you're all tools that are taken out, used and then put back in the shed. Progress has always been made on the backs of others. I don't have to remind you of this nation's history. But the fact remains, your children have abilities that will alter the face of the Earth as we know it. The coup de grace is that you, Thomas, are going to be the one responsible for all of it."

"Like hell I am."

"It's inevitable. I have you and I have your son. Now, where is your dear little Emily located?"

"Go fuck yourself." Thomas spat the words out.

"Suit yourself." Victor raised his weapon and pointed it at Laura who sat a mere ten feet away. "Remember this moment Thomas; you could have easily prevented your wife's death."

Thomas' mind burned with the utmost will to prevent Victor from murdering Laura right in front of him.

The DCI's finger began to squeeze the trigger.

Laura's face was filled with horror, along with Julie and Kim's.

Sam and Bill struggled against their bonds but were held down on their knees by the guards.

Thomas heard himself cry out in rage. His mind and body felt like they were on fire.

"NOOOOOOOOO!"

The gun's hammer snapped forward and the weapon discharged.

The bullet flew an inch to the right of Laura's head and impacted the cement floor.

"What the he..?" the DCI began to say but then everything changed.

Thomas' zip-ties flew off his wrists while he stood up.

In one fluid motion Victor's handgun was torn from his grasp, sailed through the air and ended up in Thomas' outstretched hand.

The two guards and the two bodyguards had no time to react as Thomas methodically depressed the trigger four times. At close range each guard took the round in the head and fell dead to the floor.

"...hell." Victor still had his arm extended and pointed at Laura.

A dreadful silence came over the room as the last gunshot echo faded away. Everyone stared at Thomas.

"What in the fuck was that?" Bill managed to get out.

Thomas seemed just as confused as everyone else. Instead of answering he redirected the gun in his hand towards Victor and then looked at his wife. Bill managed to get up and off his knees but Sam had grown weaker and could not get up.

"Laura, are you okay?"

She nodded slowly and stood up. "What. What's going on?"

"I...I don't know," he replied. "He was going to shoot you. I couldn't live with that so somehow I pushed his arm away."

"Yeah, but how?" Laura walked over to Thomas' side.

"I'm not sure."

"How do you feel?" She placed a hand on his forehead. "Wow, you're burning up."

"I haven't felt too good since I got stabbed with that needle during our escape."

"What needle? What the heck was in it?"

"I thought it was one of the doctor's sedation syringes."

"It works," the DCI said.

Thomas looked back at Victor. "What did you just say?"

"It works. Dr. Matsushita said he had a preliminary batch he needed to test but didn't get a chance to. It looks like you're the first test case. This is absolutely astonishing. It's everything I've ever hoped could happen. You can move things with your mind. You have telekinesis."

"Shut your mouth," Thomas warned him.

"Think of everything we could do and create together; a new breed of humans."

Thomas shook his head. "It's never going to happen."

"Hey Thomas," said Bill. "Would you mind cutting us loose?"

"Right. Sweetie, would you?"

"Of course," Laura replied. "But can't you just, well, zap them off?"

"I don't know how to do that. It just happened."

She found some clippers on one of the guards and snipped off Sam and Bill's restraints. Sam fell on his side and then rolled over on his back. Julie, Amanda and Craig rushed over to Sam's side while Kim, Sarah and Edward ran over to embrace Bill.

Bill returned the hugs. "It's good to see everyone, but Sam's really hurt. I need to help him." Bill knelt down next to Sam. "Shit, he's lost more blood than I thought. Julie, place your hand over his wound and press down."

Julie didn't hesitate and Sam groaned as she applied pressure.

Laura didn't miss a beat. "Where's Gavin?"

"He's in the last room," Bill replied.

"I'm going to get him." Laura headed for the room's exit.

"Bill," said Thomas, "go with her. And bring me back a radio."

"On it."

Laura and Bill left the room and Thomas refocused his attention on the DCI. "My family isn't for sale you sonofabitch."

"It's a small world Thomas. There isn't anywhere you can hide where I won't find you."

"Shut up."

Thomas looked down at Sam and his family that clung to him. Kim hung on to her kids tightly until Bill appeared at the door.

"I found some friends," he said with a smile.

Behind him were the five SANDBOX operators from the Cuba mission who appeared a bit ragged.

"Arm yourselves and secure the area," Bill ordered.

"We're on it," Alpha One replied and headed off.

353

Bill came over to Thomas and handed him a radio. He also held a gun in his hand and pointed it at the DCI while Thomas shoved the earpiece back in.

"Rebecca?" Thomas asked.

"Holy shit, am I glad to hear your voice. We've been watching the security feed. I... don't know what to say."

"Forget that shit for now. Sam's down and is being cared for. We're all going to need extraction as soon as possible. Aside from that, where are we with the data gathering?"

"I'm finished," Hobbes said. "I'm going to order a team to come and escort you to the airport. I'll have a jet standby to take you and your families wherever you want."

"Thanks Hobbes."

"Hobbes?" The DCI's face twisted in puzzlement.

Laura reentered the room with Gavin in her arms.

"Hold that thought," Thomas said.

"I pulled the IV drip and he woke up pretty quickly," said Laura. "He's still a little tired but the effects are fading quickly."

Thomas came over to Laura and looked down at his son and smiled.

"Hey bud, it's really good to see you again."

Gavin held out his arms and Thomas took him out of his wife's hands and he wrapped tightly around Thomas' neck. Tears flowed down his father's face. Laura moved closer and Thomas put a free arm around her. The family melded together and then she pulled back.

"Where's Emily?"

"She's safe. She's with Rebecca. You can talk with her if you want. But let's finish this up first."

Relief washed over Laura.

Laura took Gavin out of her husband's arms. "Gav, I need your help."

"Kay."

"Sam is hurt." She let him down and he headed over to where Sam lay.

"Uncle Sam?"

"Hey partner," Sam managed to reply weakly.

Gavin moved Julie's hands out of the way and saw the ragged bullet wound in Sam's shoulder. "Don't be scared," he told him as he placed his own hands over the bloody area. He closed his eyes and concentrated. Sam's wound began to close on its own. The bullet that was lodged in his shoulder emerged from out of his body and rolled off on to the floor.

Sam's color changed dramatically and his breathing became regular. Julie squeezed his hand as Sam looked up at Gavin. "Thank you."

"You're welcome." Gavin headed back to Laura and wanted to be picked up, which she did.

"Unbelievable. That ability is life changing, you know that right?" said Victor.

Bill still held his gun on Victor as Thomas walked back over and addressed him.

"It's over Victor."

"How do you figure that Thomas? What are you going to do, murder me, the Director of Central Intelligence? I don't think so. Look around you. What you've done here; hell, what all of you have participated in, especially assassinating Nikolay in Cuba, is going to net you a death sentence. It's not over for me. It's over for you. You're all through. I've won. You can't begin to touch me."

"Don't be so sure," Thomas replied. He pulled the earpiece out and unplugged it from the radio so everyone could hear. "You're up Hobbes."

That same puzzled look washed over the DCI's face again.

"Right," Hobbes replied. "Mr. Director. It's my duty to inform you that I have continuously kept dutiful records on every activity you've required Calvin and I to be involved in."

The DCI began to frown.

"Furthermore, I am duty bound to also inform you that these records include, but are not limited to, phone calls, satellite sweeps, missions, emails and anything else we could get our hands on in an effort to remain alive. I do not like you. You are a bad person and you forced me to do bad things. I take full responsibility for my part in everything but it sickens my heart to know what I've been a party to and I refuse to be threatened by you anymore. Fuck you sir, fuck you."

Victor definitely didn't like what he'd just heard. He knew Calvin and Hobbes were the backbone of his entire operation and knew absolutely everything. If even one iota of what Hobbes had been saying was true then his days as the DCI were long over. He was going down hard and he didn't like that.

The DCI lunged for Bill's weapon and got a hand on it before Bill punched him in the face with his left hand. Victor went down like a sack of potatoes and didn't get up.

"You hit him that hard?" Thomas asked.

"I barely touched him. He must have a glass jaw or something," Bill replied as he lowered his weapon.

Sam was feeling much better and with some help finally sat up. His family wouldn't let go of him. Bill's family finally was able to do the same and it felt wonderful.

"Jules, I believed you were dead. I never want to feel like that again."

She hugged Sam back fiercely. "I was dead but here I am. I don't think I'm ever going to let you go again."

"Me either."

Bill finally broke the silence. "Listen, I don't want to be the killjoy here but what's the plan? The FBI wants us and when the DCI wakes up he's not going to stop coming after us."

"I have an idea about that," Laura said.

*   *   *

Victor Bannon woke up and rubbed his sore jaw.

Bastard hit me.

A warm breeze caught his attention and he had to blink his eyes a few times for them to focus.

Where in the hell..?

He looked around and couldn't believe what he saw. A single palm tree was the only thing on the small island. It rustled as Victor looked out at the vast ocean that surrounded his new prison.

Where am I?

He put his hands down to steady himself getting to his feet and warm sand flowed between his fingers.

This is a dream, it has to be.

Victor stood up on the small island and looked around. Behind him he saw Gavin raise his right hand and extend his middle finger. A portal opened and Gavin stepped through it which left Victor all alone in a place he'd never escape or be heard from again, especially knowing that there wasn't any food or water source available.

*   *   *

Gavin emerged from the portal and Laura immediately hugged him.

"That scares me every time."

"It's okay," her son replied. "I'm getting better at it."

357

The radio came to life. "Your escort is on its way," Rebecca reported. "ETA is twenty minutes. I have two copies of the data along with Emily and Hobbes. I'm going to leave Calvin hogtied here and meet you at the airport. Is there anything else you need?"

"Yes," Thomas replied. "Hobbes, are you there?"

"Yes sir."

"Good. I want you to purge the data in the system. I can't have anyone else find it. Do you understand what I'm asking you to do?"

"Yes. You're asking what any man would ask to protect his family. The backups have everything and I can't change that now, but those can be edited later. I'll erase everything on my end. You know this is going to raise a shitload of questions, right."

"Do it. I can't take the chance that someone will see one of my children in action later on and come up with their own agenda."

"You got it Mr. Clark. Consider it done."

"Thank you Hobbes."

"It's okay, I owe you my life."

Rebecca came back on. "We'll see you when we see you."

"Thanks Rebecca," Thomas replied.

He tried to clip the radio to his back pocket and missed. Instead his finger caught on something he'd forgotten he'd placed there.

"Oh shit, I forgot about this," Thomas said as he pulled the slip of paper out.

"What is that brother?" Bill asked getting closer.

Sam leaned in as well.

"It's something my father gave me right before he said goodbye." Thomas unfolded the paper and then handed it over to Sam to look at. "I guess he kept his word. Sam, it looks like you and I are half a billion dollars richer now. I think we need to look

358

into collecting that once we've cleared your names with the FBI. I'm sure they'll be very interested to learn about Victor and his extracurricular activities."

Sam looked up from the folded paper. "At least your father is a man of his word, I'll give him that."

"Indeed." Thomas began to wonder what his father meant when he said goodbye.

52
Sunday November 23, 1997
D.C.

President Clinton looked up as the door to the Oval Office opened. In walked David Saul, the Director of the FBI, and Robert Duncan, the Deputy Director of the CIA.

"Good afternoon gentlemen," the President said as he stood up and walked around his desk. "Please, have a seat."

"Thank you, Mr. President."

"Thank you, sir."

The President took a seat on one side of the couch while the other two men sat opposite him.

"Alright, you two requested this meeting," Clinton started. "What's so important that we're all meeting on a Sunday rather than spending time with our families?"

"Sir," began the FBI Director, "yesterday I received a package at home. That package contained a slew of evidence; well a cornucopia of evidence rather, clearing indicating that Victor Bannon has engaged in numerous improprieties."

"Improprieties?" the President asked. "That's awfully vague David. You're talking about the Director of Central Intelligence and he's not even here to defend himself. You're going to have to do better; much better."

"Yes sir. The accusations against the DCI are severe sir, so severe that I immediately contacted Deputy Director Duncan as a second set of eyes."

The President turned to Robert Duncan. "Robert, what the hell is going on?"

"Sir, it appears the Victor Bannon has been involved in a variety of illegal operations that were all kept off-book."

"I'm listening."

"The evidence is quite damaging. Private Citizens held against their will in Black Sites; using military personnel for his own personal gain; attacking a private yacht, killing the protection detail, extracting the people on board and then sinking it to cover up his tracks."

The President leaned back. "That doesn't sound like Victor. Why would he engage in such activities?"

The Deputy Director shook his head. "I don't know sir. However, the evidence we've been given is very specific. There are phone logs, audio files, satellite video, emails and more. They all clearly paint a different side of the DCI and the activities he was involved in."

"To what gain?" the President asked.

"Once again, that's unknown sir."

The President stood up and walked around. "David, what's your take on this?"

The FBI Director responded quickly. "It's an open and shut case sir. I have to act on it. If this information ever got out the government would be left with a severe black eye."

"Tell me this then, where did all of this evidence come from? Who has something to gain from giving it to us rather than handing it over to the media instead?"

"Mr. President," said Robert Duncan, "that information was included in the cover letter."

"Cover letter? You have to be joking."

"No sir. Have you heard of SANDBOX?"

"They're the Private Military Company currently under investigation by the FBI," the President replied.

"That's correct sir. The owners, Sam Paige and Bill Nicholson, are taking responsibility for the evidence they have against the DCI. The package they sent also contains proof that the evidence found against them was manufactured. Victor Bannon set them up sir."

"Goddammit. What's their source? How'd they manage to get their hands on all of this evidence?"

"Strangely enough they mention that as well. A Mr. Charles Hillburg, also known as Hobbes, worked for the DCI along with his cohort James Pearlman, aka Calvin. Hobbes provided Mr. Paige and Mr. Nicholson with the necessary evidence."

"I see. What the hell do they want? Are we talking blackmail? Money?"

"No sir," replied Robert. "They only have a few requests."

"Go on."

"Yes sir. The first is that they want the charges against SANDBOX, and all its personnel, dropped immediately. The second is that they want the DCI, Victor Bannon, brought to justice. The third is that they want Hobbes exonerated from all of wrong doings, and his cohort, Calvin, brought to justice for his participation in the DCI's wrong doings. The fourth, and final request, is that they want a meeting with the person replacing the DCI."

"That's it?"

"Yes sir. No mention of money or blackmail. Although the subtext is clear; if we don't comply the media will be the next venue we'll hear about all of this."

The President walked back to the couch and sat down. "What's SANDBOX's reputation?"

David Saul spoke up. "Sir, Sam Paige and Bill Nicholson founded and grew SANDBOX from the ground up. Their company is highly regarded for their professionalism and discretion. I'm not sure you know this yet Mr. President, but Sam and Bill personally led a team of seven men to Cuba and took down Nikolay Dmitriev, the same man who orchestrated the mass bombings around our country."

"That was them?"

"Yes sir. They lost men due to the DCI's actions and yet have asked for nothing in return other than justice be served. My recommendation would be to grant their four requests."

The President looked over at the Deputy Director. "And what about you, Robert? Where do you stand with all of this?"

"Sir, we can't let Victor slide, not after reviewing the heinous acts he personally ordered. I also believe we have to step carefully. These allegations are a virtual minefield that, if the DCI were to ever come forward and talk about, would weaken the trust the people have in our government. That being said, I agree with David. These four requests are nothing compared to what they could have demanded, and that in itself speaks volumes in their favor."

"I tend to agree with both of you," the President said. "The abuse of power by Victor Bannon that's in these documents is unconscionable. We cannot let the people of this good nation think their government is out of control; that would be detrimental. This is what I want the two of you to do. First, grant their four requests. Second, find Victor Bannon and have him detained. Third, bury all of this. Nothing points back to us or gets leaked to the press."

"Yes sir. Consider it done," the FBI Director replied.

"Good." The President stood up and the two men followed suit. "One more thing."

"Sir?"

The President extended his right hand towards Robert Duncan who shook it. "Robert, as of this moment you are the acting Director of Central Intelligence. Congratulations. I wish this promotion was under better circumstances."

"Thank you, sir," Robert replied.

"One more thing before you both leave."

"Yes sir?"

"I want to be at that meeting with you to express my thanks personally."

"Yes sir, I'll make sure to tell them."

* * *

Monday November 24, 1997
D.C.

"This is Tammy Baker with CNN. Evidence released this morning name the Director of central Intelligence, Victor Bannon, as the man responsible for planting false evidence naming the Private Military Company SANDBOX as the ones responsible for the assassination of the high ranking Russian official Nikolay Dmitriev in Cuba earlier this month. Reasoning for this deception has yet to be determined due to the fact that Victor Bannon hasn't stepped forward nor contacted the CIA or FBI in regards to this evidence. The President of the United States has relieved Mr. Bannon of his duties while his second in command, the Deputy Director Robert Duncan, has been tapped as the acting DCI. All charges against SANDBOX have been dropped, although numerous questions still remain about the Hawaiian attack but SANDBOX has refused to comment on the incident.

The investigation over Nikolay Dmitriev's death continues with pressure from Cuba and Russia, but sources inside the government have told CNN that neither government has produced Nikolay's body as of yet, nor any other proof that implicates the United States in any way. Until such time the allegations against the United States, in the death of Nikolay Dmitriev, will remain just that, allegations.

I'm Tammy Baker, with CNN."

<u>53</u>

Tuesday November 25, 1997 Early Afternoon
San Francisco

The services for the fallen men were held in a cemetery not far from SANDBOX in Marin, California. There was a large contingency of Secret Service Agents that kept the service locked down tight due to the fact that the President of the United States was not only in attendance, but had offered to speak. The President stood towards in rear with the new DCI, Robert Duncan and waited.

Sam, Bill and Thomas stood together surrounded by the men and women operators that SANDBOX employed. Roberta was to the left of Sam while Rebecca stood to the right of Thomas. Gunny Malloy had also respectfully made the trip to show his respects.

The relatives of the fallen men were also in attendance. They were comforted by their extended SANDBOX family.

In front of everyone was a large pillar. On it the names of each of their most recent fallen warriors had been etched.

DAVID THOMPSON – BRAVO TWO
TONY O'NEILL – DELTA
ANDY CARTER – FOXTROT
MATT JACKSON – HOTEL
JEFF RUSSELL – OSCAR
ADRIAN SHELTON – WHISKEY
JOSEPH PICKENS – YANKEE

Sam left the group and walked up to the podium. He cleared his throat and began.

"Please, ladies and gentlemen, take a seat."

Everyone sat down. The Secret Service remained standing and ever vigilant.

Sam continued. "I would like to start out by thanking each and every one of you for coming out to pay your respects to our fallen warriors. Duty. Honor. Loyalty. These are just a few of the traits that these men, who we honor today, possessed. The call they received, that we've all heeded, is something that we all decided to follow. And what the military couldn't provide we've all found at SANDBOX. We're a family and we look out for each other. We protect those that need protecting. We go where we're needed and we get the job done. We have garnered and gained the respect of our brothers still enlisted in all branches of the service.

I worked with and I fought with these men. They protected my family and we protected each other's backs. It was an honor to know and be part of their lives. This pillar has many names on it, but never has so many been added to it at one time. A part of me feels that I have failed each man and my heart is ever so heavy because of my failure. I will never be the same nor be able to make up for their loss in this world. I will, however, be personally gifting one million dollars to each of these men's families. I can only hope it removes any financial barriers these men's absence has left behind.

I would also personally thank Gunny Malloy. He has graciously traveled here today from the Marine Base in Oahu. He, his men and six of our brothers and sisters were instrumental in defending my wife and children, along with Bill and Thomas'. Rebecca Cross is also here with us today and I want to thank her from the bottom of my heart as well.

Now, it's my distinct honor to ask the President of the United States to the podium."

D.W. Neuman

Everyone stood up as the President made his way forward. The men and women of SANDBOX saluted him as he took the podium.

The President stood there for a moment and looked out over the attendees. He snapped a smart salute, held it for a second and then brought his hand down. The crowd did the same.

"Please, be seated," President Clinton began. "At first I wasn't sure why I wanted to be here today, to honor your fallen comrades, but now I know why. All of you are a constant reminder why this country is so great. Your sacrifice is truly inspirational and I draw much strength from your selflessness. You put everything on the line and yet you ask for nothing in return other than to follow your calling. You hold yourself in such high regard and I commend each of you.

These fallen warriors, as I've been told, are exemplary; true heroes in every sense of the word. Their only fault is that I will fail and lessen the impact they each had on this world and the people each one of them impacted.

I've been told not to talk about this but I feel that it's too important not to. The American people are in your debt for what the men and women of SANDBOX have done. When our country was at the mercy of a madman, you took up the reins and did what needed to be done. Thank you.

In closing I feel it's my duty to offer an olive branch. The recent 'misunderstanding' the government had with SANDBOX needs to be put behind us so we can move forward together in future endeavors.

Thank you and God bless."

The attendees saluted the President as he left the podium and he quickly snapped off his own salute as he was escorted by Secret Service personnel to a large tent that had been erected.

Sam, Bill and Thomas were patted down for the second time and then allowed access through the tent's doorway. The inside had been set up with a large rug and comfortable chairs. Security surrounded the tent and two agents remained inside.

The President extended his hand and shook each of theirs once they were inside.

"Gentlemen," the President began, "this is the acting DCI, Robert Duncan."

Handshakes and introductions were made.

"Please, why don't' we all sit down." He turned to the two agents. "Please, wait outside."

"Yes sir." They exited the tent.

"I'll get right to the point. Your demands were paltry in comparison to what you could have requested. With that being said I was very intrigued and decided to meet the men who took down Nikolay Dmitriev. I was impressed with your speech Mr. Paige."

"And I with yours Mr. President."

"Now that the pleasantries are out of the way, what do you wish to discuss with the DCI?"

Thomas spoke up. "Sir, it was actually me who requested the meeting."

"I see. Mr. Clark, I was briefed on you," replied the President. "Your father, Michael Clark, was actually quite the CIA spook back in the days. He even met with JFK at one time."

"Yes sir."

"Our records indicate, and forgive me for saying this, that he killed himself when you were ten."

If you only knew the truth. "Yes sir."

"What can the DCI and I do for you then, Mr. Clark?"

"Mr. President. My father was the one that collected intelligence on Nikolay Dmitriev and his sleeper agents here in the United States. Before his sudden death he hid a roll of microfilm in one of the legs of my childhood chair I loved. I recently made this discovery and, long story short, brought it to the attention of Victor Bannon."

"I see."

"Victor asked me what I wanted in return and I told him I wanted only one thing. Victor then made me that promise. That's why I requested for a meeting with the DCI, sir."

The President glanced over at Robert and then back at Thomas. "You have my attention Mr. Clark. What did the former DCI promise you?"

"Sir, I formerly request that my father, Michael Clark, be awarded a star on the CIA Memorial Wall. He deserves the recognition."

* * *

Wednesday November 26, 1997 Late Afternoon
CIA

Robert Duncan finished up the Memorial Wall ceremony. Michael Clark's name was now officially inscribed under the 1967 heading. His contributions to the protection of the United States were indisputable.

Thomas stood by the wall. The gravity of so many men and women who had fallen in the line of duty was overwhelming. Robert Duncan walked over to him as people meandered away.

"You miss him?"

Thomas nodded. "Yes, quite a bit."

"May I ask you a question? It must have been hard growing up and not really knowing who or what he did?"

Thomas smiled a little. "He was one secretive sonofabitch, that's for sure. But somehow I think I've gotten to know him better through all this."

The DCI nodded. "Good for you. Closure sounds like just what you needed."

"This has helped more than you know." Thomas extended his right hand and Robert took it. "Thank you sir."

"You're welcome Mr. Clark. We should get you back to the airport; I don't want you to miss your flight. I don't want to be the one responsible for you missing Thanksgiving with your family."

* * *

Robert Duncan watched Thomas depart and then headed back to his new office. He's been very busy the last two days and hadn't had a chance to really even set foot into Victor's old office. Internal security had scrubbed the office down, looking for additional evidence of Victor's 'transgressions', and had informed Robert that he could occupy it now.

As Robert entered his office he noticed that it had a pleasant and inviting air to it.

I didn't think I'd become the new DCI this quickly or in this manner.

He walked to his new desk and sat down behind it.

Alright, time to get down to business before going home and eating some turkey.

He opened each drawer to check their contents. He found a typed piece of paper in the center drawer and he read it. Internal security had left a note letting him know that the safe's combination had been changed to the same one he had in his old office. *Delightful.* Robert turned around and opened the cabinet behind him to reveal the safe in question. He punched in the appropriate codes on the keypad. The safe clicked open and revealed a stack of folders. The new DCI took them all out and put them in a stack on his uncluttered desk.

It wasn't until hours later when he ran across an interesting file folder.

What's this? I wonder what Project Zelda is all about?

Shadows of the Heart

54

Thursday November 27, 1997 Late Afternoon Safe Location - Thanksgiving

A few days of peace and quiet had helped everyone start to relax. The families had retreated to an undisclosed, but temporary location, until they all decided what path to proceed down together. The children rarely left their mother's sides and at night they were all experiencing nightmares. The unfortunate reality is that all three wives, not to mention their children, were suffering from post-traumatic stress disorder. It would be a long time before their lives would feel normal again.

But that didn't stop the adults from trying their best to keep traditions and a sense of normalcy going. They had spent the day prepping and cooking a feast. Turkey, mashed potatoes, stuffing, biscuits, squash and both apple and pumpkin pies had all been prepared. While they ate dinner they actually all seemed to enjoy the moment. The food was delicious and there was even some occasional laughing. The mood changed quickly when someone knocked an unopened can off the counter and it hit the floor with a loud bang. As soon as that happened the children became terrified and huddled in their mother's arms, although Emily and Gavin seemed hardly affected by the loud noise whatsoever.

While Julie, Kim and Laura took care of the kids Sam, Bill and Thomas took their beers and headed out to the deck that surrounded the large property. They leaned on the railing and looked out.

"How was your father's ceremony?" Sam asked.

"I think it's the closure I needed," Thomas replied.

"That's good to hear." Sam turned and gazed out over the land and gripped his beer bottle harder than intended. Thomas noticed it.

"Something on your mind Sam?"

Sam lowered his head. "Yeah. Part of me wishes I should have put a bullet in Victor's head. But the reality is that I stopped myself because I didn't want my children to see me in that light."

Thomas nodded. "We all wanted to kill him but it just wasn't a feasible option. I'm sure wherever Gavin left him will be a thousand times worse."

"You're probably right."

Bill put his bottle down and sighed. "Listen, I'm just going to come out and say it. I'm worried about my kids. They're not doing very well."

"Mine too," Sam admitted. "I just don't get it. Emily and Gavin seem to be taking everything in stride. What do you think that's about Thomas?"

Thomas took another sip of beer before he responded. "I don't know. I can't say for sure but they've been through and seen more than any four and six year old should. And then you add their powers on top of that. It's hard for me to admit, and I hate to say it, but I think they're just used to it."

Sam and Bill took a swig of their beers and nodded.

"Listen," said Thomas. "I have an idea that might help but it's completely up to what you both think."

"What'd you have in mind?" Sam asked.

Thomas paused before he continued. "What would you say to Emily wiping your kid's memories?"

Sam and Bill looked at each other and then back at Thomas.

"Is that even possible?" Bill asked. "I mean, yes I've seen her do it, but what I mean is, specific memories?"

Thomas nodded. "Emily wiped Calvin's and those other two men's memories before they left. It's doable. But what I'm asking is, is that something you'd even consider? Remove the trauma of the past few weeks, which would also remove their knowledge of my children's powers."

Sam and Bill both nodded.

"Understood," said Sam. "We'll talk to the ladies. I'm sure that decision will be a no brainer."

"Good. By the way, how's the shoulder?" Thomas asked.

Sam smiled. "It's good. I might not ever live that down with Gavin though. I owe him."

Thomas returned the grin. "I'm sure he'll figure that out one day and use it to his advantage."

"Fantastic," Sam joked. "I can't wait."

The three got quiet and drank their beers for a few minutes as they enjoyed the view and each other's company.

Bill finally broke the silence. "What the hell are we going to do now?"

"Business as usual for us at SANDBOX," said Sam.

"Yeah," Bill said in agreement. "Thomas?"

"I think I need to spend time with my family. I have to get a grasp on my ability that I apparently have now. But I think it's important that I'm there for my kids to help guide them with theirs as well."

Sam and Bill nodded. Thomas continued. "Aside from work keeping you both busy, don't forget that you're half a billion dollars richer now."

"That's true," Sam agreed. "That reality hasn't even begun to register yet. But yes, aside from work, I need to spend time with my family too. Julie died and I thought I'd lost her forever. She and I have some issues to work through but I'll do whatever it takes to make our lives positive moving forward. The reality of what we've all been through is that we all deserve a break."

"Yeah we do," said Bill.

"And what about you Bill?" Thomas pressed. "What're you thinking?"

"I don't know. Sam's right, we need a break. But other than that we just need to make sure your back is covered, not to mention your kids are never touched again. Overall, I don't know. I guess we'll have to wait and see what the future has in store for all of us."

55

Thursday November 27, 1997 Late Evening
Safe Location

Thomas and Laura tucked Gavin and Emily in to bed. Stickers and Stir curled up next to Gavin and went to sleep. They kissed their kids goodnight and then retired to their own room down the hall. They got ready for bed and climbed in. Laura and Thomas cuddled up.

"I know you told me about what happened with your parents. Do you think we'll ever see them again?"

Thomas shrugged in the darkness next to Laura. "I don't know. Maybe. Everything's just been so damn crazy. Think about what we've been through since my father told us about his past, the microfilm, Nikolay, etc. Look at what the kids have been through. We all need a break and just spend quality time together. Damn."

"What?"

"That reminds me. We need to check in on Nick Raynes and see how little Lisa is recovering from the zoo incident."

"We can call them tomorrow if you like," Laura said. "But what I want to know about right now is what you think about your new power? You saved my life. I saw his arm move as he tried to shoot me. Your zip-ties practically burst off and his gun was pulled from his hand and ended up in yours."

"Yeah, I know."

"Does...does it scare you?"

"A little. I haven't tried to use them since then at all. I guess that makes me afraid of it. The issue is that it's all so new to me. What if I end up hurting someone with it?"

Laura shook her head. "That would never happen. That's not who you are. Our kids are learning to control theirs more and more every day. So can you. Besides, you saved my life with your new powers, thank you."

Thomas remained silent for a bit before he spoke up again. "I can't think about my powers right now. After everything our families have been through it's important to me that we concentrate on raising our children. All I know is that all they need our unconditional love regardless of what abilities they possess."

"Yes they do. But you don't understand. I'm the oddball out now."

Thomas stroked her hair to try and calm her down. "Don't talk like that. I love you. You could never be the oddball. Our family needs you and loves you just the way you are."

"That's easy for you to say."

"It's not like I asked for them. It was an accident."

"I know. If you didn't have them I...well."

"Yeah, you might not be here. It's something I don't like to think about." Thomas sighed. "You know I love you, right?"

"I do."

"Then get out of bed and come with me."

Laura was puzzled. "What are you talking about?"

"Trust me."

"Okay, I guess." She pushed back the covers and got out of bed. "Now what?"

Thomas walked her over to the bureau. He opened it up, moved some clothing out of the way, and pulled a thin object out. Laura could barely see it in the dim light.

"What is it?"

"It's a syringe. During the struggle at the lab there was a tray of them that had been knocked to the floor. I picked one up

380

thinking it could be used to sedate someone and put it in my pocket just in case. I had no idea that it held the same serum Dr. Matsushita stabbed me with during our struggle."

Laura's eyes widened. "And he's still out there, isn't he?"

Thomas nodded. "I'm afraid so. But I can't worry about him right now. Here, take it."

Thomas handed the syringe over and Laura gently took it from his hands.

"In any case, this is what he was manufacturing. He made it out of the experiments he performed on Emily and me. I was injected with one and the rest had to have been destroyed in the fire."

Laura looked up at Thomas with soft eyes. She realized what he was going to say.

"I don't ever want you to feel left out sweetie. You don't have to feel like the oddball if you don't want to. I want you to have it. It's yours now and it's entirely up to you whether you want to use it or not."

Visit my website at

http://www.dwneuman.com

If you enjoyed this novel please consider taking a moment and writing a quick review about it (on Amazon). It helps me out more than you know and fuels my motivation! Of course, word of mouth works wonders too! ;)

Thank you!

And you can look forward to book six,
Shadows of the Sand,
in the future.